ALSO BY DUSTIN GRINNELL

Fiction

The Genius Dilemma
Without Limits
The Empathy Academy

Nonfiction

Lost & Found
The Velvet Ghetto

THE HEALING BOOK

A Collection of Short Stories

A Collection of Short Stories by

Dustin Grinnell

Finishing Line Press
Georgetown, Kentucky

THE HEALING BOOK

A Collection of Short Stories

Publisher: Leah Huete de Maines
Editor: Tod Tinker & Christen Kincaid
Author Photo: Dustin Grinnell
Cover Design: Kaitlyn Gilbert

Order online: www.finishinglinepress.com
          also available on amazon.com

Author inquiries and mail orders:
Finishing Line Press
P. O. Box 1626
Georgetown, Kentucky 40324
U. S. A.

Table of Contents

Before you heal someone, ask if he's willing to give up the things that make him sick.
　　—Hippocrates

Yesterday I was clever, so I wanted to change the world. Today I am wise, so I am changing myself.
　　—Rumi

The art of medicine consists of amusing the patients while nature cures the disease.
　　—Voltaire

Preface

When I was a marketing writer for a major hospital in Boston, I wrote articles about science and medicine and interviewed experts about new treatments, research breakthroughs, and cutting-edge technologies. Through my work, I saw the awesome healing powers of Western medicine. For disorders of the body, clinicians prescribed drugs or surgeries. For diseases of the mind, mental health professionals recommended therapy or pharmaceuticals. And yet, there were few options for ailments of the spirit. In my personal experience, I've found that books are a type of medicine for the soul.

When I read *Zen and the Art of Motorcycle Maintenance: An Inquiry into Values* (1974) by Robert M. Pirsig in 2015, I was experiencing a spiritual crisis. I was working an office job writing about scientific research in Cambridge, Massachusetts. I enjoyed the work, but the exhilaration of career-finding and experimentation that had taken place in my twenties had worn off, and I was becoming dissatisfied with the monotony of office life. I was a thirty-three-year-old knowledge worker, and years were zipping by too fast. Pirsig's book was a shock to the system.

Zen and the Art of Motorcycle Maintenance is a fictionalized account of a cross-country motorcycle journey that Pirsig took in 1968 with his eleven-year-old son and two friends. It's a road-trip novel as well as a philosophical treatise, filled with soul-stirring reflections and monologues about technological progress, cultural norms, and other big ideas that provoked me. While reading the book, I realized that my life had become routine, clinical, too practical. In the city, I was cooped up and overstimulated. I needed a quest, some time for exploration. When I finished the novel, I bought a 1984 Honda Nighthawk. Six months later, I quit my job and tapped my savings to support a year of travel and writing. I spent three weeks backpacking in China, studying Traditional Chinese Medicine. When I returned home, I rode my bike across the US, like Pirsig had.

Three-quarters of the way across the country in Texas, my motorcycle broke down. I had it towed to a repair shop, where a friendly mechanic named Chris delivered the verdict. "The brakes are horrible, the suspension's garbage, and you need a new clutch. But the engine is solid." He thought it would get me to California. "I recommend you read *Zen and the Art of Motorcycle Maintenance.*" I laughed and said that I'd bought my bike after reading the book. It was clear where he was going. He knew I wasn't interested in understanding the ins and outs of the machine, nor was I inclined to repair its problems.

In his book, Pirsig categorized people into two groups: classical and romantic thinkers. A classical thinker sees a motorcycle from a technical point of view—its individual parts and how those parts work together. A classical thinker is eager to diagnose a mechanical problem and doesn't mind fixing the issues. Romantic thinkers, on the other hand, think about a bike more holistically. "The romantic mode is primarily inspirational, imaginative, creative, intuitive," Pirsig wrote. They see a bike for its aesthetic beauty and potential for freedom or adventure. You won't see a romantic tinkering with their bike.

Pirsig was a self-described classical thinker and wrote long passages in *Zen* about the inner workings of his bike and how he approaches repairs. His friend John was a romantic, refusing to get his hands dirty in the event of a mechanical problem. Relating to John, I admitted, "I'm 100% romantic." Chris smiled, "And I'm classical." His suggestion was a friendly reminder to meet him somewhere in the middle if possible. Then Chris got excited. "The author never identified the motorcycle in his book." He'd found a picture online of Pirsig and his son. "He rode a 1966 CB77 Super Hawk." He led me to a storage room and pointed to a grease-covered engine on a shelf. "Here's the motor!" He spun around and pointed to a silver engine on another shelf. "A better version." Chris said I'd done well on the Nighthawk so far, but Pirsig rode a vintage bike and worked on it every few hours. I paid the bill and strapped a duffel bag to my bike. Chris wished me good luck and asked me to email him when I arrived out West. "Or else, you know, I'll worry."

Ever since experiencing the power that *Zen* had on my life, I've been interested in how storytelling can change our lives and help us heal. At the most basic level, *Zen* had given me a distraction from everyday pressures. It took me on a journey and transported me to another world. Pirsig's novel had also given me the boost to take a modern-day walkabout—an Australian Aborigine's rite of passage where a young male enters the wilderness alone to make the spiritual journey into manhood. The year away from the workforce gave me time for self-exploration, to examine questions I hadn't had time to consider: Who am I? What do I really want? How should I live?

In this way, the book had incited me and shaken me out of complacency, prompting me to transform my life. According to Franz Kafka, we should read books that "wound and stab us," that "wake us up with a blow on the head." "A book must be the axe for the frozen sea inside us." For me, *Zen and the Art of Motorcycle Maintenance* was that ax. I had needed to pay attention to my wanderlust and discharge some restlessness, and the adventure that *Zen* sparked allowed me to do those things.

The book also made me realize that being a romantic sometimes makes it hard for me to live in the real world, as my circumstances rarely live up to the ideals in my head. I couldn't live in a fantasy, so I needed to find my place in the workforce and establish myself in a role in which I would be satisfied. When I returned to corporate America after my trip, I took the job writing for a hospital and accepted the value of being grounded in a day job that uses my skills and also gives me the financial security to pursue my creative writing in my spare time. Later, I learned that Pirsig had found a similar dynamic. He wrote technical manuals for his full-time job and wrote his creative work on the side. I'm more content than I was before I left Boston. I have a stronger sense of my place in the world.

Most of us have had the experience of feeling that a book changed our lives. Many of us can name a book that helped us navigate a traumatic experience, integrate a disowned aspect of ourselves, or perhaps even helped us gain spiritual fulfillment. This notion of reading for therapeutic effect is known as bibliotherapy, a practice that dates back to the ancient Greeks, who inscribed "healing place for the soul," over the entrance to the library in Thebes. Bibliotherapy has since gone mainstream. These days, counselors at the School of Life in London prescribe books to clients worldwide for everything from fear of commitment to a broken heart, from single parenthood to the loss of a loved one. Recent research has shown that reading therapy may benefit adults with depression, victims of sexual abuse, and traumatized refugee students.

While Pirsig's book definitely had a potent psychological effect on me, I've always been curious as to whether a book could cure a physical disease like cancer or an autoimmune disorder. My curiosity is piqued when a reader claims that a certain book healed them from a physical malady. For instance, thousands of people with chronic back pain claim their pain disappeared after reading *Healing Back Pain* by author and physician, John Sarno. According to Sarno, the cure for back pain—and various chronic illnesses including autoimmune diseases—is *knowledge*. In this case, knowledge that the mind and body are connected, and that certain powerful emotions, like anger and sadness, can convert to pain or other conditions if they remain unconscious and unacknowledged. If a book can heal someone's body, what if a novel could be written with the *intent* to heal?

This idea captured my imagination and led to me writing the short story, "The Healing Book," about a married couple's attempts to cope with a terminal cancer diagnosis. When the husband, a physician, realizes that none of his interventions will cure his wife's illness, he goes on a quest to write a book that will heal her body. As you might have expected, it doesn't work. Hours before the wife passes, she tells her husband that she wished he'd spent more time with her in her final days rather than searching for a cure. She also thanks him, though. The book hadn't allowed her to live, but the wisdom and voice of the words had comforted her, teaching her how to die.

The Healing Book is a collection of stories about people in pursuit of healing. The stories follow characters who are struggling in some way. They're searching for a cure for their chronic dissatisfaction. A way to manage their ambition, restlessness, or boredom. They want peace. In "Cured," Peter finds a cure for a terrible disease and discovers his own humanity in the process. In "An Affable Man," Sebastian's midlife crisis is triggered by the soul-deadening aspects of office life. In "Going Through the Motions," Graham is trying to manage his rebellion against self-help literature and the conventional values of mainstream society. In "The Disciple," Gabby gathers the courage to escape her life in a cult.

Most of these characters are looking for their place in the world. Their "element." A voice of their own. In their pursuits to fulfill some psychological, emotional, or spiritual void, they figure out who they are and what they want. They reconnect with others and get back in touch with themselves. In "Beyond Medicine," Allie travels to Peru to cure her depression through shamanistic ritual. In "Cubicle," a student filmmaker discovers isolation, loneliness, absurdity, and cruelty in the halls of corporate America—but also finds his artistic voice. In "The Good Parent," Kate seeks to fulfill a psychological void by leaving behind her overprotective mother's style of parenting. Instead, Kate tries a new philosophy: free-range parenting. Through this parenting method, Kate hopes to empower her child to explore the world and think for herself. In "Trail Magic," a burned-out knowledge worker struggling with depression and identity issues finds her way to contentment and freedom through therapy and the Appalachian Trail.

Although I didn't realize it while writing these short stories, many of the main characters are or become writers. The therapist in the story, "A Case of Aphantasia," writes an account of his patient's inability to picture images in his mind's eye, leaving behind the tale of a man who struggles to remain in the real world and must rely on family to free him from the grips of his mind. There's the eager journalist in "The Dark Side of Destiny," who longs to find a story that will make a name for himself, eventually discovering it in a scientist with startling intentions. In "Chasing Fireflies at Midnight," a science writer for a research institute eventually finds his journalistic voice after a night of searching for fireflies with his grandmother.

And there's the theoretical physicist in "Searching for Meaning in the Stars" who overcomes an existential crisis in his cabin in New Hampshire and writes a book about how he found meaning in his life with cosmic perspective. As Alexander writes a memoir, which also teaches readers about the universe, he realizes the power of the writing on his life and potentially the lives of others:

> "Writing was philosophy in action. Every day, I brought order to
> disorder by transforming personal insights and ancient wisdom into
> sentences, paragraphs, and chapters. Writing was similar to physics:
> they both involved discovery. I developed a strong belief that if I got

the correct words in the right order, then perhaps I could help readers make sense out of the chaos of their lives."

Having my characters find the power of writing is an example of how most of these short stories are based on personal experiences. Indeed, writing has offered me a way to examine my own life. A method for exploring ideas. A means for understanding the human condition. A way to discover the truth. These stories were inspired by jobs I've held, places I've lived, and people I've met. They explore family relationships, work experiences, memories from childhood. In short, they're all based on true stories.

In that regard, most of these short stories are autobiographical fiction, or "autofiction," a genre where the writer mines their life and presents it in a work of fiction. They are also a form of self-therapy, a way to make sense of my experiences, give meaning to my life and perhaps protect against future troubles. In my life, writing has helped me in the same way psychotherapy does, by processing and even resolving psychic conflicts. I see myself in characters and make them deal with—and eventually overcome—problems similar to my own. The process of inventing language for these characters' struggles has provided a vocabulary to understand my feelings and how to express them, even if on paper.

In "Searching for Meaning in the Stars," Alexander reflects on how writing has helped him find meaning in his life and overcome an existential crisis:

"…Writing allowed me to think critically about what I believed and helped me in my quest to find meaning—and I would share what I learned in the book: We all had to make it up as we went. We found meaning in our lives by discovering our own reasons for living. From this, I realized the book was my attempt at a second grand unifying theory: not one that searched for laws transcending time and space, but one encompassing the human endeavor. A guide for life."

Years after reading *Zen and the Art of Motorcycle Maintenance*, I learned that writing the novel had helped Pirsig make peace with himself after he was diagnosed with schizophrenia and institutionalized in the early 1960s. He began writing *Zen* after his mental breakdown, where he underwent two years of treatments that included electric shock therapy. "What I'm trying to do here is put it all together," he wrote. "It's so big. That's why I seem to wander sometimes."

And so, I invite you to immerse yourself in these fictional stories and follow characters who are on journeys of self-discovery, trying to overcome discontent or disconnection, achieve a sense of freedom, or find more meaning in their lives as they navigate the complexities, indignities, and absurdities of modern life. These characters are searching for wisdom. They're trying to become better people. They're trying to understand how to live while accepting that one day they will inevitably die. These stories were initially written to heal myself. Now, it's my hope they will heal you.

Dustin Grinnell
Boston, Massachusetts
October 2023

Beyond Medicine

When Allie's canoe tapped the dock in Iquitos, Peru, she didn't know which was greater: her exhaustion or her anticipation. After hours on the Amazon River, she was sticky with sweat, and her arms and legs itched and ached in the wake of countless mosquito bites. However, their arrival meant she was that much closer to experiencing a traditional shaman-led ayahuasca ceremony.

Allie dragged herself from her seat and onto dry land. After taking a moment to roll her neck and shoulders, which had become tight from rowing, she hefted her bags onto her back. Then she joined the rest of the group as they followed a guide along a narrow path through dense forest. When they reached an open encampment, she was directed to a private bungalow, where she dropped her bags, and then to a larger hut for dinner.

Entering the hut, Allie and the others took seats around a table made from the cross-section of a tree. She was just getting settled when they were joined by the shaman, who wore a colorful shawl and had his dirty-blond hair pulled back into a bun.

"Welcome, welcome." He removed a lit cigar from between his lips. "My name is Matteo. I am so glad you've come all this way to see us. Please eat! You've traveled a long way and must be starving."

In the dim lighting of a kerosene lamp, the group ate papayas, bananas, and breadfruit while Matteo told them about his healing practice. It centered around the potent ayahuasca brew, which had produced remarkable stories of healing in combination with his traditional ceremony.

Allie was familiar with many of these stories after months of reading about the white man who had left his middle-class life in California years before to treat his depression through shamanistic ritual here in Peru. Years of training had turned Matteo into a powerful healer, some believed, and people visited him from all over the world in search of cures for anything from addiction and asthma to depression and cancer.

As a neurosurgeon, Allie was skeptical, yet emerging research on ayahuasca was compelling. Studies had shown that ayahuasca improved the body's absorption of serotonin—the "happy hormone." Knowing this, Allie had tapered her use of SSRIs leading up to her trip lest the ayahuasca lead to serotonin syndrome.

Matteo blew out a plume of smoke. "Ayahuasca means 'vine of the soul.' The ayahuasca concoction you will drink during the healing ceremony contains a chemical that will produce visions. These visions will allow you to bypass your mental defenses and access deeper layers of your subconscious, which will help you reorient the way you perceive yourself."

"Die to the flesh; awaken to the spirit," someone remarked.

Matteo nodded. "We call it *ego death*." The wrinkles in his face lifted. "The ceremony will also allow you to purge any bad spirits that might have attached to you throughout your life. During the ceremony, I'll protect you from harmful spirits, but you will need to be brave for the shamanistic healing to work."

Allie raised an eyebrow. "Spirits?"

"People who have passed on but haven't yet left the earth. There are many: proud spirits, spirits who are envious of our human forms, despondent spirits. Some can be harmful, and I'll fight those off if they appear. However, not all spirits mean harm. During the ceremony, pay attention to what you see—images of loved ones or strange figures—as they may have some significance."

Mentioning the healing center—which sat behind the hut they ate in— Matteo instructed them to meet there by nine that night for the ayahuasca ceremony.

After dinner, Allie trudged along a narrow dirt path to her bungalow. She washed her face and lay down on her bed. Exhausted as she was, she didn't dare close her eyes lest she invite in a rush of unwanted images: the sixty-pound body of her older sister, Vera, writhing on a hospital bed, gasping for breath in her final hours, eyes sunken, skin loose, papery-skinned hands reaching toward Allie in desperation.

A talented engineer and pride of the family, Vera had been destined for her dream job at NASA when she'd been burdened with a mysterious chronic disease that affected the connective tissues and led to severe malnutrition. Allie had tried so hard to work with her sister's doctors to help diagnose and treat Vera's disease, but it hadn't been enough. She even feared all her efforts had somehow complicated matters, leading to Vera's untimely death.

Right at nine, Allie entered the healing center, not sure what to expect. Everyone else was already present, seated quietly on meditation cushions. Behind them, empty yoga mats splayed out in several rows. Standing at the front of the room, Matteo sang in a language Allie didn't recognize, and he smiled and nodded to her when she met his gaze. Beside him sat a large barrel that no doubt contained the ayahuasca brew.

A petite man with a soft face, who'd been introduced to them earlier as Matteo's apprentice, led Allie to a cushion. He collected her cell phone, offering to take pictures if he could. He placed a cup in front of her, as well as a plastic pail for vomit.

"What is he singing?" Allie inquired.

"Songs that call forth the plants' healing properties," the apprentice explained.

Matteo continued singing as he ladled a thick, brown concoction out of the barrel into cups. He handed the cups to his apprentice. While Matteo only filled most of the cups halfway, the one he filled for Allie was filled to the top.

The apprentice set the cup down in front of Allie and winked. "Those who need the most healing get the most brew."

Allie's neighbor eyed her cup. "You must be teeming with demons."

Demons. Just another word for trauma.

As she waited for Matteo's command to drink, Allie examined the awful-smelling sludge. By drinking this disgusting potion, she hoped she would stop obsessing over her sister's death. Stop calling the hospital where Vera had died, demanding to review her medical records so she could check her glucose levels leading up to the heart attack. Stop writing op-ed pieces about how deadly medical errors were in the United States.

A few days before Vera died, Allie had requested the services of a renowned eating disorder specialist from a prestigious hospital in New York City who, after evaluating Vera, hadn't had much to offer. Why hadn't she instead consulted a rheumatologist, who could've assessed Vera's connective tissue? She could've brought in a talented diagnostician to try to determine the root cause of her vexing illness. Why hadn't she just checked Vera's electrolyte balance herself before she left for the night?

Allie had put her medical career on pause and left her chic apartment in Boston's Back Bay to travel to Peru in the desperate hope the ceremony would help her accept that she couldn't have done any more the night Vera died. Maybe then the images of her sister would stop keeping her awake at night. Maybe then Allie could move on.

Once all the filled cups had been handed out, Mateo scanned the room and nodded, giving everyone permission to drink. Allie closed her eyes, lifted the cup to her mouth, and drank the brew in three gulps. Putting the cup down, she watched the others swig the sludge.

Matteo instructed his apprentice to turn down the lamplight. Allie sat calmly and watched Matteo dance and sing in the dim light. After about twenty minutes, her head felt fuzzy, and her arms and legs tingled. Her vision filled with globs of light: first red, then green and blue. A kaleidoscope of shapes appeared: triangles, rectangles, and shapes she didn't even know names for. Then they blurred into streaks of color.

Allie tensed as the colors transformed into horrifying images: an anaconda bloated from feeding; a tarantula; a flash of piranhas shredding a horse flailing in shallow water; a caterpillar losing its legs; a mangled hand in a blender.

Then Allie saw Vera in the hospital bed, more malnourished than ever. Her skin was loose from the severe weight loss. Her back contorted, her thin arms reached out, and her fingers wrapped around Allie's neck.

"Why couldn't you just leave me alone?" Vera screamed. "You brought in your fancy doctors, but how did any of them help?"

Allie gasped for breath, struggling against her sister's hold. "Help me!"

"I'm here, Allie," Matteo called, singing louder. "I am protecting you."

Allie didn't feel protected. She felt alone in the darkness. Both Matteo's words and her own thoughts sounded far away.

In the next moment, the walls closed in, and she fell backward into a cloud of thick smoke. She climbed a rope slippery with grime—climbing, slipping, climbing, and finally slipping off altogether. She fell, tumbling end over end, and splashed hard into glacial waters. Then her skin burst into flames. She was submerged in water, but still, somehow, her skin was ablaze.

Allie reached blindly for the pail beside her and vomited.

Even as she retched, Allie was back in the hospital, watching her sister suffer a heart attack, as if she'd been in the room that night. A faint heartbeat sounded from a distant monitor. It was cut short by a long, high-pitched whine. The doctors pressed on Vera's chest, snapping her brittle ribs.

Allie drifted into a memory from later that night. Vera's doctor stood before them in a waiting room. "We resuscitated her, but she has no brain function."

Her sister was a vegetable.

After days of deliberation, hoping Vera would defy medical science and awaken, Allie decided to withdraw care. Her father nodded in agreement, but he couldn't remember why they'd come to the hospital. Most days, he forgot about the shell of a person Vera had become. The Alzheimer's was too far advanced.

Allie vomited until her stomach was empty.

Questions swirled. The day before Vera's heart attack, Allie had brought one of the best cardiologists in New York City to see Vera. When they had entered her room, Vera had hissed and told them to leave and never come back. What if Vera had allowed the specialist to consult on her case? They might've diagnosed the issue that led to the heart attack. They might have caught a medical error before it led to catastrophe.

Suddenly, the scent of smoke overwhelmed Allie. Her breathing became less shallow, and slowly, she returned to her body.

Matteo knelt over her. "Welcome back."

Allie searched his face. "Where was I?"

"In a place beyond names."

Allie closed her eyes and sobbed.

When she returned to her bungalow, Allie crashed into bed. Her body ached, and her head throbbed. Being so out of control during the ceremony had been terrifying. She'd never felt such profound fear. In the grip of the hallucinations, she had thought she would go insane.

Ego death, Matteo had called it.

As Allie stared up at the ceiling, she slowly realized her mood was different. She felt calmer than she had in years. Lighter. She allowed herself a soft smile.

When handing Allie back her phone, Matteo's apprentice had told her he had managed to take a picture of her during the ceremony. Now curious, she pulled her phone out of her pocket to see what he'd captured.

The image she found showed her sitting upright on her cushion with her eyes pressed shut. She frowned. There was something strange about the image. She peered more closely. Above her head hung a bright streak of light.

The flash of light ended at the crown of her head.

***

A month later, in Boston, Allie sipped a smoothie on the patio of her studio apartment in Back Bay while she contemplated the complex brain operation she would lead in a few hours. She thought about the brain scans of the elderly man whose life would soon be in her hands. She visualized the brain tumor trapped within a tangled knot of blood vessels in his left occipital lobe. The tumor had paralyzed the man's right arm and caused him to lose sight in his right eye.

Most neurosurgeons wouldn't have even touched the surgical case. The patient was too old and had too many underlying medical issues that increased the risk of complications. It wasn't even clear how the tumor could be removed.

Yet Allie never shied away from a challenge. She had an encyclopedic knowledge of the human brain and the uncanny ability to focus for ten to twelve hours during a marathon surgery. While she would be the first to admit she lacked a talent for diagnosis, her technical skills made her a distinguished member of the neurosurgical team. She was a proficient mechanic, possessing "gifted hands" that made difficult surgical maneuvers possible. And she could improvise in sticky situations, if necessary.

That morning, Allie had awoken feeling fresh and energetic. For the past month, she had slept well, no longer needing medicine to knock her out every night. She had been more social, attending get-togethers with her fellow surgeons. She had even found time in her hundred-hour work weeks to go on a couple of dates.

She recalled that rainforest village in Peru. Whatever had happened that night, the clouds of depression had parted. The ayahuasca had caused a surge of serotonin in her brain, but unlike antidepressants, the effects had lasted, no additional dosages needed.

Yet even though Allie felt better she still didn't feel "healed." She remained anxious and tense at a level just below conscious awareness. Even weekly massages couldn't dissolve the tension in her shoulders, neck, and back. She often joked with Olivia, a junior neurosurgeon, that the anxiety had turned her body to stone. Olivia would tease her, saying Allie was like a quivering rabbit, always monitoring her environment and emitting a nervous energy everyone could sense.

Worse, every time a Code Blue blared over the hospital's intercom, indicating a patient was experiencing a life-threatening emergency, dread would surge through Allie. She could hear Vera's fragile ribs snapping with every forceful push on her chest. She would picture a doctor standing over Vera's head and shoving a rigid tube down her windpipe. She would even replay the conversation with her father after it had become clear Vera had no neurological function.

Allie had told hospital administrators that such alarms were triggering for people like her. She had asked them to find a different technology to notify teams that a patient had coded, but her pleas had gone nowhere.

An hour later, Allie stood at a large stainless-steel sink, using a visualization technique to keep her mind as calm as a mountain lake as she scrubbed her hands. Once done, she pushed the door to the operating room open with her hip, keeping her hands high and in front of her.

In the center of the room, the man lay unconscious on the operating table. Before Allie had arrived, Olivia had spent an hour preparing the patient for the tumor resection. She had cut into the man's scalp and skull and had peeled back a triangle-shaped patch of skin and bone, revealing the gray convulsions of exposed brain tissue.

Ten minutes into the operation, Allie's gloved hands were covered in blood. Beside her, Olivia managed the patient's bleeding.

"Suction," Allie requested.

Olivia moved in with a suction pump. It sucked loudly as the area drained of blood.

Using the microscope attached to her surgical glasses, Allie navigated the contours of the patient's brain. She paused when she found the bundle of rope-like blood vessels she was looking for. Her eyes switched from the microscope to a computer screen that everyone in the room could see.

"Our brain tumor's in there."

Olivia vacuumed up a tiny blood clot. "That's quite a mess."

"Let's go digging."

A nurse handed Allie a tweezers-like instrument, and she picked at the densely packed area. Allie shook her head, frustrated. "These vessels won't come loose."

Suddenly, the brain region filled with thick, red blood. "Intracranial bleed,"

Olivia whispered.

"Clip that bleed, please."

Olivia placed a clip over the lesion, pinching off the bleed. Allie used an instrument to cauterize the broken blood vessel. The operating room filled with the odor of burnt brain tissue.

Allie examined the area. "So much scarring."

Olivia nodded as she continued to suction the area. "He's lost a lot of blood."

Allie glanced at the neurosurgeon who was frowning at the patient's vitals on a nearby monitor. "Please prepare a transfusion bag, Dr. Simpson."

He nodded and hung a blood bag on a stand.

Allie continued trying to untangle the knotted mess, but she felt a tinge of worry. Some of the blood vessels were stretched dangerously thin.

"If any of those blood vessels burst, the patient will hemorrhage," Dr. Simpson announced.

"Keep your eyes on vitals, please."

"We're not far from calling it?"

Allie glared at him. It was far too early to give up on the patient. She knew Dr. Simpson wouldn't mind if her patient died on her watch. Every surgeon had statistics: wins, losses, surgical complications. Dr. Simpson was the best diagnostician in the department and loved decrypting complex medical cases, but he envied Allie's technical aptitude and had often tried to emulate her surgical techniques—without success. It's why he didn't accept complex cases. Still, he wanted to be chief of neurosurgery, so stats were important to him, and if Allie lost this patient, it would be his win.

Allie, on the other hand, didn't care about titles. She was determined to save this patient, but she was stuck. Should she accept that the tangled mess of blood vessels was inoperable? Was Dr. Simpson correct?

Allie closed her eyes as the night Vera died flashed through her mind.

Her mind swirled over the medical errors that had occurred. So many people had cared for her sister, and a lot of information had gotten lost in the shuffle. Her blood glucose level had been low when she'd been admitted to the hospital, and it was zero during the cardiac arrest. Had they not been monitoring her glucose levels? Had they forgotten to do blood work? Either would have been a tragic oversight. An intravenous sugar solution would've brought Vera's blood glucose back up to normal levels.

No one from the hospital had been held responsible for the errors that had led to her sister's death. Sometimes, while lying in bed, unable to sleep, Allie would imagine ways of hurting the doctors who'd botched Vera's case. She'd whisper words that would cause them the terrible pain they deserved. Allie would say, "Crumple," and the lead doctor's head would ball up like used tissue paper. She'd say, "Choke," and the uncaring hospital administrator's throat would tighten until he couldn't breathe. Or she'd say, "Fire," and the nurse who'd forgotten to check Vera's blood glucose levels would ignite.

The idea that she could do such things with just a word might have been silly, but her patient's condition was dire, and she needed a miracle. Allie closed her eyes and whispered, "Untangle."

Opening her eyes, she examined the mass of vessels. Before her eyes, something impossible happened. It was subtle, like a flower turning to follow the sun's rays throughout the day, but the knotted blood vessels loosened, allowing Allie to pick away at them until they were all freed.

Untangled.

Allie scanned the eyes of those around her. Had they seen what she saw? Surely they had, yet no one looked awestruck.

Olivia smiled in admiration. "Well done, Dr. Watts."

"Please close him up, Dr. Simpson," Allie demanded.

She scrubbed out and stumbled into the hallway in a daze. Surely she'd just witnessed a coincidence. What had happened couldn't have had anything to do with the command she'd whispered. Maybe she'd imagined it—or gotten lucky, something doctors didn't like to admit.

Allie burst through the front doors of the hospital, startling a crow off the branch of a nearby tree. It swooped past her as she headed for one of the hospital's gardens. Just as Allie went to sit on a wooden bench overlooking the garden, a loud thud filled the air.

Jerking around, she hurried over to the window from which the sound seemed to have come. In front of it lay the crow, twitching, its scalp bloodied.

"Oh no."

Allie knelt beside the bird as a wave of sadness washed over her. She held back tears, pushing down the grief that tried to break through. Without knowing why, she cupped the bird in her hands and watched it die.

She thought back to the miracle that had happened in the operating room. Could that "power" work here? Could she bring the crow back to life? She shuddered.

Keeping her eyes trained on the bird, Allie focused her attention on the weight in her palms. "Fly."

The bird jolted in her hands as if shocked by a bolt of electricity. Its eyes snapped open and darted back and forth, and its wings fluttered. Unable to hold onto it, Allie lifted her hands, and the bird burst into the sky. It swooped down, cutting through the garden and the leaves of the tree it had left just before it died.

It banked into a strong wind, lifted high above the hospital, and disappeared into a cloud.

Oh my God. What is going on?

For a moment, Allie entertained the thought of a miracle, but miracles didn't happen twice, back to back. Allie remembered the bolt of light that had appeared above her head during the healing ceremony. She could've chosen to believe she'd been possessed by a rainforest demon, but she didn't. How else could she explain what was happening? Maybe an explanation lay somewhere in the middle ground between science and spirituality. She wondered if she possessed something else: a peculiar ability—a psychosomatic power, so to speak—that had been enhanced somehow in Peru.

In medical school, Allie had suffered from medical students' disease, frequently experiencing symptoms of the many diseases she studied. While studying dermatology, Allie had developed painful warts on her knee. In orthopedics, she had experienced a clicking in her hip socket. She had developed tension headaches during neurology class.

The strange occurrences had always brought to mind Allie's favorite book, *Travels,* an autobiography by Michael Crichton, who had written best-selling science-fiction novels while studying to become a doctor at Harvard Medical School. Crichton's literary success had led to an existential crisis: Should he pursue writing or continue with a medical career?

As the decision weighed on him, he had developed a troubling weakness in his arm. Crichton had been convinced it was multiple sclerosis, but doctors had found nothing physically wrong. One doctor had even suggested it might be hysteria or conversion disorder—names given for physical symptoms that seemed to be based in emotional troubles.

With no other explanation, Crichton had accepted it as psychosomatic, or "somatization of psychological stress." He had gone on with his life, and his symptoms vanished six months later as mysteriously as they had appeared.

Through reading about Crichton's background and experiencing her own ability to manifest symptoms, Allie had developed a strong belief that the mind was linked to the body in subtle, less conscious ways that her medical training hadn't prepared her to understand. If she didn't address some psychological trouble, her body would speak. If she buried anger or sadness, her lower back might spasm, causing excruciating pain, or a dull ache might develop in her abdomen.

Sometimes, Allie's psychosomatic symptoms had resolved in anticipation of an intervention. The wart on her knee had gone away before the dermatologist could freeze it off. The tightness in her back had unwound before she visited a physical therapist.

Had Allie enhanced these tendencies during the healing ceremony? Had she unlocked some latent gift?

***

Later that night, in Allie's apartment, Olivia listened as Allie told her everything that had happened. And as Allie had expected, she didn't believe a word of it.

Olivia topped off Allie's glass of wine. "So, when do you start levitating and speaking in tongues?"

Allie rolled her eyes. "I'm not possessed! I'm just saying it wasn't skill that saved our patient's life today." She bit her lip. "It was something else."

"This false modesty is unbecoming. We all know you're a rock-star surgeon."

Allie frowned and scanned the kitchen. She needed to demonstrate the power for her friend. It was the only way Olivia would be convinced.

"What's wrong?" Olivia asked.

Allie walked across the kitchen and pushed a shoulder against the refrigerator. "I just need to find—"

A centipede flitted across the kitchen floor.

Olivia shrieked, leaning back in her seat and jerking her knees up toward her chest. "It's your damn basement! It's so damp, it's a breeding ground for these devilish creatures. Call your landlord and get that taken care of." She pulled out her cell phone.

"Wait."

The centipede had darted to the center of the floor and stopped. Allie tiptoed to a cabinet and pulled out a glass. As she moved toward the insect, she flipped the glass over in her hands, and the centipede remained motionless. Lunging, Allie covered the insect with the glass.

"Gotcha!"

The bug scurried back and forth, butting up against the glass.

Olivia squinted and stuck out her tongue in revulsion. "It has so many legs. Too many legs!"

Allie grabbed a sheet of paper and slid it beneath the glass. Then she slipped her hand beneath the paper, keeping the glass sealed as she lifted it from the ground.

"I need to show you something."

Olivia quivered in her chair. "Don't come near me with that beast!" As Allie placed the paper and glass on the table, Olivia shook her head. "That's officially your side of the table."

"Watch carefully." Allie stared at the centipede and whispered, "Freeze." When the centipede stopped moving, she lifted the glass away.

"Allie!" Olivia screamed.

"Don't worry. It's dead." Allie shook the table, but the centipede didn't move.

Olivia leaned in closer. "Did you poison it?"

"No, I killed it." Allie cleared her throat. "With, well . . . my mind."

Olivia tilted her head. "I'm going to need a few more glasses of wine before—"

"Watch this." Allie covered the centipede with the glass again. "Awake."

The centipede sprung to life and flitted across the paper.

Allie explained that as hard as it might be to believe, something miraculous must have happened in Peru. Allie now had the power to give and take life with her mind.

Olivia brushed her face with her hand, clearly having trouble with the information. "Didn't I tell you not to go to the Amazon to deal with depression?"

"Nothing was working, Olivia. I was desperate. The pain was always there."

"You mean Vera was always there."

Allie nodded. "That ceremony allowed me to finally look directly at her."

"But so many things could've gone wrong—and something did indeed go wrong." Olivia scratched her chin. "Maybe the ayahuasca triggered a psychotic break."

"Come on, Olivia."

Leaving the kitchen, Olivia grabbed a massive red textbook from a shelf in the living room—the DSM-IV, a reference for psychiatric disorders.

Allie followed her. "What are you doing?"

Olivia skimmed the index, then flipped the book open to the page she was looking for. She dropped it on the coffee table with a thud.

Allie read the headline of the section she'd opened the book to. "Dissociative identity disorder?" She grimaced. "You think I have a split personality?"

"What some might consider demonic possession is considered dissociative identity disorder in some psychiatric circles."

"No, something happened in the rainforest, Olivia. I can't explain it, and it's not in that book. You saw what happened, didn't you?"

Olivia folded her arms across her chest, appearing stumped. Then she shook her head, walked to the closet, and grabbed her jacket. "Let's go."

"Go where? It's the middle of the night."

"To the hospital. We'll use all the tools at our disposal to figure out what's going on with your brain."

***

In an exam room in the neurosurgical department, Allie reclined within an

MRI machine while Olivia controlled the imaging machine from an adjacent room.

Through a speaker, her friend instructed, "Okay, Al, try to get yourself in a centipede state of mind."

Though the tight space was making her anxious, Allie closed her eyes and took a deep breath, allowing her shoulders to release some tension.

"No lesions in your brain. That's good," Olivia commented.

"Did you examine the temporal lobe?"

"First place I checked. Nothing out of the ordinary."

Allie thought for a moment. "Maybe this thing doesn't originate in the brain. Maybe it's in the mind."

"Could be the default mode network—the part that's active when we're daydreaming. Maybe you're using it to a fuller capacity?"

Allie exhaled slowly. "Maybe we're looking at this too much like scientists?"

"How else should we be looking at it?"

"What if the problem is spiritual? Like a spiritual disease?"

"You're not about to go all Deepak Chopra on me, are you?"

"This isn't a bad spirit, and maybe it isn't a structural issue or a physical disease," Allie said. "It's a sign of deeper, unresolved issues. And maybe if I bring what is troubling me into conscious awareness, this power—this pain—will go away."

Allie thought about her father and his fading memory. When she'd visited for Christmas last year, Dad had retrieved a book and shown it to her. It had been a collection of Allie's published scientific papers. He'd read every paper, yet when he showed it to her, he asked her why he was only seeing it for the first time.

It was crushing to see him so forgetful, so dependent on others to help him remember where he was and who he was. But Allie's pain went beyond her father's dementia. She was that quivering rabbit because of Vera. If only she could let go of the guilt, maybe she could rid herself of this power.

Suddenly, an announcement rang out over the hospital intercom: Code Blue.

Allie twitched.

"Come on." Olivia skipped into a jog.

Olivia led Allie down the long corridor and used her key card to access the intensive care unit. They rounded a corner, and Olivia opened a door to an exam room. Inside, Dr. Simpson stood at the patient's bedside, leading the code by shouting orders at a group of nurses.

Olivia watched as the team worked. "Should we help?"

Allie scanned the room and shook her head. "They've got everything handled."

She knew the patient's history. A year earlier, Dr. Simpson had removed a tumor from the man's brain, but the cancer had come back, and the second operation hadn't gotten everything. Most doctors, Allie included, thought the man was terminal.

Just then, Dr. Simpson shook his head. He tapped the shoulder of the nurse who was compressing the patient's chest. "Stop compressions. I'm calling it."

One by one, the doctors and nurses quietly left the room. As Dr. Simpson walked past Allie, he shrugged. "You win some; you lose some."

Visibly upset, Olivia said she wanted to stay behind to check the patient's chart before he was brought to the morgue. The room cleared out, leaving only Olivia and Allie. Olivia approached the patient's bed and motioned for Allie to join her.

Olivia raised her eyebrows. "If you really have this power, why not try—"

"No, absolutely not." Allie shook her head, not budging.

"What's the point of having this thing if you're not going to use it?"

"This isn't a game, Olivia."

"Don't you think it's significant that a doctor got this power?"

Allie chewed on her lip, conflicted. It was beyond unethical to do what Olivia was suggesting, yet her nerves were still frayed over the triggering code. She thought of Vera and how she hadn't been able to save her. Why not save this man?

"Fine," Allie said. "I'll try."

She stepped closer to the patient's bedside and wrapped her hands around the patient's lifeless fingers. She inhaled deeply and closed her eyes.

"What are you going to say?"

Allie exhaled. "Breathe."

Suddenly, the patient twitched. Then his back contorted, and he inhaled a massive gulp of air. Allie and Olivia stepped back in awe—and horror.

"Oh my God, what did I just do?"

Dr. Simpson flew through the door, mumbling to himself. "Those nurses always forget to—" He stopped short, looking surprised to see Allie and Olivia beside the patient's bed. His eyes grew wide when he saw the patient flexing his fingers. "What in God's name happened here?"

Olivia turned toward Allie and shrugged. "Magic."

Allie ran out of the room without saying anything. Olivia followed as Allie sprinted down a hallway and burst into the hospital garden.

Olivia caught up to her. "Allie, wait!"

"That was *not* okay, Olivia," Allie said, out of breath. "I just messed with something no person should mess with."

"You just gave that man the best thing a doctor could give a patient: time.

He always talked about wanting to see his daughter get married. Now he might be able to see that happen."

Allie thought about the countless ethical questions. "Where does it end? Should I bring others back? And how would I decide who to use it on?"

Allie shuddered as she considered the flip side: the ability to take life. If she had had this power the night Vera passed, she could've brought her back. It was a horrifying thought. This "power" was a burden. A curse. And she needed to get rid of it.

"I'm going back."

"I agree; let's go. My shift starts in—"

"To the rainforest," Allie clarified. "To see the shaman again."

Olivia breathed deeply. "Maybe you should just stop all this self-analysis. Why continue examining your pain? Maybe this thing will just go away."

"No, I can't just forget what happened with Vera, or push it aside. And this power—whatever it is—isn't going away. I left something unfinished in Peru. If I don't deal with it, I'll be living with this pain, and this power, for the rest of my life."

***

Back in the rainforest camp in Iquitos, Allie found Matteo sitting cross-legged near the river, smoking a cigar. Without turning, he blew out smoke and addressed Allie.

"I knew your healing journey wasn't over, but I didn't expect you to come back."

"Something happened after the ceremony, Matteo." Allie cleared her throat. "Something . . . strange . . ."

Matteo reached for a leaf and cupped his hand around a colorful caterpillar, which crawled onto his fingers. Holding his hand out to Allie, he dropped the caterpillar on her palm and nodded at her. "Go ahead."

Allie knew what Matteo was asking her to do. He knew about the power. Had he once had it himself? Either way, if the shaman were to help her, Allie knew she needed to show him she was afflicted.

Allie closed her eyes and barely breathed a word. When she opened her hand, the caterpillar was still. Then, without closing her eyes or saying anything, she willed the insect alive. The caterpillar twitched and scurried to the edge of her hand. It tumbled to the ground and disappeared beneath blades of grass.

"The spirit attached to you that night," Matteo said.

"What is it?"

"We don't know, but we've seen it attach to those who are in the most pain."

"Is it evil?"

Matteo pulled at his cigar. "It's beyond good and evil."

"I don't want it. It's more power than any person should have."

"You may be right."

"What happened during my ceremony, Matteo? You were supposed to protect me."

"I tried. I swear, I tried to protect you. But the spirit was too powerful. It was beyond my abilities."

"Or maybe my trauma was too strong for you."

"You were very vulnerable that night."

"You asked me to kill that caterpillar. That means you . . . ?"

Matteo nodded. "When I first came here, I, too, was very vulnerable to this spirit."

"But you were able to get rid of it?"

Matteo took a puff off his cigar and nodded.

"Please tell me how."

"You will have to be very brave."

Allie shivered at the thought of living with this power forever. "I'll do whatever I need to do. Go as deep as it takes. Look the trauma right in the eye."

Matteo stood and motioned for Allie to follow him. He led her onto a muddy path, and they meandered through the dense rainforest. He looked up at the sunlight poking faintly through the canopy above.

"How much of my story do you know?"

"I know you used to live in the United States. San Francisco, I think."

Matteo nodded. "You'd probably be surprised to know I was an advertising executive. I was pretty good at it, too. Had clients from all around the world. Had more money than I knew what to do with."

Allie sidestepped a large mud puddle. "What happened?"

"I was miserable. I tried so many medications and interventions to relieve my depression. But I couldn't find relief with Western medicine. Like you, I began to seek relief from nontraditional sources. I came to Peru to try ayahuasca."

"And that's when . . . the sprit attached?"

"Yes. I was very scared at first, but with my shaman's help, I was finally able to break free of it. That healing experience is part of the reason I decided to stay here."

"Why ayahuasca?"

"Because it made me feel better the first time. I didn't just have mental health problems, you see. I had thyroid disease, which made me tired all the time. I'd even had my thyroid removed, but that didn't treat the underlying disease. I was too sick to work, so I did something radical: I quit my job and came to Peru to understand the true nature of my problems. I found a healer here who has since passed. I took a workshop with him and then apprenticed for several years. I eventually realized I wasn't expressing my true self in the United States. I was a healer who hadn't found his path yet. Now, I'm on the right path."

Matteo's words resonated with Allie. She, too, felt like conventional medicine had failed her. He wasn't a doctor but a healer. Perhaps he offered a better medicine than she could.

"Ayahuasca called to me," Matteo admitted. "It has called to you as well, Allie."

"Can you teach me what you were taught?"

"Yes, but you are not ready." He placed a hand on Allie's shoulder. "Before you can heal the pain of others, you must finish healing your own."

"I'll do whatever you think I should. I can't continue living like this."

The following morning, Allie lay on a wooden table at Matteo's request, resting her head on a pillow.

"We're going to engage in a therapy known as tapping," Matteo declared.

"I don't remember seeing that in my medical textbooks."

Matteo chuckled. "It's an alternative therapy aimed at releasing buried emotions. I'll ask you to recall traumatic memories while I physically tap areas on your face that correlate with meridian points."

"What's it supposed to do?"

"It helps you become aware of unconscious emotions and release them."

Matteo asked Allie to choose a painful event to focus on for the session. She chose Vera, of course.

"I'm going to tap twelve areas twice—each of your eyebrows, the outside of each eye, under your nose, your chin, both sides of your collarbone, and each of your underarms. As I tap, I want you to say, 'Even though I have guilt surrounding Vera, I deeply and completely accept myself,' and 'Even though I couldn't save Vera that night, I deeply and completely accept myself.'"

As Matteo tapped each place he'd mentioned, Allie repeated the phrases again and again.

"Even though I couldn't save Vera, I deeply and completely accept myself."

As Matteo continued tapping, Allie closed her eyes. She was transported back to the exam room where Vera had died. Her emaciated body lay motionless in the hospital bed. A deep well of sadness rose within Allie, and she began weeping.

"Keep going, Allie. You're doing great."

Matteo's words and touch were gentle and caring, triggering a sense of calm within her. Remarkable. Allie had access to the best healthcare in the world, yet she found comfort not in any technology or cutting-edge intervention but in the nurturing care of a rainforest shaman.

After the session, Allie felt like something had been dislodged. She speculated that it wasn't the striking of the meridian points that had made her feel better but rather the speaking aloud of emotions that had been troubling her beneath conscious awareness.

As Allie left for her bungalow, Matteo encouraged her to sit with her emotions and dwell in the happiest memories she had of Vera.

Once in bed, Allie flipped through pictures on her phone. She paused on one image of her and Vera at their family's beach house on Martha's Vineyard. Vera looked healthy: a normal weight, rosy cheeks, her face bright with joy. Their arms were wrapped around their smiling parents. They hadn't known then how much pain was to come. They had taken such happy times for granted.

Over the next few days, Allie and Matteo spent time unearthing painful memories as they walked forest paths, cooked, and canoed down the river. Allie wanted to do another ayahuasca ceremony, but Matteo was adamant she wasn't ready yet. There was too much she still needed to discover within her subconscious.

At Matteo's request, Allie meditated in the morning and before bed. She knew the basic science of meditation and its potential healing benefits. A rheumatologist she knew hadn't been able to relieve the pain a certain patient had been experiencing from lupus. On a whim, the doctor had referred the patient to mindfulness-based stress reduction (MBSR), which had been scientifically proven to reduce anxiety, depression, and some pain conditions. Allie had never forgotten what the doctor had told her.

"MBSR didn't cure my patient's pain, but the pain no longer ruled their life."

After several days of meditation, Allie realized she had seldom felt calm or peaceful because of her chaotic mind. She was always preoccupied with plans or anxieties. Her mind controlled her. At any moment, a painful memory could crop up, and she'd be swept into it, lost in the reverie, a prisoner of her mental activity. After only a week of meditating twice daily, Allie felt like she was more in control of her mind, less vulnerable to letting her thoughts take her emotions for a ride.

At the healing center, Matteo led Allie through a gentle form of massage called craniosacral therapy. "It eases tension in the bones and muscles of your head, neck, back, spinal column, and the sacrum, thereby lowering stress levels."

Matteo moved around Allie's body, expertly placing his hands on the tightest areas. Tension melted from her neck and shoulders.

"Allie, you could become a healer if you wanted."

"You know I'm a doctor, right?"

Matteo nodded. "A patient comes to you with a brain tumor, and you remove it. They are fixed, but are they healed? Have you addressed why they developed the tumor?"

"The development of cancer—any disease, in fact—is multifaceted. It's often driven by one's biology—one's genes and the predispositions one may have."

"Indeed, but why are those genes expressed? What causes them to turn on? Isn't it true you could have a genetic predisposition for a certain disease but never have it manifest without the appropriate conditions?"

"That might be correct. It's often uncertain what triggers a patient's illness."

"Could it be stress? Emotional troubles? Unaddressed trauma that disrupts our mental activity and changes the chemistry of our bodies, causing the release of stress hormones that tip the balance toward disease?"

Allie couldn't argue. "I guess that's what we're doing here?"

Matteo nodded as he gently slid one hand beneath Allie's neck.

"My whole life, I've wanted to help people," Allie acknowledged. "And what you do here seems to offer a powerful path toward healing. But I can't just throw away a Harvard education and become some rainforest healer."

Matteo instructed Allie to flip onto her stomach. He pressed both hands to Allie's upper back. Her back warmed beneath the touch. "Why not?"

"I'd be a joke among my colleagues! They'd think I was delusional. That I was joining an industry full of self-help gurus and snake-oil salesmen."

"And what would you think?"

"I would most likely agree with them. But I'd also be curious to learn other methods of helping people get better."

A few days later, Allie was drinking coffee by the river as she thought of Vera: all the agony her sister had suffered over many months because of her chronic illness; the countless specialists she'd visited; the hospitalizations, exams, and surgeries she'd undergone to diagnose her or treat her disease.

A few days before she passed, Vera had asked Allie to do something. "I can't spend more time in hospitals, Allie. No more doctors. No more surgeries or procedures. Please give me something. Please help me stop this."

The request had been Vera's last resort. Death would've ended her physical and existential pain, but Allie thought there had to be another way to help. She had squeezed Vera's hand. "We'll get through this."

Days later, the hospital had called late at night to inform the family that Vera's heart had stopped. They had been able to resuscitate her, and they were calling to verify whether they should continue resuscitating her if her heart stopped again.

"Resuscitate?" Allie's father had asked, confused. "What do you mean?"

Allie had grabbed the phone from his hand. "Continue, goddamn it!"

By the time they had arrived at the hospital, Vera was a vegetable.

Allie had demanded to see Vera's chart. One detail on it continued to haunt Allie: Vera had awakened while being resuscitated. That must have been terrifying for her.

Sitting by the river, Allie pictured Vera lying dead in the hospital bed: Her slim fingers clenched into fists. Her ribs bruised and broken. A tube holding her jaw open.

A salamander on the riverbank caught Allie's attention. She narrowed her eyes and projected her pain onto the creature, aiming to kill it, but the salamander didn't die. It leaped from the muddy shore into the brown water.

Allie pointed a clenched fist at where the salamander had disappeared into the water and shouted, "Die!"

A second later, the salamander bobbed to the surface, floating on its back.

Later that evening, Allie told Matteo she'd experienced a delay in her "power."

"That's a good sign. You're opening up, becoming less emotionally blocked. I believe the spirit can only hold onto pain."

"And without the pain, it might have to move on?"

"That's the idea."

The following morning, Matteo led Allie through an analysis of her dreams, which she'd been recording in a notebook for weeks. They were searching for possible connections to her waking life.

"When you start picking apart your dreams, your mind shies away from it. If you stick with it long enough, your mind will submit and reveal its secrets."

To start, Allie told Matteo about a reoccurring dream that terrified her. "I'm an astronaut moving along the side of a space station with a colleague. Suddenly, the other astronaut becomes untethered and starts floating away."

"What happens then?"

"I'm still attached to the station by a cable, so I push toward them. When I get close, I reach my arms toward their outstretched hand. I get so close, but they're always just out of reach."

"Do you know this other astronaut?"

"I can never see their face."

"What do you think you want in this dream?"

Allie thought about it. "I want to grab the astronaut's hand."

"Keep exploring the dream for meaning."

As Allie took her morning walk the next day, she felt lighter.

Referring to Hippocrates's belief that walking was the best medicine, Matteo had encouraged her to establish a walking routine. He urged her to reflect and deliberate problems as she walked. Though exercise had many health benefits, such as lifting one's mood, Allie had never previously practiced the deliberate rumination Matteo had prescribed. Now, she strolled the rainforest each morning, deep in thought.

During that morning's walk, she came across a snake lying dead on the path and slowed to a halt. She pointed a finger at the snake's lifeless body. "Slither." When the snake didn't move, Allie repeated the word, but again, nothing happened.

Frustrated, Allie shouted, "Slither!"

The snake twitched to life and slithered across the forest floor.

Days later, Allie underwent another session of craniosacral therapy.

"Your energy is much calmer than it was during our first session. When we first met, your aura was only around your head. Now, it surrounds your entire body and radiates outward."

Allie didn't know whether to attribute it to the treatments, the meditation, the journaling, the dream analyses, or the walking, but Matteo was right. She'd never felt more grounded.

Allie lay face down, and Matteo pressed lightly against her lower back.

"I've been thinking about depression," Allie whispered.

"How so?"

"In the West, depression is just a chemical imbalance. And sure, certain chemicals are imbalanced when someone is in a depressive state, but that's a result, not the cause. Depression is a signal—an alarm bell—telling us something needs to change."

Matteo instructed Allie to flip onto her back.

"My depression was a teacher," Matteo agreed. "It taught me I was ignoring something I desperately needed to address."

When the session ended, Matteo kept his hand beneath Allie's head. He smiled. "I think you're ready."

"Ready for what?"

"Another ayahuasca ceremony. But this time, it'll be different."

"How so?"

"This time, you'll learn how to prepare the ayahuasca."

Allie was reading in her room later when her phone rang. The caller ID showed it was her father. She hesitated. Would he be lucid? Would he remember the anger he had toward her for not saving Vera?

Allie swung her legs over the edge of the bed and answered. "Dad?"

"Allie, hi." His voice was upbeat, almost cheery. "How are you?"

"Hi, Dad, I'm fine. Is everything okay?"

"Where are you?"

"I'm traveling."

"Please come home, Allie."

"I can't yet, Dad. There's still something I need to do."

"Well, please try to come home for Christmas, will you? It makes me happy to see you and Vera together underneath the same roof."

Allie's stomach dropped. There was so much she wanted to say, but she couldn't find the words. She wanted to remind him Vera was gone. She wanted to tell him she was sorry she hadn't been able to save her that night. She wanted her father to say Vera's death wasn't her fault and that she didn't need to carry the guilt any longer.

A bell chimed, indicating it was dinnertime. "Dad, I need to go. But I'll come home for Christmas dinner, okay?"

"That sounds great, Al. Please take care of yourself."

As Allie ended the call, she burst into tears. She ran out of the bungalow toward the river. Once she reached the shore, she screamed as loud as she could.

Between sobs, the despair turned to anger. She scanned the water and spotted what looked to be a school of piranhas just below the surface. Squinting, she pointed at the fish. "Float."

She searched the water's surface for activity. Nothing.

"Float!" she yelled. "Float! Float! Float!"

Still nothing. Had she lost her powers?

Footsteps approached from behind her, and Allie spun around to see Matteo, tears in his eyes. He walked over and wrapped his arms around her.

"Tell me what's wrong, Allie."

"I don't know!" Allie cried out. "I'm in so much pain. I lost my sister. And now, I'm slowly losing my dad."

"If your dad were here, what would you wish he could say to you?"

"That I did my best? I don't know. That he's not mad at me. That even though I couldn't save Vera, he still loves me. That everything's going to be okay."

Lost in the fog of dementia and still believing Vera was alive, her dad would never be able to say those things, but it felt good to say them aloud. If she couldn't get absolution from her dad, she'd have to get what she needed from herself.

Matteo rubbed Allie's back. "It may sound cheesy, Allie, but it's not about other people forgiving you; it's about you forgiving yourself. And if you can't get there, at least come to terms with there being nothing more you could have done."

According to something Matteo had once told Allie, his shaman had taught him that the shaman's healing practice wasn't just about using plants to promote healing through inward exploration. The most powerful healing practices involved an outward, social journey. Connecting with others was just as healing as ayahuasca.

And that's what Matteo had given Allie. He'd spent the last few weeks listening to Allie and letting her story come alive in his mind so she didn't feel so alone with her pain. With him, she felt seen.

In Matteo's embrace, Allie finally realized why Vera had been so angry with her in the hospital. Vera hadn't wanted to be poked and prodded anymore. She'd wanted to go peacefully and on her own terms. But Allie had kept forcing specialists and interventions on her sister.

Why?

Allie hadn't been able to help herself! She was a doctor with a mandate to help the sick. If there was a problem, she fixed it. If someone had a brain tumor, she took it out. If her sister were sick, she'd find a way to help her. Anything short of solving the problem was a medical failure. A failure of the doctor.

Allie's failure.

"I didn't listen to her!" Allie shouted. "She didn't need another doctor. She just needed me to let go. But I couldn't. I was always trying to save her. I watched her waste away. And now I'm watching my dad waste away too. I couldn't do anything for Vera, and I can't do anything for him."

Matteo stepped back and looked into Allie's eyes. "Sometimes, there isn't anything we can do, Allie. When there's nothing we can do, we have to let go."

"I couldn't let go." Tears welled in her eyes. "I still can't."

"It's the hardest thing to accept, but some things in life are incomprehensible. Some things remain a mystery no matter how hard we try to figure them out."

Allie wiped her eyes and nodded. She knew Matteo was right.

"The hardest thing for me to accept is that some things are beyond my control," Allie said. "Beyond the limits of medical science. Beyond my limits. As a physician. As a sister. As a daughter."

Behind her, Allie just made out the *glub* of something breaking the surface of the water. Then a frenzied splashing erupted, and she knew the piranhas were feasting.

***

Matteo swung a machete at the dense vegetation ahead of them to clear a path. Allie followed, carrying a ladder in one hand.

She wiped sweat from her forehead. "How long until we get there?"

"It's not much farther."

"Do I really need to learn how to make ayahuasca?"

"Think of it as one more tool in your doctor's bag."

Finally pausing in a clearing, Matteo examined a tall tree with green leaves and took the ladder from Allie. He stood the ladder against the tree.

"Two plants are needed to make the ayahuasca brew: the *chacruna* leaf, which contains the natural psychedelic—DMT, and the ayahuasca vine, which protects the DMT from being metabolized before it can activate."

Allie held the base of the ladder as Matteo climbed and used his machete to hack at the tree's branches.

Hours later, he showed Allie how to combine the leaves and vines in a large pot heating over a fire. When the brew was ready, Matteo handed her a ladle, which she used to fill her cup with the brown liquid. Then he led her to the healing center, where she sat on a cushion, crossing one leg beneath the other.

When Matteo nodded at Allie, she took a deep breath and gulped down the bitter liquid. He rested a hand on her shoulder. "Tonight, go to Vera."

For the first twenty minutes, Allie felt relaxed, like she was floating lazily on her back in a quiet pond. Then she groaned as the world began to crumble beneath her. Nausea turned her stomach, and she tasted bile. Retching, she grabbed the bucket next to her and vomited into it. She rocked back and forth as reality swirled.

"Don't fight," Matteo whispered. "Surrender. Go toward the pain."

Matteo helped her stand and led her to a yoga mat so she could lie on her back. As soon as she was horizontal, the ayahuasca slammed into Allie with the force of a hurricane.

The night Vera had asked her to help her die came rushing back.

Vera's eyes were sunken and dark with hopelessness. "Help me, Allie, please. If you love me, help me end this."

Allie couldn't meet her eyes. "Vera . . . I can't . . ."

Vera exploded in anger. "You can't help?" She pointed to the door. "Fine! Get out of here and don't ever come back."

Another wave of nausea overwhelmed Allie, and she vomited into the bucket. The scent of smoke blew over her, and Matteo began singing, filling the healing center with his deep voice.

Allie floated over the intensive care room. Doctors and nurses were resuscitating Vera. One doctor stood over her, compressing her chest with both hands. Another charged a defibrillator, called "Clear," and once the others had stood back, delivered a shock to restart her heart. The team watched the EKG machine, but the rhythm had flatlined.

Allie threw up again. Matteo sang louder.

Allie stood before the doctor who had told her they'd been able to resuscitate Vera, but she no longer had any brain function.

"I want to see her," she pleaded. "I don't want her to be alone in there. Please, I just want to hold her hand."

Allie emptied her stomach again.

Matteo's singing faltered. "Go to Vera, Allie."

Allie was attached to the space station from the dream she hadn't been able to escape since Vera's death—a dream that felt like it had been surgically implanted in her brain. Allie was tethered to the space station while the other astronaut floated, unattached, a few hundred feet away in the inky-black sky above Earth.

Vera's voice sounded in her headset. "I'm floating away, Allie."

"Vera!"

Allie tugged on the cable to make sure it was secure, and then she pushed off in Vera's direction. She was only a foot from Vera's outstretched hand when her cord pulled taut.

"No, no!" Allie reached with all her might. "Vera, I'm sorry. I can't reach you."

Vera smiled through the visor. "It's okay, Allie."

"I tried everything! But I just made it worse." Allie sobbed. "Maybe if I weren't your sister, you'd still be alive."

"You go too far, Allie. So much was beyond your control."

Anger and sadness welled up within Allie, and she decided to make one last effort. She unclipped herself from her cable.

"What are you doing, Al?"

"I can't let you go again!"

Allie held the end of the cable with one hand and reached toward Vera with her other. Their hands touched at last, and Allie wrapped her fingers around Vera's wrist. They were face-to-face. The glass of their visors touched.

Vera held Allie's gaze. "You have to let me go."

Allie shook her head. "No! I'm never letting you go."

"What happened wasn't anyone's fault. Not the doctors', not the hospital's, and certainly not yours."

Back in the healing center, Allie lay flat on the mat. Tears streamed down her face.

To her sister, Allie shouted, "I'm sorry, Vera. I'm so, so sorry!"

Vera smiled. Always edgy, Vera almost never smiled that way. She looked so sweet, like a child. Like someone forgiving a sister.

"You've got to let me go now."

It was what everyone had been saying all along. Allie needed to accept that in life, some things happened that defied explanation. She needed to let go of the guilt she'd clung to since Vera's death. She could let her go and still love her.

Allie mustered a nod within her helmet. "I love you, Vera."

"Love you too, Sis. Do something for me, Allie?"

Allie sniffled. "Anything."

"So many people suffer in this world. You can help them heal."

"I will." Allie knew it was her destiny to practice a new kind of medicine.

Over Vera's shoulder, Allie watched a gigantic, yellow sun rise, but it didn't sting her eyes to look at. Allie exhaled heavily and opened her hand, releasing her sister. Vera smiled softly as she floated away.

A beam of light pulsed from Allie's chest, aimed at Vera. Vera opened her arms, and the beam entered her chest, merging with her body.

Time seemed to accelerate as Vera floated away from Allie. Faster and faster, she navigated toward the sun. Then there was a tiny splash of orange as Vera fell into the bright star and vanished.

In the healing center, Allie opened her eyes.

An Affable Man

For his annual performance review, Sebastian sat in a cramped office across a desk from his boss, the director of marketing. She told him he was a valued employee and one of the department's highest performers. "You should apply for the open marketing manager position," she said.

Sebastian respectfully declined. "I like staying behind the scenes, managing the company's website." Though he didn't admit it, Sebastian had no intention of climbing the ladder within the organization. He felt that he was paid reasonably enough. Plus, managing people sounded like a headache. Sebastian "worked to live," and he used his personal time to hang out with friends and travel, most recently to the Galápagos Islands.

By all accounts, the review was going great. It was Friday afternoon, and Sebastian couldn't wait to start his weekend with friends. Then his boss reiterated how much his colleagues enjoyed working with him. "You're such an affable guy."

Sebastian knew the word *affable* was intended as a compliment, but it didn't sit well with him. With only a vague idea of the word's meaning, he looked up the definition after the meeting: "friendly, good-natured, easy to talk to."

Why did that word irk him so much? He liked being known as a nice guy around the office, but to him, *affable* sounded pathetic. It meant he was passive, docile, housebroken. If he were honest with himself, though, that's exactly what a decade of working in a modern office had made him: a people-pleasing company man who always colored within the lines.

After work, Sebastian and his friends went out for beers at their favorite bar. While his friends talked, Sebastian was quiet, lost in thought. He realized that he had all the trappings that came with a white-collar job: a studio apartment downtown and a BMW he liked driving fast. But his soul was restless. At thirty-five years old, he'd realized that his job wasn't giving meaning to his life, and yet he spent more time at work than anywhere else.

"What's up with you, Sebastian?" a friend asked.

"Do you ever fantasize about draining your savings account and leaving your stupid life behind?" Sebastian asked.

Everyone at the table turned to confirm whether Sebastian was being serious. He took a sip of beer and began talking excitedly.

"I've been reading about people who shook up their routines and escaped the rat race," he said. "There's a primary care doctor who closed his practice, bought an RV, and lived on the road with his family. A man who ditched his corporate job and walked the earth for seventeen years without talking to another soul. And a New York City bus driver who blew through all his stops one day and drove to

Florida, becoming a folk hero in the city."

These stories had inspired Sebastian, and he fantasized about leaving it all behind someday. He'd hop on a plane to anywhere, or he'd walk to the end of his driveway, then to the edge of town, and continue on without a plan or destination in mind.

Having worked in corporate America for over a decade, Sebastian always wondered why his coworkers didn't feel a similar need to escape. Why wasn't there more despair in modern office settings? It seemed so absurd that he and his coworkers traveled to the same building every day, sat in the same chairs, tapped keys on their keyboards, rearranged symbols within computer software, and never objected to such monotony. No one rebelled against their lack of freedom. Instead, most of his coworkers expressed gratitude for having the security of salary and health insurance that their work provided.

Such a work life might be justified if people enjoyed the work they did every day, but most of his coworkers had little enthusiasm for their jobs. No one jumped for joy upon entering the office each morning. In fact, Sebastian didn't know one colleague who found their work meaningful.

Why doesn't anyone rebel against such conditions?

"We aren't in prison," Sebastian said to his friends. "At any moment, we could stand up from our desks, walk away, and never return. We all have that choice. Why don't we? Why don't I?"

It wasn't complicated, his friends explained. They all needed a salary to support life's necessities, and even if they wanted to go without health insurance, they were legally obligated to have it.

"The truth?" Sebastian said. "I have no clue what I'd do if I quit my job and struck off on my own."

People needed things to do, Sebastian explained, and a job provided structure and a ready-made purpose. What would he do without the routine and responsibilities his job offered? Such an uncertain path was terrifying. His job wasn't a constant source of joy, but at least it gave him a way to spend his days. It limited how he could use his freedom. Without it, wouldn't he lose his way?

Plus, without work, he'd be bored, and boredom bred trouble. He'd seen bored coworkers fill up their time with gossip, just to make life more interesting. The routine also appealed to Sebastian because it was common. Everyone he knew worked for American corporations. If Sebastian dropped out of society, what would people think? What would he think of himself?

Sebastian was ruminating on these issues when his friend suggested he take a break from work. "You know, a vacation." A long weekend somewhere warm to escape the New England winter. It sounded like a good idea to Sebastian. He'd find a beach, bake in the sun, and forget his existential worries.

That night, he bought a plane ticket to San Diego, California, and a month later, he was checking into a hotel and searching online for things to do. He'd visited California once as a child, but he'd never seen Cedar Springs, a marine zoological park. It sounded like a good enough idea.

Within fifteen minutes of walking into the theme park, Sebastian was overstimulated and annoyed. Shouting kids ran in all directions while their parents tried to corral them. He decided to give up and leave early when he saw a sign: *Experience the Magical World of Killer Whales.*

Intrigued, Sebastian walked to Watson Park. A massive water tank stood before rows of seats filled with onlookers. As he watched, a killer whale broke the surface and rose out of the water. The whale was the size of a pickup truck and gorgeous. Its sleek black skin glistened in the hot sun. Sebastian's jaw dropped in awe as he noticed a man in a wet suit balancing on the tip of the whale's nose. As the whale reached its peak of maybe fifteen feet, the man hopped off its nose and ducked into a forward roll. He flipped twice and sliced through the water in a perfect dive. The crowd erupted with cheers and applause.

The scene compelled Sebastian to explore Watson Park and try to learn more about this majestic creature. On the side of the tank, a plaque explained that Watson was a thirty-nine-year-old male orca whale, or *Orcinus orca,* colloquially known as a killer whale. Sebastian walked into an exhibition hall. He read a few panels, learning that Watson was more than twenty feet long and weighed over ten thousand pounds.

Leaving the area, Sebastian spotted a crowd standing in front of a glass panel that offered a look into Watson's tank. He walked to the window and found a spot to peer into the tank. He came in close to the glass, looking for movement. All of a sudden, the killer whale glided past.

"What's wrong with Watson's fin?" a child asked, pointing to the whale's dorsal fin, which was flopped over.

The whale slowed his glide, and Sebastian stepped closer. He locked eyes with the beast. As he stared into Watson's eye, he felt a presence looking back. This animal had a wild soul, but he was also a thinking creature, and Sebastian even sensed an emotional life. Yet Watson's eye looked drained—as close to lifeless as possible while still having a heartbeat. He wondered if the whale had forgotten the ocean's vastness. Did he remember the exhilaration of diving deep to the ocean floor on a mighty breath? Maybe he longed to return but realized he'd never again have the freedom it once had. Sebastian saw his reflection in the glass as if he were looking in a mirror. His eyes were the same as Watson's: lost and spiritless.

Had Sebastian not met Watson, he never would've returned to Cedar

Springs the next day. A bunch of wide-eyed tourists pointing and shouting at incarcerated sea creatures wasn't his idea of fun. Reading a paperback thriller on the beach sounded a lot better. But something about Watson intrigued him.

Standing at the glass the next day, Sebastian searched for Watson. After a few minutes, the killer whale swam past. As he watched, Sebastian wondered again about the animal's inner life. Watson seemed docile, broken. As he watched Watson twist through the water, Sebastian compared himself to the killer whale and realized they differed in one very meaningful way: Sebastian hadn't been snatched from his home and forced to live in captivity. Sebastian could leave the office every day. If he wanted, he could leave it behind forever. He didn't want to, but at least he had that choice. Watson didn't.

"This one's nuts," a man's voice announced from behind him. The man wore a tight-fitting swimsuit and a name tag that read Landon.

Sebastian shook his head. "Nuts?"

"Yeah, crazy, bananas, cuckoo."

"How so?" Sebastian asked.

"He bit my foot during training yesterday and dragged me to the bottom of the pool." He glared at Watson through the glass. "I probably would've drowned if I hadn't poked him in the eye."

It seemed unfortunate that Watson had been hurt, but Sebastian guessed it had been the trainer's last resort. "What's wrong with him?"

"Orcas can get funky in captivity. Watson's been acting up a lot: biting trainers, ramming the glass, not to mention that little stunt he pulled yesterday."

Sebastian thought he'd probably be agitated too if he were confined to a concrete cell and forced to twirl, jump, and flip for park-goers his whole life. "Maybe he just needs more space?"

Landon ran a hand through his blond hair. "I think about that sometimes."

"Have you ever considered taking him back to the ocean?" Sebastian asked.

"I once asked my boss if we should just put Watson back."

"What'd they say?" Sebastian asked.

Just then, a short woman shuffled into the area, wearing a Cedar Springs polo, white shorts, and foam shoes. Her name tag read Allison. "I told him he was paid to entertain, not make executive decisions." She glared at Landon. "How many times have I told you to leave the visitors alone?"

Landon stepped back and looked at the floor.

"Show starts in ten minutes, Landon. You better bring your A game today." Allison huffed. "Otherwise, you'll be giving tours in the aquarium again."

"Got to go." Landon flashed Sebastian a nervous smile and jogged away.

"Sorry if our trainer was bothering you, sir," Allison said.

"Oh no, of course not," Sebastian said. "It was nice to learn more about Watson."

Allison had turned to walk away when Sebastian cleared his throat. "Um, ma'am, is it really true that orcas can go crazy in captivity?"

Allison looked around to see if anyone was watching. "It's not *not* true."

Interesting way of putting it. Sebastian could see that Allison was less conflicted about Watson's neurotic behavior than Landon. It was clear why Landon had had trouble summoning the courage to stand up to her.

"Watson has two strikes," Allison said. "One more, and we'll have to put him down."

Sebastian squinted. "Down?"

She made a gun with her hand and then a *bang* sound.

Sebastian thought it was odd that Allison had been so open about euthanizing Watson. Once he returned to his hotel, Sebastian read online about killer whales in captivity. One news report said that Cedar Springs only euthanized killer whales for health reasons, not for behavior. Would Cedar Springs euthanize Watson for his behavior and blame it on his health?

Sebastian read for hours and learned that orcas were friendly and seldom harmed humans in the wild; in fact, orcas had never killed or intentionally hurt a human in the wild. But they were renowned for handling confinement with difficulty, and many displayed neurotic symptoms in places like Cedar Springs. The phenomenon of a collapsed dorsal fin only happened in one percent of killer whales in the wild.

In captivity, some agitated orcas had eaten trainers' arms or even killed and eaten them. Various organizations had sued Cedar Springs over such incidents, arguing that performing with orcas was too dangerous and should be stopped. The incidents had created a public-relations nightmare for the park. PR professionals at Cedar Springs twisted facts and often blamed trainers when such incidents happened, avoiding discussions of how the animals' conditions had caused the behavior.

This discovery led Sebastian to learn about Watson's living conditions. When the whale wasn't training or performing, he was housed in a pool with a metal floor and concrete walls that was far too small for comfort. At night, the lights were turned off, and Watson was kept in total blackness.

Sebastian's reading dredged up troubling memories that had taken place within his company. His organization was in the business of breeding and selling research animals—such as rats, mice, pigs, monkeys, and even dogs—to academic labs and the pharmaceutical industry. Like most employees, Sebastian had convinced himself that science and medicine wouldn't have created lifesaving treatments for diseases had they not been tested on animals first. However, it still bugged him that they were breeding millions of animals a year to essentially act as lab equipment. At lunch, he would often bring up how he sometimes had trouble with the role the company played in the world.

A few weeks before, a virus had infected a colony of ten thousand mice. Since the mice were no longer usable for research, they were euthanized. Just like that, ten thousand mice, dead. He'd tried to talk about the event with his boss, but she had only given him an amused look.

"You're not going soft on me, are you, Sebastian?"

Had she thought he was starting to identify with the animal activists who protested outside the company's entrance? The "crazies," as she called them, who carried signs and called employees evil as they drove into work.

That night, Sebastian tried to sleep, but his mind raced. He thought about how hard he worked for the company, often ten hours a day, but did any of his work fixing glitches on the website really matter? What did all that activity add up to? Sebastian wasn't ambitious, but he'd always wanted to be a part of something bigger than himself.

Recently, he'd read about a revolution in a foreign country. In a strange way, he envied the oppressed citizens. They had resisted their authoritarian government and toppled a dictatorship by unseating a tyrant.

Meeting Watson had brought up feelings Sebastian had been avoiding for years. He, too, was trapped in his environment. He, too, had become nervous and high-strung. His desk was located in the center of an open-office environment. With his back facing half the office's activity, he often flinched when someone passed by because he couldn't see them walking toward him. He was often startled by his boss slamming the door when she wanted privacy.

In a constant state of low-level stress, he had trouble falling asleep and would sometimes wake up gasping in panic. The antidepressant he swallowed each morning seemed to keep the anxiety at bay, but how long could his body and mind put up with the stress? Surely, he'd relax if he left the dreadful open-office environment and moved out of the city, maybe to a wooded area outside of Boston. Yet he'd convinced himself the action was in the city. He was closer to opportunity, and everyone was at the top of their game, making him better, so he chose to stay.

Sebastian hadn't planned to go back to Cedar Springs the next day. He had fallen asleep thinking he'd explore San Diego, maybe try a restaurant or visit the beach. But he was drawn back to the park, this time to see Watson perform.

The website had advertised a show starting in ten minutes, but the entrance to the stadium was blocked. There was no one inside, not even the trainers. Confused, Sebastian walked around the stadium, hoping to see Watson, but the tank was empty. He thought back to his conversation with Allison. Had Watson gotten his third strike?

Sebastian jogged to the middle of the park and scanned the crowd for someone of authority. He ran to a hut with a *Trainer's Den* sign and knocked on the door.

Allison flung open the door, holding a small, white box of Chinese food. "No visitors allowed in the trainer's area!"

"Sorry to disturb you, but I was wondering if Watson had a show today. Your website says—"

"Show's canceled," Allison interrupted. "Try the giant sea turtles." She reached for the door, but Sebastian stepped closer, stopping her from shutting it.

"If I may ask, where's Watson?"

Allison exhaled heavily. "You one of those animal rights freaks? You think every animal should be treated like a child of God, hmm?" She set her food on a table. "Watson has been endangering our staff and other orcas for years. But he was removed from circulation because of his health problems, not for almost having Landon for lunch."

"What health problems?"

"I'm under no obligation to tell you that." Allison scowled. "Look, it wasn't my call to take Watson out of circulation."

"What does being removed from circulation mean?"

Allison squinted. "Hey, buddy, I only get an hour away from these little snots called children, so—"

Sebastian raised his hands, preparing to back off, but then he steeled himself and squinted his eyes. "Where are you taking him?"

Allison shook her head in disbelief. "He'll be put to sleep at a facility out of state." She jerked her chin toward one exit. "Landon's loading the whale onto the truck now."

Sebastian's eyes widened. "Really? Thank you. Sorry to bother!"

Sebastian sprinted toward the exit, not sure what his plan was. Did he want to say goodbye? Was it foolish to think he'd created a bond with the orca? Or maybe all those mice being killed had upset him enough that he wanted to do something. But what? He was going to protect an animal he'd met in an aquarium two days before?

His heart pounded. It was an exhilaration he hadn't felt since he visited the Galápagos Islands. It had been so exciting to see all those incredible animals in their natural environment. It made him believe that Mother Nature was an artist. If reincarnation had existed, he would probably come back as a sea creature, like one of the dolphins that had swum around his boat, doing what they pleased.

Anger filled him as he considered that Watson had been free until he was taken from the ocean against his will. And now, because he'd had a few tantrums, he was to be killed? Sebastian's hands balled into fists as he reached the edge of the park.

Sebastian walked through a door that led to a private parking lot and heard the rumbling of a vehicle's engine. He ducked behind a wall and saw Landon and another Cedar Springs employee walking around an enormous truck carrying a green tank. Landon tugged on straps to make sure the tank was secured.

"All right, let's get this show on the road." Landon slapped the tank with one hand. "Time for Watson to meet his maker." He hopped into the driver's seat of the truck.

Sebastian was horrified by how casually Landon talked about the murder of such a beautiful animal. He thought about how often he or a coworker suffered an indignity at work and no one said or did anything. Even if he witnessed cruelty among his coworkers, he never dared to speak up. *Don't rock the boat*, he'd always thought. Not today.

Suddenly, a voice called over the loudspeaker, "Dear visitors, we'd like to invite you to the west side of the park to watch the dolphin performance in fifteen minutes."

Sebastian had an idea. He ran back into the park, toward the ticket building at the front entrance, thinking that was where the loudspeaker controls might be. Looking through the window of a ticket booth, he saw a man with a microphone sitting next to a speaker.

The man stood up and walked toward an exit. "I'm going to have a smoke." Sebastian circled the building and pressed his back against the wall beside the door. The door opened, and the man emerged. Just before the door closed, Sebastian slipped through and moved toward the front.

The ticket agent was assisting a woman with two kids. "I'd like one adult and two children's tickets," she requested.

Sebastian didn't think. He grabbed the microphone, pressed a button at the base, and brought the microphone to his mouth. "Landon, please report to the trainer's hut at once. Landon, please report to the trainer's hut. Thank you."

His voice reverberated throughout the park. The ticket agent glanced over her shoulder curiously and then quickly spun around, shouting for Sebastian to stop. Sebastian dropped the microphone, ran to the exit, and burst through the back door, passing the smoking employee.

As Sebastian jogged toward Watson, Landon was walking toward him, shaking his head. "If this cuts into my surfing time, I'm going to be pissed."

Sebastian needed some luck now. He hoped Landon was so hurried, he'd left the keys in the truck. In the parking lot, another employee was fiddling with something at the rear of the truck. Sebastian opened the driver's door and stepped into the big machine. The key was still in the ignition. Closing the door, he put his hands on the wheel.

Wait. What am I doing? Stealing a truck from Cedar Springs? He'd never even violated a traffic law, much less committed a felony. Even if he somehow got out of the park, where would he even go?

"Stop thinking," he told himself. This was the right thing to do. He started the engine, put the truck in gear, and drove toward the main gate. In the side mirror, Sebastian could see staff members scampering after him.

When Sebastian reached the gate, it opened without any trouble. He waved at the guard in the security hut, who stared, perplexed, as he passed. On the road, Sebastian could hear Watson squealing in high-pitched tones. The sloshing water in the tank rocked the truck from side to side. Adrenaline surged through Sebastian's body as he drove along the California coast. For the first time in his life, he was standing up for something. No longer was he that pathetic, "affable" man his boss had admired. Now he was an outlaw. He'd spend time in jail, but how much worse could it be than the prison of his open office?

Maybe it was better to burn out in an exciting act of justice than to fade out in monotony. And maybe, just maybe, he would help Watson get back home.

Spotting a sign for a beach, Sebastian prepared to turn, until he noticed the line at the gate was backed up. He'd never get his truck through, so he kept driving. A few minutes later, he watched a pickup hauling a motorboat turn onto a road leading to a marina. Sebastian followed and slowed to watch it enter the marina.

When he realized there were no security checks, he put the truck in park and watched the driver spin the pickup around and back it down a concrete ramp into the ocean. When the boat met the water, a man jumped into knee-high water and unlatched it. The truck moved forward, and the boat slipped off the back, bobbing in the water.

Was there enough room for Sebastian's truck? It looked possible, so he entered the marina and turned the truck around.

Just as Sebastian started backing the truck up, an employee burst out of a building, shouting and flapping his hands. "Are you crazy? That truck's way too big to be in here!"

Ignoring the man, Sebastian continued backing toward the ramp. Had he lost his mind? Maybe going crazy was an appropriate response to knowing that an intelligent creature like Watson was going to be killed. How many people did nothing when they encountered injustice? More than organizing a book club or writing a letter to the editor of their local newspaper, anyway.

Maybe Watson needed a crazy person.

Why did it usually take a radical—a criminal, sometimes—to wake people up to what was so obviously wrong? Watson had been a puppet in the games people played for their amusement. If Sebastian's actions woke people up to that fact, then maybe it was worth going to jail.

Sebastian used the truck's side mirrors to make sure the wheels were aligned with the ramp. Slowly, the truck backed down the concrete, and the back of the tank dipped into the water. When half the tank was submerged, Sebastian parked and leaped into the water.

Behind him, the marina employee was hysterical. "I called the cops!"

Sebastian didn't respond. Instead, he climbed the side and hovered over a hatch at the top of the tank. He spun the latch until the hatch cracked open. Through the crack, Sebastian saw Watson writhing, sloshing water, and making high-pitched squeals. Sebastian looked into Watson's frightened eye, reached a hand into the tank, and stroked the whale's head. Tears welled up in Sebastian's eyes.

"I don't know what I'm doing, Watson. I'm in so much trouble. When this tank goes under, I just need you to swim like hell, okay?"

Sebastian heard sirens in the distance. Knowing he didn't have much time, he hopped off the tank, reached the door, and climbed into the driver's seat. The parking lot filled with police cars. Breathing heavily, Sebastian put the truck in gear and backed it farther into the water.

A dozen or so police officers leaped from their vehicles, guns pointed.

When the tank was submerged, he saw a button labeled *Back hatch*. He was reaching down to press it when he heard a voice through a loudspeaker.

"This is the San Diego Police Department. Stop what you're doing immediately. Shut down the engine, put the keys on the dashboard, and step away from the vehicle."

Sebastian pressed the button and heard a loud whir as the back hatch opened. He looked for Watson through the back window, but he saw nothing. Another voice blared through the loudspeaker.

"Sebastian, this is Landon. I told the cops we'd met at the park, and they let me speak to you. Look, man, I get what you're going through—I went through something like it too—but you've made your point, so let's all take a breath, okay?"

Landon held out his palms as he approached the truck. Sebastian kept scanning the water. No Watson. Had the whale been in captivity for so long, it now preferred a cage?

Landon walked into the water until it was up to his knees. He grinned. "Even I don't get crowds this big."

"C'mon, Watson," Sebastian whispered.

"We can't just let the whale swim away," Landon said.

The cops inched forward as Sebastian searched the water for movement.

Just then, a jet of water shot into the air. Sebastian threw his hands up. "Watson!" Behind him, the cops froze in place and lowered their guns. Landon shook his head in disbelief.

As Sebastian watched Watson, the reality of what he'd done sunk in. He wasn't excited about seeing the inside of a prison cell, but maybe it would offer a respite from the insanity of corporate America. Sure, he'd lose his physical freedom, but his mind could still travel.

In prison, he'd have time to think of a new career that didn't deaden his soul. No way would he return to his current job when he got out. Sebastian had traded so many hours of his life for a paycheck without ever asking whether it was a fair deal. If he rejoined the workforce, he'd only do so if he found meaning in the work. He just couldn't tolerate the idea of giving over the better part of his waking hours if the time wasn't well spent.

Maybe he'd go back to the Galápagos Islands and become a naturalist guide. Like the guides he'd met, he'd swim with sharks, orcas, and sea lions. He'd move from island to island on sailing boats. He was no doubt minutes away from capture, yet the vision filled him with hope.

Sebastian opened the door and jumped into the water. The cops raised their guns, but Sebastian waded through the water until it was up to his waist. Landon followed until they stood next to each other.

"Is it true that orcas can't survive without a pod?" Sebastian asked.

Landon nodded. "But pods often accept lone orcas. Watson'll find a family."

Sebastian turned to Landon. "Doesn't Cedar Springs put a tracking device on these animals?"

Landon nodded. "Every orca's got one. It's protocol."

Sebastian suddenly felt anxious for Watson and wished the whale would dive deep and disappear. Landon reached into his pocket and pulled out a device about the size of a tack.

"Before we loaded Watson onto the truck, I removed his tracking device. *Also* protocol." Landon grinned and tossed the device into the ocean.

Just then, Watson's dorsal fin pointed toward Sebastian and Landon. The orca came closer, and Landon backed away in fear. Watson turned at a sharp angle and glided past the two men. As it glided past, Sebastian reached out a hand and let it slide along the whale's smooth skin. When Sebastian's hand reached Watson's tail, the whale turned toward the horizon and sprayed water from its blowhole. Then it dipped below the surface, leaving a swirl of water behind.

With his eyes trained on the horizon, Sebastian felt the click of metal handcuffs tightening around his wrists, and he smiled.

The Good Parent

Weston, Massachusetts

Sitting on the couch in her living room, Eleanor reads a letter from her daughter. It's been ten months since she last saw her, and apparently, Kate has been living at a retreat in Portland, Maine, the entire time. It didn't surprise Eleanor when the twenty-nine-year-old left without a goodbye. It was just another act of defiance from her "pathologically rebellious" daughter.

"It's not exactly a clinical diagnosis," the psychiatrist had told Eleanor at McLean Hospital. "But Kate tried to organize a coup within the psych ward."

"She doesn't much care for authority," Eleanor had agreed.

"She tried to plan an escape with the other patients," the psychiatrist had added. "She went on a campaign to convince everyone that the doctors were feeding them lies about their childhoods, that we were planting false memories in their minds."

Eleanor sets Kate's letter down and turns on the television, trying to distract herself with the nightly news. She can't stop wondering, though, where she went wrong as a parent. She gave Kate the best tutors, enrolled her in the most prestigious schools, rewritten essays for her. Kate is her firstborn. Her heart. The family's pride. She was supposed to be an academic, a writer, yet she became the neighborhood dog walker.

Eleanor was also troubled by her daughter's "relationship" with an egotistical businessman named Patrick. When Kate accidentally left her phone unlocked in the living room one night, Eleanor took the chance to read some of the texts from Patrick. She was mortified to see him treating Kate like an object, labeling her his submissive.

Patrick wrote in one text: "You are my most treasured and loyal lost girl, a steadfast pet. I wish you were a doll that I could slip into my pocket and take out to play with or groom. You would wear a tiny collar to keep you from straying."

Eleanor tried to shake off thoughts that something terrible had happened to her daughter in Maine.

Leo, Eleanor's boyfriend of three years, walks into the living room and kisses the top of her head.

"I'm going to make a sandwich," he says. "Want one?"

Eleanor bites her lip. "Am I a bad parent?"

Leo looks caught off guard.

"All the attention I gave Kate? All the resources I devoted? Maybe it did more harm than good. Maybe some people are born without parenting skills. My mother said she lacked the 'parenting gene.' Maybe I'm missing it too."

"Parenting is hard," Leo says. "You never know if you're doing it right."

Eleanor thought Leo was a fabulous parent. His boys were so great. A doctor and an engineer. He let them do whatever they wanted when they were young. Roam in the woods. Play in mud puddles. Swim in the river alone. They didn't even have a curfew. Leo trusted that they would do the right thing. He didn't text them to ask where they were or where they were going.

Eleanor sighs. "The kids who were free as children seem to flourish as adults."

"Kate will find her way," Leo says.

Eleanor wasn't so certain. Kate wasn't like other kids. That's why Eleanor stuck close, especially during a crisis. If she saw Kate struggling, she mobilized. Sometimes her interventions only made the situation worse, but it was compulsive. A similar compulsion kept her mindlessly chewing at the ends of her fingers until the skin wore off. Whenever Eleanor's control weakened, she would nibble her fingers raw. It gave her worried mind a place to fixate.

"Kate's anxious, because I'm anxious. It's a cycle." Eleanor looks at Leo. "Your dad left you, but you were determined to be a better parent, to break the cycle, and you did."

Leo looks out the window at the Audi in the driveway. He squeezes Eleanor's hand.

"You sure you don't want me to come with you?"

She stands up. "No, I need to do this alone."

Leo smiles. "Go get your daughter back, then."

As Eleanor pulls out of the driveway, she thinks about the moment when she will see Kate again. She'll unload a series of confessions: "It's not you, it's me," she'll tell her. "Your troubles as a daughter are my failures as a mother."

Portland, Maine

After two hours of driving, the sun has set, and the Maine forest hums with the rising and falling rhythm of the cicadas. Deep in the woods, Eleanor smells pine through her open window. She chews at the ends of her fingers on one hand and worries. What if something terrible has happened to Kate?

Eleanor sees a sign for the Free-Range Center and turns the car onto a bumpy dirt road. Parking, she leaves the car and walks along a dirt pathway, passing tiny cottages, gardens, and a pond where fish nip at insects on the water's surface. She can hear the faint sound of chanting. The distinct, drawn-out "Om" comes from a brown barn with a crimson roof. Eleanor approaches slowly, branches cracking under her feet. In the distance beyond the barn, she sees a young woman scribbling in a notebook. The woman flicks a cigarette into the dirt. It's Kate!

Eleanor rushes toward her daughter. "Honey! I'm so happy to see you." She tries to hug Kate, but her daughter recoils, turns her back, and walks toward a roaring campfire. She throws her notepad onto the ground and folds herself into an alpine-style chair.

Eleanor notices that Kate has gained some weight. Healthy weight. There's even some definition in her arms, and her skin is a pinkish color, not the veiny, bluish hue it took on after years of starving herself. She must be eating, Eleanor thinks as she lowers herself into a chair beside Kate.

Eleanor struggles to find something to say.

Suddenly, Kate stands up and walks toward the barn. The door closes behind Kate, and Eleanor picks up Kate's notebook and flips through pages of her daughter's writing. She stops at a page and reads a poem. There is something radiant in Kate's words. Something alive. Has Kate awoken from a long sleep? It makes Eleanor smile. A few minutes later, Kate walks out of the barn, clutching an object covered in a blanket. The object moves, squirms. In the faint light, Eleanor squints at it, and then she realizes it's an infant. Eleanor leaps from her seat.

"Oh, Kate!"

Kate says, "I came here when I found out I was pregnant."

Eleanor lowers her eyes. "Is it . . . his?"

"She's Patrick's, yes, but he's no longer in my life."

Eleanor stretches out her arms. Kate carefully hands her baby to Eleanor. "Her name is Jenna."

Eleanor supports the baby's head as she reclines in her chair. "Hi, Jenna."

Kate looks at her baby in her mother's arms. At the Free-Range Center, she has listened to thought leaders, authors, and researchers lecture on free-range parenting, which the founder of the Center calls "a commonsense reaction to parenting in overprotective times."

"Kids aren't physically and emotionally fragile," Kate has heard him say, "and we shouldn't treat them that way." The founder has admitted that he's rebelling against a culture of overprotection to "future-proof our kids." It wasn't long before Kate committed to raising "a free-range child."

Kate has learned about the link between play in childhood and creative capacities in adulthood. She's been told that children can—and should—roam and play unsupervised. The same is true for walking home after school by themselves or riding the subway alone, if necessary. One impassioned author even told the group: "For the love of God, can we stop loading our children's brains and bodies with Adderall, Ritalin, and Prozac? Instead, let's try the hard work of parenting."

She's particularly fond of the talk given by Laura Dekker, who became the youngest person to sail around the world in 2009.

"Jenna is going to be different," she says to Eleanor. "Different from me. Different from you. Better than both of us. She's going to climb trees, fall, scratch her arms and legs. I'm not going to scold her for running in flip-flops. She can ride the train when she's a teenager. I'll give her freedom. Space. Opportunities to make mistakes. To fail. To learn responsibility. Independence. And, most of all, my worries will not become her worries."

The last time Eleanor saw Kate, she was impetuous. Immature. Lost. Kate appears more dignified now, not just in speech but in the way she carries herself, how she smartly pulls her shoulders back and softly examines her baby. She has clearly done some growing up.

Eleanor chokes up as she thinks about all the ways she inhibited Kate in childhood.

"I shouldn't have hovered over you or smothered you, shouldn't have stopped you from playing and trying new things, from finding out who you were and what you wanted." She shakes her head. "I should have let you go to that damn writing conference."

"I've been hard on you, Mom. I'm sorry. I was really lost for a really long time. To be fair, I was a loved kid. I have you to thank for that."

A young man walks out of the barn then. Kate smiles as he approaches the campfire. The twenty-something has a beard and wears a flannel shirt—a hippie, without seeming grungy or dirty. He smiles and stretches out his hand toward Eleanor.

"You must be Kate's mother. I'm Bradley. I'm—"

"He's my fiancé," Kate blurts out.

"Um, okay, hi. Bradley."

Bradley laughs. "It's sudden, I know." He looks at Kate affectionately. "But I care about your daughter very much."

Kate rolls her eyes. "Please. This is gross. Mom. We're in love, okay?"

Bradley doesn't appear to be anything like Patrick, who saw the world through cold, detached eyes. Bradley appears softer, kinder, humbler.

Eleanor asks, "Are you sure about this, honey?"

Kate smiles tenderly. She had spent the last several years unable to feel anything, and now, that "deadness" has dissolved, leaving in its place something that looks like—feels like—happiness. Joy, even.

Kate shakes her head. "I'm actually good, Mom."

"Well, we have an extra bedroom for Jenna." Eleanor smiles clumsily at Bradley. "And Bradley can stay with us too."

We're leaving, Mom."

Eleanor looks confused. "Where are you going?"

"California."

Bradley speaks up. "I have an apartment in Seal Beach."

"I'm going to finish my degree at Long Beach State," Kate adds. "Study history. I already spoke with the dean. I'm enrolled for the fall semester."

"And Jenna will stay there? Is it safe? Who will—"

Kate laughs. "There you go, worrying. Everything will be fine, Mom."

Bradley eagerly adds, "And she has a job interview with an animal shelter next week."

Eleanor glances at Kate's notebook.

"I see you've been writing too."

Kate nods.

"So, this is goodbye?"

"You can visit, Mom."

Eleanor gently hands the squirming infant to Bradley. Then she wraps her arms around Kate and squeezes.

"We should get going," Kate says. "We want to visit Mammoth Cave National Park in Kentucky tomorrow."

Eleanor reaches for Kate's notebook and opens it to the poem she'd read.

"Can I have this one?"

Kate tears the page out and hands it over. She walks toward a Subaru Outback and spins around to give her mother one last smile. Kate loads Jenna into the car seat, and Bradley starts the car. As the car merges onto I-90 West, Kate turns and playfully sticks her tongue out at Jenna. Then she lowers her window and rests her arm on the door. Closing her eyes, she lets the wind blow her hair in all directions.

Heading east in the opposite direction, Eleanor also enjoys the warm air on her face. Without a worry in her mind, she closes her fingers tenderly around her daughter's poem and smiles.

The Dark Side of Destiny

After several years of writing the obituary column for *The Boston Globe*, I longed to dive deep into more interesting topics and write more significant stories. I wanted to write exposés that revealed injustices for the public good, like the investigative journalists I admired. I pitched many article ideas to my editor, but it wasn't until a chance encounter at a dinner party that I got the big break I desired.

At the get-together, I sat next to a newly married man who confessed his wife had tried many interventions to rid herself of a troubling problem. In times of stress, she would pick the skin around her fingertips until they were raw, leaving them damaged and hardened, sometimes bleeding. The issue seemed rather insignificant, but his wife had been disturbed that she couldn't control the behavior. She knew she shouldn't do it, yet she had found the habit irresistible.

Her primary care physician had referred her to cognitive behavioral therapy. There, she had focused on identifying the underlying thoughts and feelings fueling the problem. Regrettably, it had done nothing to change her behavior.

She had then gone to a psychoanalyst to understand the cause of her dermatillomania, also known as chronic skin-picking. Despite ten therapy sessions, nothing was ever found, and the habit had persisted.

"Hypnosis cured her," her husband claimed. "In fact, after one session, she was free of the burden."

His wife had been delighted to have put the quirk to rest. That is, until a few months later, when she developed a condition known as Raynaud's disease, which reduced blood flow to the fingers in cold temperatures.

"How does that affect your family?" I asked.

"She can't spend long periods in the cold," he admitted. "She spends most of our ski vacations in the lodge, huddled next to a warm fire with a book."

The cause of her Raynaud's disease was unknown, but he speculated that the hypnosis had caused his wife's new malady, having "crossed some wires" in her brain, perhaps. Regardless, they believed Raynaud's disease was a small price to pay to avoid the alarming sight of bloody fingertips.

The tale stuck with me for several days. Hypnosis had alleviated the intended problem but might have replaced it with another. Having undergone some psychoanalysis myself, I wondered if the woman's neurosis might have been the result of some underlying anxiety. Had hypnosis simply bypassed the unconscious forces at play, causing them to manifest elsewhere in her body?

Given the stigma against medical conditions being "all in one's head," I didn't dare suggest to the man that his wife might have been suffering from psychosomatic symptoms. However, I did wonder if exploring the dark recesses of her mind might have helped relieve her physical symptoms. Had she expressed some deep-seated anger or sadness, would she have been free of both health issues?

A quote by the English psychiatrist Henry Maudsley came to mind: "The sorrow which has no vent in tears may make other organs weep."

I felt darkly stimulated by the encounter one Saturday morning. Over coffee, I grabbed my phone and wrote a pitch for my editor about the "dark side" of medical interventions, in particular, alternative therapies like hypnosis. During our one-on-one meeting on Monday, I voiced the idea, but it was met with lukewarm enthusiasm. Undeterred, I followed up with a more formal proposal via email.

"The idea has promise," her responding email said the next day. "You can begin research for one article."

I finished the three obituaries I had to do for the day in record time and began looking for centers in Greater Boston that offered alternative or integrative therapies. My first call was to the Eureka Center in Williamstown. I told the naturopath I spoke with that I was a reporter looking for stories of individuals who might've resolved one health problem only to find themselves dealing with another.

When I mentioned the woman with Raynaud's, the naturopath said she knew of several similar cases. One had undergone hypnotherapy to quit smoking but then developed a chronic respiratory condition known as chronic obstructive pulmonary disease. Another had undergone acupuncture to get a handle on his migraines, but while the migraines were diminished, he developed severe acid reflux that inflamed his throat, causing it to constrict while he slept.

When I spoke with the man, he said a neurologist thought one of the acupuncture needles might've gone too deep and struck a bundle of nerve fibers in his neck or scalp. This may have caused the nerves in the esophagus to become hypersensitive and thus overreact with swelling when acid regurgitated from the stomach.

With this information, I wrote the story enthusiastically. It was published in the bottom right-hand corner of the front page. There was my name, Winston Solomon, beside my very own column, The Dark Side, with the catchy subtitle "What are the costs of our healing therapies?"

The one-thousand-word piece generated hundreds of letters from all over the state from people with similar experiences. Elated, I dove headlong into my work, writing obituaries during the day and the column at night.

For my next story, I interviewed a man who had undergone a year of existential psychotherapy, or philosophical counseling, to cure nihilism—a sense that life was insignificant. He thought life had no intrinsic meaning, so why should he go on living? The existential therapist, trained in dealing with such hopelessness, argued that the innate meaninglessness of life shouldn't stop people from living.

Why couldn't life's shortness itself inspire them to wisely choose how they spent their time?

After some time, the man finally found his antidote: the realization that the onus to manufacture a purpose in life was on him. He no longer searched for a meaning of life; rather, he understood that meaning was found in living.

What was the "dark side" of the story? The man discovered he'd spent his whole life working at a desk, enriching other people, and never learning his individuality. Realizing he hadn't lived his life, he quit his job, sold his belongings, and literally walked the earth.

The story was a sensation. Encouraged by the public's delighted response to my column, my editor urged me to continue exploring and writing. Deciding to pivot, I began to seek stories of unintended consequences in conventional medicine.

I spoke with an oncologist at a major hospital in Boston who specialized in managing the cardiovascular side effects of cancer therapies. Many of the doctor's patients had beaten cancer but now lived with life-threatening heart rhythm disturbances. I told her about my grandmother, who had succumbed to lung cancer years earlier after chemotherapy wreaked havoc on her body, scarring her heart and shredding her gastrointestinal system.

"Should we have taken her home when she was reasonably healthy," I asked, "so she could check a few items off her bucket list before her inevitable death? She had always wanted to visit Nantucket, yet she spent her last few days suffering in a hospital. Wouldn't beach walks have been their own form of medicine?"

"As a doctor, I have an obligation to do everything I can to save patients like your grandmother," the doctor replied. "But deep down, in my heart of hearts, I would agree with you. I wish more families would do just what you described."

As I dove deeper into conventional medicine, my column became unpopular among clinicians and researchers around Boston. No one liked having their livelihoods publicly criticized; many professionals saw my articles as blatant attacks on their fields. Hundreds of emails poured into my inbox, including a response to my exploration of the side effects of cancer therapies in which a physician insisted the drugs they used saved hundreds of lives every year.

"If you knew anything about medicine or pharmacology, you would know every drug has side effects."

I hesitated to reply that he had just proven the point of my column.

Though it certainly wasn't my intent, some of my stories put companies out of business. One story explored the effects of a nutritional supplement reported to extend people's life spans by "optimizing metabolic circuits." While some customers who had taken the supplement for years had more energy and sharper focus, many had suffered unusual symptoms, from malaise to nausea. One individual had developed a severe autoimmune disorder known as Still's disease and took a handful of pills each morning to control the chronic illness. A few folks had heart attacks. One had even died from a massive stroke.

The story made the nightly news, and *60 Minutes* even began investigating it. The company that produced the supplement closed its doors a few months after the publication of my story.

Weeks later, in a meeting with my editor, I mentioned my desire to take my column in a new direction. I thought it would be interesting to explore the potential dark side of basic scientific research. I had grown up reading dystopian novels like *1984, Brave New World, and Fahrenheit 451*, cautionary tales that explored the consequences of man's inventions. I also read science fiction, which explored future possibilities within fictional scenarios. In the film *Jurassic Park*, Dr. Ian Malcolm criticized the scientists who resurrected dinosaurs to create an amusement park for tourists.

"Your scientists were so preoccupied with whether or not they could that they didn't stop to think if they should."

This staggering line had never left me. It both haunted me and darkly inspired me to consider not whether we could but whether we should. I'd always felt there were certain types of people who would try anything, no matter how dangerous or morally complex, as long as it would get them the immediate results they desired. Maybe this was humanity's innate curiosity—our explorer spirit. Maybe it was rebellion: If certain people were told they couldn't do something, they wanted to do it even more.

Or maybe it was just that humans had trouble feeling the threat of something if the potential consequences wouldn't appear until far in the future. At best, this might be caused by wishful thinking: "That won't happen to me" or "Even if it does, we'll figure something out." At worst, it was caused by complete disregard for possible long-term consequences: "So what? I won't have to deal with the fallout."

I reached out to a biomedical research institute in Cambridge. According to its website, the institute comprised about two dozen labs dedicated to improving human health through curiosity-driven research to understand the biological mechanisms that drove intractable diseases, such as cancer, heart disease, and Alzheimer's. Most of the principal investigators were world-renowned in their scientific fields. Many had received the National Medal of Science and were members of the National Academy of Sciences, and two had a Nobel Prize each in physiology or medicine.

After researching the institute, I was most interested in speaking with a Dr. Oscar Black. I was intrigued by the mission of his laboratory. All the lab's inventions and medical devices—he claimed to have seventy inventions to his name—were inspired by nature.

For instance, research into the use of echolocation by bats had led to a potential cure for blindness, which was currently in phase II clinical trials. Another fascinating project, funded by the US Department of Defense, studied the mind-boggling speed with which hummingbirds flapped their wings. Though it seemed ridiculous, no doubt the military aimed to give soldiers the power of flight.

At the front desk, it was apparent the institute was a highly creative and intellectually vibrant environment. While I checked in, a woman with red hair and thick glasses passed by, discussing an upcoming meeting with venture capitalists. Scientists walked by engaged in intense discussions that may as well have been in other languages. In the elevator, a pair of researchers discussed what sounded like a scientific experiment. They used strange terms, like *sestrin2, leucine sensor,* and *mTORC1.*

Once I'd entered Dr. Black's suite, the secretary confirmed the schedule and knocked on his door. A raspy voice shouted, "Come in!"

When the secretary eased open the door, Dr. Black was hunched over his desk, his fingers strumming over his keyboard. He didn't make eye contact. Instead, he took a bite of a sandwich and squinted at the computer screen through white-rimmed glasses. Unlike other investigators, who wore sports jackets or suits in their online pictures, Dr. Black wore jeans and a dark-red flannel shirt. His office was cozy, and the walls were covered in photos of him at barbecues and beach parties. On the windowsill sat a picture of the cabin he'd built in New Hampshire (he mentioned it in his memoir, *Nature Is My Guide*).

"What do you want?" Dr. Black asked.

"I'm the reporter who called about the Dark Side column."

He scoffed. "So you're the one assassinating doctors and scientists around town."

"I assure you, that isn't my intention. In fact, my column protects people from the unintended consequences of the therapies they seek." As an example, I told him about a reader who had canceled her appointment to get breast implants after one of my articles profiled a patient who had experienced horrific side effects.

That seemed to disarm Dr. Black, who moved his sandwich to the side. "I'm well aware of the harm modern medicine can do, despite its lifesaving accomplishments," he offered. "My wife passed away a few years ago."

With some probing, I learned his wife had developed a brain tumor that had enveloped the major artery in her neck. It had been an impossible case, and most surgeons wouldn't touch her for fear of her dying on the table, no matter how skilled they were.

The only neurosurgeon brave enough to take on the case managed to extract the tumor, but Mrs. Black suffered a massive stroke during the ten minutes the artery had to be blocked. She was cancer-free, but the stroke impaired the function of her right arm and leg and left her with a speech impediment. Unable to form sentences well, she could no longer enjoy conservations with her husband as she had before. To make matters worse, the cancer returned five years later, and Dr. Black was left with the vague notion that the benefits of the risky operation may not have outweighed the costs.

"I have to finish this grant proposal before the end of the day," Dr. Black said, shaking off the memory. "Let's make this quick, Mr. Solomon."

"Do you mind if I record our conversation?"

Dr. Black agreed but asked me not to write about his lab. Disappointed, I set my tape recorder down on the table, promising never to write a word without the source's permission.

"Can you explain your work, Dr. Black?"

He nodded and pushed his chair back away from the desk. "As you're no doubt aware, my research is inspired by Mother Nature and all her magnificent creations." He pointed to a glass container on a nearby table. Inside, mounds of sand teamed with ants. "Among our many projects, we are currently studying the organizational complexity of ants. An ant colony is a perfect society."

He explained that they were organized into groups, almost like castes, and that each ant had a unique role within the hierarchy of power. The queen produced the eggs while the workers performed various duties to maintain order. Some worker ants monitored the eggs, while others left the nest to find food.

"Every ant has a job to do," he mused. "Each is suited for a role in their colony, and each does it well. It's a happy republic—a utopia, in fact."

Dr. Black's explanation reminded me of my time playing football in high school, where a player's position was determined mostly by their physical characteristics. The linemen, who protected the quarterback, were almost always muscular and above average in size, often overweight but still athletic. On the other hand, wide receivers, who had to sprint for passes and evade defenders, were usually slender and fast runners. Having been stocky but quick on my feet and able to withstand collisions with powerful linemen, I had been put in the fullback position.

Intrigued, I asked Dr. Black how studying ants had translated into useful knowledge for humanity. It was somewhat surprising to hear him suggest that *Homo sapiens* could learn a great deal from ants. He believed we could use the knowledge to perhaps organize a perfect, harmonious society.

"Look at the misery most people suffer because they are ill-suited for their roles. For example, a litigator who prefers legal research and writing briefs to performing in courtrooms or securing clients for the firm through constant networking. What about teachers who have no aptitude for working with kids? Or a senator—a public servant—who has no intention of serving the public, only themselves?"

Dr. Black explained that most people were mismatched. "Square pegs in round holes," he called them. "They fulfill roles in society inappropriate for their skills, temperament, intelligence, and personality."

"How would you solve the problem?"

"I have created a machine that can match an individual with a role best suited to them based on seventy-five unique factors."

Dr. Black pulled a book out of a drawer. "In *The Republic,* the Greek philosopher Plato imagines a perfect society in which each citizen satisfies the role they were born to fulfill. For example, large and strong men would be society's warriors and protect the public in the military. The pensive and philosophical would write society's laws. And the sensitive and empathetic would be healers in their communities."

"We are all born to do one thing," Dr. Black insisted. "How many individuals are unsatisfied because they don't like their place in the world? My machine, which I call Element—as in 'finding one's element'—solves that."

Dr. Black's grandiosity was startling. "Surely a person is more than their size, shape, intelligence, and temperament?"

"My technology accounts for *all* the unique components of a person."

I nodded slowly. "So, how did this idea develop?"

Dr. Black smiled wryly. "To be honest, Element never would've come about if not for my son's struggle to find his own place in the world." He pointed to a picture of a handsome man in a black gown holding a medical school diploma.

"Nathan spent many unhappy years as a primary care physician," Dr. Black explained. "He thought his patients complained too much, and most didn't get better. Worse, he felt he couldn't help them because many of their problems were stress related—usually psychological or emotional, not physiological."

Nathan had a vivid imagination and exceptional linguistic skills. For years, Dr. Black had told him he had enough talent to be like the great physicians who also wrote fiction. Nathan admired Michael Crichton, who had also attended Harvard Medical School, and had grown up on novels like *The Andromeda Strain* and *The Terminal Man.* To expand his palate, Dr. Black had introduced him to the greats: Anton Chekhov, Arthur Conan Doyle, and Mikhail Bulgakov.

When the idea hadn't taken, Dr. Black built the prototype of Element for Nathan. "Testing showed that my son scored off the charts on verbal and written intelligence. He was also way above average on the creativity scale. This suggested that perhaps he was well suited for life as a writer."

To Dr. Black's delight, Nathan had accepted the results and began writing short stories about his clinical encounters, with the permission of those involved. As Dr. Black had expected, they were often derivates of Crichton: thrilling, science-based tales, the first of which was about an infectious disease outbreak and was clearly modeled after *The Andromeda Strain*.

To Nathan's amazement, most of his stories were published in science fiction journals. While he didn't leave his clinical practice, Nathan was expressing his inborn talents, which made Dr. Black proud. That said, Nathan did admit to feeling guilty; as a doctor, he should focus on his patients' health rather than thinking about one day fictionalizing his experiences with them. Nevertheless, he continued writing and improving his craft.

I knew such details would add color to my story if Dr. Black agreed to go on the record, but now wasn't the time to pressure him. Instead, I asked more about how Element worked. It sounded a lot like a personality test, like the Myers-Briggs or other such services that companies subjected their employees to during company retreats.

"The Myers-Briggs is nowhere near as sophisticated as my machine." Dr. Black bit his lip. "Perhaps it would be best if you saw it."

We walked out of his office, through the suite, and down a hallway. He opened a door to the lab space, and we walked through a lobby with white walls and lab rooms on either side. He used a key card to open another door, revealing a cramped, dimly lit space. In the center of the room was the unmistakable donut shape of an MRI machine. The bulky cylinder had a hole in the middle, into which the bed slid.

We circled the machine as Dr. Black articulated that it was, indeed, a wide-bore 3 Tesla MRI scanner that could evaluate brain anatomy, neurochemistry, and a host of other physiological factors. It measured brain activity while a person responded to a proprietary list of behaviors, questionnaires, and cognitive tests. The prompts, questions, puzzles, word association tests, and brain games helped assess the patient's intellectual abilities, creative capacity, emotional intelligence, and what were known as the five broad personality traits: extroversion, agreeableness, openness, conscientiousness, and neuroticism.

"We can also do a full genetic analysis," he added, "including ancestry."

"How does that matter in the context of helping a person find their place in the world?"

"Well, for example," Dr. Black replied, "some individuals with the 'warrior gene' are more likely to show aggressive behavior and thus might do better as soldiers or athletes. We also account for the nature of work in the twenty-first century. We can use the data obtained by Element to predict a domain or area in which the subject could flourish."

With a kind of reverence, he ran his hand along the machine. "Astrologers and mystics have been trying to predict people's futures for centuries. Science has made that a reality at last."

Dr. Black walked me into an adjacent room, from which we could see Element through the window. "I believe every person knows, even if only subconsciously, what their talents are and what they should be doing with their life. It can take a long time to figure out what you're good at. It can take even longer to figure out how to translate those faculties into a practical role in society.

"Element quickly identifies inborn talents and matches them with a vocation. It's as simple and uncomplicated as that."

I frowned. "But how does the machine account for someone's values? I mean, say you're good with numbers. Should you become an accountant or a mathematician? If you work in finance, should you work for a nonprofit or on Wall Street? For a small firm or large? Or perhaps you would be better suited for self-employment. Would you rather work on the sales side, with people, or the analytical side, with data?"

"We're still working on that aspect, but we're almost there," Dr. Black shot back. "Indeed, values are nothing more than what arises from the combination of a person's biology and psychology and the culture they live in, perhaps in combination with other factors, like socioeconomic background, race, gender, and others."

Dr. Black appeared certain that if he knew these aspects of someone's personhood, he would know what that person stood for. I remained skeptical until he probed into why I had chosen a career in journalism.

"My knack for words, I guess. I've always loved to read, and writing came naturally."

Dr. Black nodded. "And why not choose advertising? You could've expressed such natural talent in that field." He scoffed. "If we can even refer to advertising as a field."

He had a point. It was, indeed, a question of values. To me, journalists held an essential role in society by keeping those in power accountable. "The job of the newspaper," as the saying went, "is to comfort the afflicted and afflict the comfortable."

"It is something of a thrill to write the first drafts of history," I admitted. "And I hope to write a first draft of your work, if you'll let me."

Upon returning to the newsroom, I told my editor about Dr. Black and his work. Intrigued, she pushed me to get the scientist's consent to write about his work, but she also urged me to write about the science through the lens of my column: to find Element's unintended cost.

At first, none came to mind. In fact, the technology seemed to provide a good deal of benefit. I had read somewhere that only 15 percent of people were engaged at work. Who wouldn't want to identify their place in the world with such speed and efficiency?

My editor didn't care about the perceived benefits, though. "Go dark on Element. And for God's sake, get the man's consent to write about him."

That night, I went home and sat on the back porch with a beer. I pressed play on my recorder and listened to my conversation with Dr. Black. I started typing and had a thousand words within half an hour.

Dr. Black's main philosophy appeared to be that most people's talents were squandered, their gifts untapped, leading to untold misery. Element, it seemed, could be a boon to humanity. Nevertheless, I had to "go dark" on the machine, which centered on whether the technology did indeed do what Dr. Black said it did.

Of course, I was putting the cart before the horse by writing a story without Dr. Black's consent. With a first draft almost finished, I called him that night, buzzed from three beers.

"The American public needs to know about Element," I told him. "I promise, I'll write a balanced article about your work."

"I'll think about it," he replied before hanging up. I was sure my story would never see the light of day.

The next morning, though, Dr. Black called me and said I could publish. "The world would be a better place if more people learned about my work and took it seriously."

"Mind if I spend some time in your lab to learn more about Element and your philosophy?"

I spent a week doing just that. Dr. Black even had me undergo the testing, which was quite enjoyable. Reclined, with my head and neck covered by the machine, I performed a series of word games and memory tests and free-associated while looking at beautiful and grotesque photographs. When the testing was over, Dr. Black handed me a twenty-page document of results.

Unsurprisingly, it noted I was well suited for my chosen career. It detailed my linguistic aptitude versus mathematical skills. The results suggested: "Subject shall thrive in the field of communications, particularly as a producer of content versus more administrative roles." Another page said: "High idealism suggests a strong match for the betterment of the public, i.e., journalism."

Element had shown I was well matched for my career, an outlier in Dr.

Black's mind. "Most people are lost," he reminded me. "You are not, Winston."

The story turned out to be my longest yet, so my editor published it as a three-part series. The article went viral, and it didn't take long before everyone in Boston was discussing Dr. Black's invention.

Two days after publication, I traded emails with Dr. Black. The institute's technology transfer office had arranged meetings with biotech companies that had agreed to commercialize Element. Dr. Black said he didn't care for this level of attention—"fame and tranquility are not good bedfellows"—but he eventually agreed to conduct a clinical trial on a dozen undergraduate students at Harvard University. I pleaded with my editor to let me follow his clinical research. She agreed but reminded me the newspaper was paying me to write obituaries and maintain the Dark Side column.

The Harvard students were eager to participate in the trial, claiming such technology was a godsend. Who wouldn't want a machine to reveal their best traits? With all the pressure they were under to find their "thing"—and fast—Element could cut down the uncertainty.

In a *Harvard Crimson* article, one student said she was "insanely envious" of individuals who'd realized their passions at a young age. Another student agreed, joking that he wished he would experience a natural disaster or illness, as it would probably give his life laser focus.

"In a world where Element exists," one parent was quoted to have said, "I won't have to watch my child flit from job to job in his twenties."

The study revealed that nearly all twelve students were headed for careers that didn't align with their skills, temperaments, or intelligence. Most changed majors after breaking down the results with their parents and friends.

Cassie, a biology major, discovered she had little to no aptitude for science or mathematics. Instead, she became a dance major, having scored off the charts in kinesthetic abilities. Incidentally, she had always loved to dance. In a follow-up *Crimson* article about the study, she claimed, "It feels like I have to move to think."

Beatrice, a culinary arts major, had been inspired by the movie *Burnt* to become a pastry chef. She thought being a chef was badass, but she had little passion for food ("my friends ate tapas in Spain; I found the closest Subway"). Beatrice also had inferior taste buds and low creativity scores. She scored high on mathematical abilities, however, saying in the *Crimson* that numbers had always come easy to her. When she was a little girl, she had played with equations while her friends played with dolls. So she became a math major.

Another student, Wells, opposed Dr. Black and his machine, publicly rejecting his results. He believed all the machine did was make him feel bad about being different. "I will follow my intuition," he proclaimed. "If I take some wrong turns, so be it. That's part of life."

Every student except Wells aligned their futures in accordance with Element's predictions.

After the clinical trial, my editor and I decided I had to move on from Dr. Black. I continued the Dark Side column for a few years and wrote many feature stories, one of which earned me a Pulitzer for Feature Writing. Not long after, I was tapped by a major newspaper to be a senior reporter. A couple of years later, I became the managing editor of *Boston Magazine*.

Dr. Black made bold career moves too. Several years after the Harvard study, he founded his own company, The Black Center for Human Advancement, which sold his machines to the public.

By then, Element had made its way into schools across the country. Parents anxious about their children's futures had them tested by the thousands. Guidance counselors had little to do in the age of Element; they simply sent students to the nearest machine for testing.

To reduce turnover and absenteeism, many employers throughout the United States began requesting applicants' Element results. Others would sponsor testing for attractive candidates, and entire departments paid for the testing as part of annual retreats.

Commercials ran on TV with slick lines like "Do you love your place in the world?" or "Do you feel lost in your career, unengaged at work, or unhappy in life?" Dr. Black was on the cover of countless magazines, including *The New Yorker*, which featured a cartoon of a silhouetted figure falling backward off a building, at the bottom of which stood the doctor holding a safety net.

A decade after meeting Dr. Black, I had mostly forgotten about him. I was in the middle of a pitch meeting when one of my reporters talked about a retired physician who had attempted suicide. He pitched a piece on burnout among healthcare providers in the age of industrialized medicine, which I thought was a good idea.

"What's the doctor's name?"

"Nathan Black."

I paused, not expecting the name to be familiar. "As in the son of Oscar Black?"

The reporter nodded.

"Pursue the story. I'll interview Nathan Black to get his side."

Wasting no time, I visited the hospital where Nathan Black had been admitted, and a social worker led me to his room. When I entered, Nathan sat on the edge of the bed with his knees against his chest. He was pale, and his eyes were wild with fear. I introduced myself, saying I knew his father.

"I know who you are," Nathan assured me. "You made my father famous. Made him *obsessed*." He shivered. "I haven't spoken with him in over a year because all he ever talks about is Element and the impact it's having on society." His voice dropped to a whisper. "But Element is cursed."

"Can you elaborate on that?"

"Leaving medicine to start writing was a terrible idea. Sure, my patients weren't always easy to deal with, but at least the hours were steady and I was a respected member of society. People looked up to me, admired me."

But his father's machine had "infected" him with the notion that his destiny was to become a writer. And while Nathan might have had a natural facility with words, Element hadn't accounted for certain intangibles Nathan would need to tolerate the rigors of a creative life.

"It's shameful to admit, but I don't have the guts for writing. It's like driving down a winding road at night with just one working headlight—or even no headlights and with the car in need of an oil change too. But I'm someone who needs two headlights. Hell, I'd much rather drive during the day, anyway."

It took a certain level of courage to sit down every day and "feel one's way" through a narrative and then prune it to give the reader the impression the story could only have turned out the way the author designed it.

As a journalist, I could relate. One of the hardest things to accomplish as a writer was to build a piece that was clear and hung together. I considered my favorite authors who discussed how they had managed the uncertainty that accompanied the early stages of a writing project. Though I hadn't written fiction, I knew fictional stories often began with almost infinite possibilities, yet they ended in what appeared to be the only way fathomable.

"Kurt Vonnegut," I told Nathan, "wrote numerous versions of his novel *Slaughterhouse-Five* before he finished, even abandoning it countless times."

Nathan smiled. "After writing the first two parts of *Siddhartha*, Hermann Hesse realized he had no way to conclude the book's third section, and it took him years of soul-searching to return to it."

He shook his head. "What patience! It drives me crazy just not knowing where a short story is going. Too much uncertainty, and I implode."

Had Element missed an important aspect of Nathan's personality? And what part of him were we talking about? Was courage, grit, or guts assessed by his father's machine? Was it temperament? What about one's nature or essence?

Element predicted a path that suited cognitive strengths, but it seemed it might be incompatible with various indefinable aspects of character. And despite being a talented writer—his short story about a rheumatologist who cured his own autoimmune disorder with laughter by prescribing himself funny movies was fantastic—Nathan was unhappy. Clinically depressed, even.

"Have you given up medicine?"

"I cut my clinic hours a few years ago to commit myself to writing fiction full-time, even though I'd only published a few short stories and my unpublished novel had been declined by dozens of agents. I bought a small office space in Concord, not far from Walden Pond, and would go there to write all morning."

After receiving mostly rejections, Nathan had realized it would probably take him another decade to excel at fiction writing, and he had no intention of making that level of commitment.

"I'm good at writing, but it takes a hell of a lot more than talent to have a career."

Indeed, I had seen many people with similar problems: one might have an aptitude for something yet still not make money from it or be recognized for it.

Nathan supposed those Harvard kids had wanted his father's machine to guarantee them successful futures. They might want to be rich and famous, but for the most part, they just wanted security.

Who didn't?

"I was thinking about all this—going too deep into my thoughts—when my mood started to dip," Nathan said. "The antidepressants helped for a year before they lost their effect."

All the alone time and introspection needed for writing well had messed up his neurochemistry. His father had him admitted to a psychiatric institution when Nathan confessed he'd been fantasizing about not being around anymore.

"That was the appeal of suicide," Nathan said. "The second the lights went out, all my worries, all my problems, all my silly ambitions just went away. I would be able to 'rest in peace,' as the saying goes."

As I drove home from the hospital, I grew increasingly disturbed by my meeting with Nathan Black. It was a shame to see such a bright young man fall so hard. Plenty of people never climbed out of such a hole, and I wondered if he would ever recover. Should he have stayed in medicine? He hadn't been as passionate about medicine as he had about writing, but at least he hadn't been suicidal.

My mind drifted back to my old Dark Side column, which had launched my journalism career. Was this the "dark side" of Dr. Black's machine?

Thousands of individuals now designed their lives in accordance with Element's predictions. And everyone seemed to be thriving. Some even claimed their lives consisted of two parts: life before Element and life after Element. They didn't have to experiment with various jobs or careers. They didn't have to hire career coaches or read business books to navigate the complexities of building a brilliant career.

What misery it must have been to drift from job to job, to get a graduate degree to secure a career in a field that was only of slight interest, only to never find one's calling and toil in a job that made one unhappy. That was a life of floundering.

With Element, people had a purposeful existence.

Yet were there others like Nathan?

That night, I searched online through articles about the first batch of Harvard students who had undergone testing. First, I looked up Cassie, who had begun Harvard as a biology major but switched to dance. It turned out she owned a dance company in Marlborough, about forty-five minutes from my apartment in Brighton.

The next morning, I drove to the address listed for her business. I walked through the main entrance and saw maybe a dozen young girls twirling on the hardwood floor. In front of a large mirror, a woman I guessed to be Cassie was barking orders. I was surprised, though. She appeared much older than her photos online. She was trim, but she was no longer the vivacious dancer I'd seen in my research. She looked haggard, and gray streaked her brunette hair.

I introduced myself and asked if we could talk someplace quiet. As she led me down a hallway to her office, we passed large posters that showed her in starring roles in Broadway productions. She walked with a slight hobble, favoring her right leg. An injury, I guessed.

Once in the office, Cassie closed the door, grabbed a glass, and began making herself a drink. "Do you want one?" The clock on the wall read half past eleven in the morning. I shook my head, and she poured herself a whiskey. "So, what do you want to know?"

"I'm trying to track down subjects from Dr. Black's original study of Harvard students to see how their lives have unfolded since then."

Cassie scoffed. "Look, without that machine, I'd probably be teaching high school biology somewhere, and I'm grateful for the life Element has given me. But I might not have taken the test knowing what it would lead to."

When I tilted my head questioningly, she took a sip of her drink and pointed to a poster of her performing a pirouette. "Look, I was the hottest dancer on Broadway, highly sought after by the best producers and choreographers in the business. For a while, it was lifestyles of the rich and famous."

"So why do you seem conflicted?"

"Because I was successful, but fame and money were all I had. I got everything I ever wanted, but I would've liked to share it with someone, to have a witness."

"Did you never get married?"

"I got close a few times, but my relationships couldn't bear the weight of my responsibilities. Just like this knee." She stuck out her right leg and shook her head in disappointment.

"What do you really want to do with your life?"

She took a swig, finishing her drink. "I'd trade all the money and fame just to be able to bring a child into this world. Element gave me a great career, but all I really wanted was a baby. Maybe I'm not beyond my fertile years, but I feel like that ship has sailed."

I had to get back to the office to run the magazine, but I was compelled to track down the other subjects of Dr. Black's first study.

The next was Beatrice, the undergraduate who'd wanted to be a chef but switched her major to math. After exchanging several emails with me, Beatrice agreed to meet me in Boston Common. After we exchanged greetings, she walked to a bench and eased herself onto it, gingerly holding her swollen belly. I sat down beside her and pulled out a notepad, while she kept an eye on her two children.

Never one to beat around the bush, I dove right in. "So, I'm wondering what you've been doing since you graduated."

"I've become a real baby factory." She was currently on maternity leave, pregnant with her third child. With her husband on a business trip, she was delighted to be talking to an adult for the first time in a few days.

She'd gotten married in her mid-twenties, and her husband, who had just received an MBA from Harvard, helped her get a job at his father's accounting firm. "The math comes easily, but I mostly just move little symbols around on the computer screen all day."

"Do you wish you were doing something else?"

"I'd rather be doing something purer, like teaching math or doing research at a university. Not using my math skills to help rich people get richer."

Beatrice yelled at her son to stop running after pigeons and then turned back to me with a shrug. "To be honest, I'm bored as hell on the job. My boss doesn't give me enough assignments, so I spend a lot of time shopping online. My friends complain about burnout, but no one ever talks about 'bored out.'"

Beatrice insisted that 'bored-out syndrome' was common among white-collar office workers and believed it was more soul-deadening than being overworked. She hated office life too: the politics, the colleagues jockeying for power, the gossip, the backstabbing.

"What do you think of Element?"

She chuckled. "I'm happy to have a job I'm good at, so I shouldn't complain. But I wish that machine could've warned me about my inability to tolerate the modern workplace."

As I returned home, I couldn't help but think of the one student from Dr.

Black's study who hadn't followed Element's results. It didn't take long to find Wells online. His website said he was a motorcycle mechanic in Northampton. His profile picture showed a handsome man with a warm, easy smile.

It was a lovely Saturday afternoon, so instead of calling Wells, I decided to drive an hour and a half to the address listed on his website. Reaching my destination, I found a charming cabin nestled in the forest. To reach the front door, I passed over a shoulder-wide bridge that crossed a brook. When I rang the doorbell, no one came and I peeked through a window to find no one inside.

Stepping off the porch, I walked around the cabin toward a small shop, perhaps two hundred square feet in size. As I got closer, I heard metal clanking against metal. The door was up, and I saw a man lying with his head and shoulders underneath an old motorcycle.

"Hello," I began, trying not to scare him.

The man pushed himself out from under the motorcycle, stood up, and said hello. It was Wells. He was lean and tall, with brown hair swirled with gray. He invited me inside his shop, using a rag to wipe the grime from his hands. After we shook hands, Wells went to the refrigerator, grabbed two bottles of beer, popped off their caps, and handed me one. I accepted it happily, and he struck mine with the top of his before taking a sip.

"So, what brings a city slicker like yourself out to the sticks?"

I cleared my throat. "I'm following up with students from the original Element study."

Wells laughed. "Dr. Black's 'destiny machine.' If only a person could find their purpose so easily. Forty-five minutes in a big donut and presto: all your existential questions are answered."

I pulled a tape recorder from my pocket. "Do you mind if I record our conversation?"

"No problem." Once I had the tape recorder set up, Wells continued. "The trouble is people can't stand not knowing their fate. Element absolves them from the agonizing work of finding one's vocation." He was a Harvard grad, a philosophy major, yet he tinkered on old British motorcycles for a living. "You won't see a profile piece about me in *Forbes*, but I couldn't be happier with the way my life has turned out."

"Oh? And what does *happiness* mean to you?"

He chuckled. "Happiness? What does that word even mean? I'm not interested in happiness. Well-being or fulfillment is more important than happiness."

"Then what would you say happiness *isn't*?"

"I'll tell you: Happiness isn't sitting in a tightly packed, temperature-controlled office with twenty other primates, staring at a screen for eight hours a day." He leaned against the motorcycle and took a sip of beer. "Happiness isn't opening and closing Word documents all day. It isn't flooding the internet with an organization's digital products. And it's definitely not going home every day wondering why I'm exhausted when I barely moved my body."

"To me, happiness is working with my hands. It's diagnosing a problem on an old motorcycle." He patted the surface of the machine beside him. "It's rebuilding the engine of this old Nighthawk."

"Happiness is the manipulation of *things* versus ideas. It's having the time and space to think, to read, to write—to do nothing, if I please. It's unstructured time to play. It's solitude."

"Happiness is agency. It's being who I am in a world that tries to make us into anything but ourselves."

"Does it feel weird being a graduate of one of the best universities in the world and not being, well, more . . ."

"Successful? My classmates have such a narrow definition of success. They all want to be the next Jeff Bezos or Elon Musk. I mean, don't get me wrong; I wanted that too, and I played the game early on. I got a high-status job at Fidelity after graduating, and my boss said I'd be a vice president in five years if I kept my head down, worked hard, and paid my dues."

"But I'd rather have a hole in my head than float in the shark-infested waters of corporate America. In my opinion, most of my white-collar friends wear golden handcuffs. They're soulless careerists climbing ladders that lean against the wrong buildings."

"Do you earn enough money to survive?"

Wells laughed. "Okay, maybe I feel a twinge of jealousy when I see what they make in a year, but whenever I do, I just lie down for a bit, and the feeing goes away fast. A couple of friends mock me for doing manual labor, but fixing these vintage bikes is just as demanding as developing a marketing strategy or writing a legal brief."

To Wells, discovering the cause of a mechanical issue was exhilarating. "It took me four hours yesterday to learn why this bike wasn't idling. When I finally figured it out, it felt like I'd discovered King Solomon's mine."

"How did you find your way?" I asked, referring to both his job and his life.

"I experimented, took risks, and listened to my gut. I took a job, didn't like it, and took another. I lived in a few different states. I dated and found someone whose company I enjoyed. Eventually, I decided to come back and call Massachusetts home; I'm originally from Beverly."

"It wasn't easy, though. I quit a job, was fired from another—well, another two." He laughed. "The smartphone app I tried to develop never got off the ground, and my law school application essay is still sitting on my hard drive."

"You followed your intuition," I offered.

Wells took a sip of beer and nodded. "The media calls Dr. Black's machine 'elegant in its simplicity,' like one of Einstein's equations or something. Personally, I think you should be deeply skeptical of someone who claims to be able to simplify a problem as complex as deciding what to do with your life."

On my way home, I contemplated Wells's criticism of Dr. Black's machine. How many people did I know who were quite talented in their professions and made obscene amounts of money yet were miserable? Or perhaps the right word was *unfulfilled*. I thought of a friend who taught kindergarten. She wasn't always joyful, teaching five-year-olds, but she was nonetheless fulfilled. Over beers, she would often lament she was too intelligent to be a caretaker of young children, that it somehow wasted her intelligence. Yet she was gifted in interpreting the emotional lives of children, and her facility with children made her the best teacher in the school, praised by parents. When she quoted funny things the kids said and shared how she'd brought joy to a young mind, it was obvious that teaching was her calling.

Once home, I went to my bookshelves and found *Man's Search for Meaning* by Viktor Frankl. Lifting it off the shelf, I began flipping through its pages. An author and psychotherapist, Frankl had a lot to say about what made humans happy and gave their lives meaning. He knew humans weren't just machines, not just packets of chemicals; each individual was a unique animal with a mind, body, and spirit—or whatever one might call the immaterial aspect of the human being we cannot deny exists.

As a Holocaust survivor himself, Frankl observed that the survivors of concentration camps had one thing in common: They had something to live for. For some, it was the thought of loved ones that gave their lives meaning or hope. The survivors of that nightmare were those who chose a positive attitude, even when they had every reason to despair.

Such observations formed the foundation of Frankl's conception of what drove humans. People needed meaning in their lives. They needed a purpose to get out of bed in the morning. It gave them a way to orient themselves, a place to channel their energy each day.

Could Dr. Black's machine know what gave a person's life meaning? Did it assess one's values? I began to wonder if Element overlooked these harder-to-define aspects of humanhood.

I walked out onto my deck, sat in my favorite chair, and kicked my legs up on a stool. It also wasn't clear how Dr. Black's machine accounted for the changes that occurred in people's personalities over time. Indeed, sometimes it felt like my own personality fluctuated every month, maybe even every day. The student who had taken a Myers-Briggs personality test in high school was not the same individual of today.

For instance, I was much more aware of my emotions now than I was in my twenties, likely a result of years of the self-examination I'd done in therapy. As I'd gotten older, my taste in entertainment had shifted, too. I now preferred classical music over rock, comedies over dramas, and philosophy over self-help. In fact, looking at pictures from my twenties was almost like looking at an entirely different person.

Yet Element's predictions were supposed to last a lifetime?

One friend of mine had been a newspaperman for a decade until he "just grew out of it." Over the years, he had become disenchanted with the media's penchant for sensationalism. After a vacation in Maine, he gave his two weeks' notice and told our editor he would write fiction from then on. He was now a New York Times best-selling author of horror novels.

My gut instinct was that Element wouldn't have been able to account for the sea of change in my friend's heart. Obviously, I had questions, and there was only one man who could answer them.

The next morning, I called The Black Center for Human Advancement to arrange a meeting with Dr. Black. Years prior, I had been able to simply walk in the front door of the institute he worked at and take the elevator to his office. Now, Dr. Black's calendar was full for two weeks.

While waiting for the appointment, I read everything I could find on the man the media had deemed an eccentric genius. Dr. Black permitted interviews only to perform demonstrations of Element. He was quite the showman; he would walk journalists, investors, and politicians through his labs and dazzle them with laboratories full of hardworking scientists and high-tech equipment.

Every reporter asked to see the inner workings of Element—how it functioned. Though he would discuss the machine's panel of seventy-five personality factors, Dr. Black always replied that his technology was proprietary. When asked if he dated, he answered that he was like every other entrepreneur he'd ever met: married to his business. Legend had it, he slept four hours a night.

The Black Center was about fifteen minutes northwest of Boston. The perimeter was lined with high-voltage security fences. The Dr. Black I met that day was a different man than the one I'd met in a cramped, windowless office at his old institute. His new office was almost the size of a tennis court, with finished hardwood floors and a wall of massive windows behind his desk. He wore a turquoise suit tailored to fit his body. He smiled when his secretary opened the office door and shook my hand.

"Glad to see you, Winston. You look well. I was thrilled to see you're running a magazine now. Well deserved." He led me to the chair in front of his desk. "I hope you're not here on assignment like last time," he joked.

Why was I visiting? I was curious to know more about his machine, but maybe I just wanted to see how he was doing.

"How does it feel to have achieved worldwide acclaim, Dr. Black?"

"Please, Winston, we're old friends." He patted me on the shoulder. "Call me Oscar."

"Okay, Oscar." I smirked. "So, how's it feel to be rich and famous?"

Dr. Black laughed. "I'm an accidental billionaire. I think I preferred the life of obscurity, when I could tinker quietly and worry about trivial matters, like whether my ants have been fed for the day. Now, there are television and radio interviews, commencement speeches, TED Talks, and on-camera interviews for documentaries. I can't understand how celebrities deal with having cameras follow them around."

I reminded him of the words he once shared with me: "Fame and tranquility are not good bedfellows."

He nodded ponderously. "So true."

After some more pleasantries, Dr. Black showed me a new ant colony that was three times the size of his original. Watching the ants scurry in and out of their nests, I mentioned my meetings with some of the subjects from the original Harvard study. Dr. Black seemed surprised, even concerned, which piqued my curiosity. When I promised not to write a thing, he seemed to calm down.

"That original Harvard study seems like a lifetime ago. How are all those students doing now? Running the world, I imagine."

"Well, while many of them seem well matched for their current stations, they're not as content as the press lets on."

Dr. Black squinted. "Oh no, are you going back to that dull Dark Side column?" He lifted his hands and mimed framing words. "I can see the headline now: 'Wildly Successful, Deeply Unhappy.'"

I laughed, thinking that was a decent headline, though I didn't tell him I might prefer something like "Why Are Oscar Black's Patients Miserable?"

Dr. Black pressed for an example of someone's discontent. I brought up Cassie, the dancer who felt like she had missed her biological window to procreate (not to mention, she might've been an alcoholic). Then there was Beatrice, the math whiz who seemed to be dying of boredom as a knowledge worker.

"Then there's Wells out in Western Mass. He turned his back on corporate life and seems content fixing motorcycles in his shop. I find it curious that he ignored Element's data, yet he seems happier than anyone."

"Element doesn't guarantee happiness. Anyway, I bet if you dug a little deeper, you'd find this rebel isn't as happy as he seems."

With so much to do at the magazine, I had to return to my duties. But Wells remained in my thoughts for days. And I couldn't shake the sense that something was off with Dr. Black, the Black Center, and Element. I had always had a nose for a good story, and I felt compelled to explore the matter further, but I didn't know where to begin.

Throughout my career, whenever I felt stuck with a story, I would stop new reporting and reexamine old material, maybe even return to a subject to interview them again. As such, I called the hospital looking for Nathan, only to learn he'd been released.

When I knocked on the door of his house, a woman greeted me with a toddler in her arms. She introduced herself as Nathan's wife and welcomed me in after I explained why I was visiting.

"So many folks have stopped by to visit Nathan since he left the hospital," she said as she took me to his office. "It was great to see Oscar yesterday. He's been so focused these past few years, we hardly ever see him."

Before opening the door to Nathan's office, she mentioned he didn't like to be interrupted while working, but he'd probably make an exception for another writer. When I entered, Nathan was slouched in a chair at his desk. He was holding a pen and staring at a pad of yellow paper that only had a few lines scribbled on the first page. He glanced over his shoulder, then spun around and shook my hand. He explained he'd been trying to write at least one thousand words a day, but for some reason, the words weren't coming today. He invited me to sit on the couch.

"I visited your father yesterday."

"So he said. You were poking around for a story again? Or 'probing,' as he put it?"

"I feel like he's holding something back. Maybe you could provide some insight?"

Nathan shrugged. "My father came to apologize. He said my fall—my depression—was his fault."

"Why do you think you've struggled with the career Element assigned you?"

He stared at the floor. "One of my favorite songs is 'Bohemian Rhapsody.' The line at the end resonates with me—that nothing matters. I realized that even if I wrote fifty novels in my lifetime, what difference would it make when you consider my work and life from a cosmic perspective?"

"That's what Element never gave me or anyone else: *significance*. When I understood that anything I produced would ultimately mean nothing in the grand scheme of things, I tumbled into a deep depression, out of which I'm still trying to climb."

That evening, as I edited a feature article, I explored the website of Dr. Black's company. In the leadership section, I scanned the bios of the people on his illustrious board of directors. Two were Nobel Prize-winning biologists. They also had a Pulitzer Prize-winning novelist, a former national security advisor, and a retired four-star general. The most startling member, however, was Wells. In the displayed headshot, he wore a suit and tie and was cleanly shaven—a far cry from the bearded, grease-covered man in a flannel shirt I had met a few weeks ago.

The following weekend, I drove out to see Wells at his home. I found him revving the engine of an old motorcycle with Bruce Springsteen blaring on the radio. He smiled at me in greeting.

"This bike is a 1966 CB77 Super Hawk, the same kind ridden by Robert Pirsig, author of *Zen and the Art of Motorcycle Maintenance*. The owner of this beautiful machine put about two quarts of oil too much into the engine, and now everything's gummed up."

"I'm sure it's nothing you can't fix."

He laughed and nodded. "Too many riders are like this guy. He'll never get his hands dirty with repairs. If something breaks, he wants nothing to do with it. He brings it to me and goes to a bookstore for a few hours, knowing it'll work fine when he returns."

"Listen, Wells, I noticed you are on the board of directors for The Black Center for Human Advancement. I'd like to talk more about that, if you don't mind?" When he agreed, I asked how he'd gotten to know Dr. Black and come to serve on his company's board.

"When I rejected the results of my test, Dr. Black reached out to me. He told me it took guts not to follow the herd. Said he admired my spirit. Felt I had what so few people had: gumption. He wanted to stay in touch, and we did. I was a rising star at Fidelity when he asked me to join his illustrious board."

Wells chuckled dryly. "I was quite outspoken during board meetings, a thorn in everyone's side. Eventually, Dr. Black rounded up the board and forced them to kick me off." He shrugged. "I always suspected Dr. Black didn't want a part-time motorcycle mechanic on his precious board. But that wasn't the actual reason I was ousted."

He invited me into his house for a steak dinner. Afterward, we sat out on the porch, overlooking a pond, and he finally whispered, "I'll tell you what I think you want to hear."

I was astonished by what he proceeded to tell me.

Two hours later, I sat in my car in the Black Center's parking lot. I pressed record on my digital tape recorder and slid it into my jacket pocket. My heart racing,

I checked in with the security guard in the main lobby. It was eleven at night when I walked into Dr. Black's office. Despite his secretary's efforts to stop me, I walked in to see Dr. Black typing at his computer in almost the same crouched position he had been in when I first met him.

"Winston," he greeted in a guarded tone. "Back again so soon? Now, what's so urgent that it couldn't be taken care of over the phone?"

"Is there something you want to tell me, Oscar? Anything at all? About you, the Black Center, or perhaps your machine?"

Dr. Black's face scrunched up in confusion. "What are you getting at? If you have a point, make it."

I told him about my illuminating conversation with one of his former board members.

"*That's* what this is about?" Dr. Black cackled. "Wells? That radical? He was removed from the board rather dramatically. Though I am sorry to hear it hasn't yet been reflected on the center's website."

"It doesn't work, Oscar." When he didn't seem to understand, I added, "Your destiny machine: *Element*. It's fake. It doesn't work, never did."

Dr. Black balled his hands up into fists. "It's obvious you're on another smear campaign. I'd kindly ask you to leave my—"

"Why did you lie? Was this your way of proving to everyone you're the hero scientist you imagine yourself to be after years of being marginalized and mocked?" I questioned if he had falsified Element's data for the money, or perhaps the fame so his name would be remembered.

Glaring at me, he pressed something on the side of his desk, likely calling for security. "You have no idea how much good my machine has done—is doing!— in the world." He pointed a finger at me. "Right now, thousands of Americans are pursuing careers that highlight their strengths, that allow them to reach their full potential, perhaps even reach a state of self-actualization."

"Ah, yes," I drawled sarcastically, "a perfect society. Like your organized ant colony or Plato's perfect republic, hmm? This might have been a noble pursuit had Element been effective, but your machine's no better than any other imperfect personality test. Did it ever work?"

He sat motionless, searching for words. He glanced at the door, perhaps hoping the guards would burst in and carry me off the premises.

"It didn't, right?" I pressed. "Yet you packaged it up and rolled it out into the world." I shook my head. "Did you fake the data from the Harvard study?"

Dr. Black exploded. "I'm sorry. Is that dancer—what's her name? *Cassie*? Is she or is she not world famous? The people who listen to Element are some of the highest performers in their fields. That wouldn't have happened if their gifts hadn't been identified. Element put them on the path to reaching their full potential."

As Dr. Black screamed at me, his face red with rage, I thought of Cassie, who just wanted a baby, and Beatrice, who was restless in her job. Then Wells came to mind.

"Indeed, while many of your 'loyal subjects' were quite well matched for their vocations, that didn't make them happy. Following Element's predictions didn't give their lives significance. And isn't that what people *really* want: meaning?"

It was clear Dr. Black wasn't going to confess to fabricating his data, so I tried a different tactic. "What about Nathan? Your first patient, your son. He's miserable."

Dr. Black became somber. "I built Element for my son. When Nathan was in junior high, he took a personality test; the results recommended he become a physician. That day, he came home from school and said he was going to be a doctor. He fixated on it through high school and college. For over a decade, every decision he made—studying for the MCATs, becoming an EMT—revolved around medicine. All because of a stupid personality test. And it turned out to be wrong! How could someone decide their entire future after answering ninety questions? He turned out to be a mediocre doctor who detested clinical practice. I gave him a new life."

"That's right," I said. "*You* gave him a new place in the world, *not* your machine. Wells discovered your secret—that you meddled with patients' data when you realized your machine didn't work."

"Element will work, I can assure you," Dr. Black declared. "We just need more time for research."

I had him in his lie now.

"So you're admitting your machine doesn't work, then? That you doctored thousands of people's results. That it was you who chose those people's futures?"

Dr. Black stood up, stomped around his desk, and pointed a finger in my face. "It's the media's fault. *Your* fault. The technology wasn't ready, but the opportunity was there for a sensational story, hmm? Competitive journalists like you fell all over yourselves for the story of the decade, putting me at the top of the nightly news and on the cover of every magazine. My story made your career!"

He pointed to the bust of Plato on his desk. "This is why Plato banished writers from his ideal society. Their powerful lies can capture the public's imagination and manipulate them to believe whatever they desire. You were part of the machine that built me into some mythical figure in a story of heroes and villains, and now you're salivating at the opportunity to destroy me."

I didn't need Dr. Black's lecture. Plato had banished writers because he thought they were propagandists. Indeed, a story of Dr. Black's fall would make me a household name; I would be interviewed on talk shows, news segments, and documentaries. I'd be offered a book deal and perhaps even awarded another Pulitzer for my investigative journalism.

But it was no longer the pursuit of fame that drove me. In *my* interpretation of Plato's *Republic*, the writer had a mandate to tell the truth, and in that regard, Element had matched my personality with the perfect career. In Dr. Black's republic, I was fulfilling the role I was destined for—doing my duty—by exposing his invention and showing society that the emperor had no clothes.

I lifted the tape recorder from my pocket and pointed to the red light indicating it was recording. Knowing he was caught, Dr. Black uttered a growl of frustration. "Element would have been ready by the time it went to market, but we just didn't have enough time. The vision for the machine was ahead of the existing technology."

"You lied," I said. "Wells has agreed to blow the whistle, and if my instincts are right, Nathan will go on the record, too."

Dr. Black hesitated, and tears filled his eyes. "Tell on his own father?"

"He thinks Element ruined his life." I shook my head. "It won't be tomorrow or even next week, but the public will know you're a fraud, Oscar."

"Don't do this," he pleaded. "We just need more time! Most people were adrift before they came to us. They only cared about wealth and fame before we gave them another vision for their future. The forecasts weren't outright lies. They were educated guesses, and not everyone is unhappy with their results."

Dr. Black held out his hands pleadingly. "Take you, Winston. I was right on the money with you."

"Except I already knew my place in the world before Element. You didn't get it right; I did. And for all those other folks who underwent testing, you didn't give them direction. You didn't help them decide their fate. You stole it."

At that moment, two security guards stormed into the room, and I raised my hands in surrender. As they pushed me toward the door, Dr. Black dropped his face in his hands and wept.

As I stepped into my car, I pressed stop on the recorder. Then I pressed record and spoke an insight I'd just had.

"What was the biggest draw to Dr. Black's machine? That it could show a person a path to their life's meaning. Yet finding meaning in one's life isn't so simple, and it varies for each of us. Like Wells, like me, we must find our own way in life. We must find our own reasons for living, our own meaning, our own destiny."

A couple of days later, I interviewed Nathan. I then spent three days vigorously writing an investigative article that would expose his father's criminal behavior to the public. When the story was published, numerous media outlets piled on and took Dr. Black apart. The avalanche of reporting led to an FBI investigation, and all testing with Element was quickly stopped. The Black Center was dissolved, and Dr. Black was banned from ever doing science again. Eventually, the disgraced scientist went to prison. Not long after the article was published, I left the magazine to work as an independent investigative journalist devoted to telling stories about the unintended consequences of people's actions. By exploring the dark side of humanity, I believed we could sidestep the pitfalls before us and keep our civilization from destroying itself.

At the core, I was an idealist. I wished things weren't broken and inefficient. I wished a technology like Dr. Black's could solve all our problems and make our lives and society better, safer, more just. But it wasn't that simple. Reality was more complicated than that. Making the world a better place took people who were willing to look at the worst to get to the better.

So, I would continue peering into the darkness so we could reach the light.

Cured

Peter Spaulding removed his sunglasses and squinted through the sunlight as he hesitated outside the hospital—a massive, dark green tent covering a patch of Kenyan earth. His stomach rumbled. Hungry, he glanced at his watch. Five o'clock.

He was thirsty, too, but he'd run out of bottled water. Everyone told him not to drink well water unless he wanted to spend the next two days in the bathroom, a putrid hole in the ground at the edge of camp.

Back at Harvard, Peter probably would have had a salad, but the lettuce would have to be rinsed with water, so that was a no-go. Who knew how much longer he'd have to survive on protein bars as he played what his doctoral advisor described as an "advocate for the malarial initiative" and flexed his "adventure muscles"?

Adventure muscles? I don't have a single adventure muscle in my body.

Peter inhaled deeply, dipped his head as he entered the tent, and gazed up. Two gigantic trees, covered in chop marks from the handmade axes that had cut them, pierced the thick canvas, stretching the material high into the air. Kenyan men and women talked among themselves and exchanged words with the nurses, doctors, and scientists who tended to patients. The tent smelled of disinfectants and sanitizing solutions. Secondhand hospital equipment hummed and displayed vital signs. Patients hooked to beeping machines suffered in their cots, soaking their beds with sweat and other bodily fluids.

One brightly dressed Kenyan woman caught Peter's attention. She was speaking with a tall, dark-haired German doctor he'd come to know in the past couple of months—Dr. Leon Becker. The woman was cuddling a squirming infant and pointing to a tiny red mark on the child's arm.

Peter watched Dr. Becker's angular face as the doctor nodded and pressed the soft skin around the inflamed bump. As a scientist, Peter could only watch and let the doctors do their work, but he approached the bed, curious.

"My daughter was bitten by a mosquito." She rubbed the child's head, which was covered in a thin layer of black hair. As the woman explained her child's worsening condition since being bitten a week before, Dr. Becker examined the infant. He stared at the ground absently as he gently pressed the baby's belly, checking her spleen.

"You can help her?" the woman asked, finishing her explanation.

"Yes," Dr. Becker began, avoiding the mother's eyes, "we can help your daughter." The mother showed no signs of noticing Dr. Becker's detachment. Her expression told a story of absolute faith in the West's seemingly infinite knowledge and magical technology.

Dr. Becker noticed Peter and waved him closer. "This is Peter Spaulding," he told the mother. "He's from the Harvard Department of Immunology and Infectious Diseases."

"*Jambo*," Peter said, immediately regretting using the Swahili greeting.

His presence felt foolish. He wasn't a doctor here to treat patients, and it would be three years before he obtained his Ph.D., assuming he made some inroads with his research on antimalarial drugs.

"Your daughter has malaria, ma'am," Dr. Becker explained as he fiddled with a bag of intravenous solution. "This bag of fluid contains medication that'll make her feel better."

Once he'd finished hooking up the IV, Dr. Becker stripped off his latex gloves and threw them in the trash. He turned to Peter and whispered, "It's *Plasmodium falciparum*."

Of the five species of malaria, *P. falciparum* was the most lethal. Peter had swirled colonies of the parasites around in a beaker hundreds of times, trying to find a way to beat them, but he'd never been able to. It had always been an abstract problem for Peter. He'd never seen the parasite's effects up close, so tragically effective in the human body. The child couldn't have been more than a year old.

As Dr. Becker discussed the child's condition with her mother, speaking of her enlarged liver and inevitable demise, Peter studied the mother's face. He expected her to cry or maybe get angry and shout like other parents had, like the ones who now clutched at their children, understanding they had only hours to live.

But she didn't get mad. Nor did she cry. Something did change, though. Hope drained from her face, and her faith in the doctor crumbled.

She glanced at Peter, and their eyes locked.

What can I do for her? Nothing.

Peter wanted to leave. He wanted to go back to where things made sense—a life of quiet experiments, exams, presentations, and beers with friends after the lab.

"Well, I'm going to check on the others," Dr. Becker announced, scribbling notes on a chart. "We will do everything in our power to help your daughter, ma'am." He then walked to the far corner of the tent, leaving Peter with the mother and patient.

"My name is Amara," the mother said.

Peter introduced himself. "What's her name?" he asked, glancing at the infant.

Amara was still caressing the child's head. "Her name is Malia."

"The doctors will do everything they can," Peter echoed.

Even as he spoke, Peter knew the medication flowing into Malia's arm probably wouldn't stop the infection; the parasite had likely developed a resistance. The doctors were smart, but for as long as Peter had studied the disease, malaria had proven itself smarter.

"The doctor does not believe anymore," Amara said, looking down at Malia.

"Believe?"

"He does not believe he can help us. I can see it."

Peter carefully searched for words. "Malaria is a challenging disease."

Amara tilted her head. "Do you believe?"

If she had seen through Dr. Becker, she would see through Peter. She likely knew this tent, this conversation, was agonizing for him, and that Peter had wanted to leave ever since he'd arrived.

"I'm not really a doctor," Peter muttered, feeling uncomfortable.

Malia coughed and scrunched up her face. The soft pout turned into a breathless cry. As the mother began to rock Malia, her eyes filled with tears. "Please help!"

"U-um," Peter stuttered. "I-I-I will try."

Malia started wailing, provoking other children to cry as well. Voices lifted all through the tent, trying to calm the sobbing children. Tears streamed down Malia's face.

Peter ran through the tent, hurrying past distressed families consoling the unwell. He burst through the exit and into the hot African air. Gazing up at the sky, he inhaled deeply.

The aroma of meat roasting over a nearby fire filled his nose, but the odor of a cigarette tainted the fragrance. Peter turned his head to see Dr. Becker staring idly into the village and smoking. The doctor inhaled and blew out several smoke rings.

"So, do you believe?" he asked without turning his gaze from the sunbaked huts. Blowing out more smoke rings, he chuckled. "She asked you that, didn't she?"

"Yes," Peter replied.

"Of course she did. They all do. And you know what? When I got here three years ago, I believed. I thought we could stop this thing. But people like you have been working on the malaria riddle for decades. And what have you got to show for it? A few drugs, many of which the parasites evade."

Dr. Becker shrugged. "Let them have their faith, I say. It's all they've got. Now, if someone asks if I believe, I say yes and move on."

"Will Malia die?" Peter asked.

The doctor nodded. "I doubt she'll make it a week. Two, if she's lucky." He threw his cigarette on the ground and crushed it underfoot. "But you don't have to worry about that anymore."

"What do you mean?"

Dr. Becker reached into his coat pocket and handed Peter an envelope. "Your advisor sent this letter. You're going home early."

Peter opened the envelope and pulled out a plane ticket to Boston.

***

It had been a few days since Peter returned from Kenya, and he hadn't yet recovered from the seventeen-hour journey. If the brown coffee stain on his lab coat hadn't expressed his fatigue, his messy hair, the bags under his eyes, and his general dim-wittedness certainly would have. While he often reveled in the emptiness of the lab—in particular, his isolated section of bench space—it had been difficult to focus lately. The soft ticking of the machines, usually relaxing, only added to his malaise.

The spreadsheet on the monitor didn't help lift his spirits either. It displayed the results of an experiment he had run the day before, showing quantities of *P. falciparum* cultured in Petri dishes. In addition to the standard cocktail of nutrients the parasites needed to thrive, experimental populations were subjected to a drug formulation he'd developed from medical literature. Nonetheless, the data presented high rates of growth in all populations, including those subjected to Peter's compound.

Another failure. What's new?

Since he had begun as a doctoral student in Harvard's Department of Immunology and Infectious Diseases two years before, every one of his antimalarial formulations had failed. A few dozen unsuccessful experiments were considered normal, but two years of disappointment had put him at his wit's end.

Frustrated, he closed his notebook and shoved it across the granite-topped lab bench. It bumped an opened cylindrical bottle and tipped over a large tray of pipette tips, spilling them across the bench and onto the floor.

"Someone's a little hungover from their African adventure."

Andrea Malloy and Chris Livengood, two of Peter's lab mates, strolled into the lab. Andrea walked by a mosquito-crossing sign and pulled a flyswatter off the wall. She stepped over the pipette tips on the floor and smacked the swatter on the bench just to annoy Peter. He rolled his eyes.

Andrea was a fifth-year grad student and a hippie intellectual: big brain and superior attitude cloaked in a deceptively laid-back disposition. She wore a flannel shirt and baggy jean shorts, with socks pulled up to her calves. As she leaned over to squint at the numbers on Peter's computer screen, the scent of body odor and sweat assaulted his nose. He knew she must have come from the insectary, where she bred mosquitoes.

"You know, you're right," she stated, inspecting the spreadsheet. "You should have been a doctor." She smirked. "Looks like another letdown."

Andrea studied the genetics of the malaria parasite. Her work generated mini successes every day, discoveries like new genes and molecular mechanisms—publication-worthy stuff. She seemed to delight in reminding Peter of his fruitless doctoral concentration—career path, even—and that medicine would have been easier. She loved to recap how impossible basic research was, as well as how much soul-crushing disappointment was involved. The work was dismally funded, and they were always battling for hard-to-win grants to back experiments that, in all probability, would fail and, if successful, would have only a slight impact on the scientific community. Meanwhile, a friend had graduated from medical school and just finished his residency; in two years, he'd be making six figures. With two post-docs ahead of him, Peter would be lucky if he earned that in ten years.

Nonetheless, every time Andrea had Peter thinking about the challenges of their chosen professions, he reminded himself of his passion for the puzzles science offered. While he liked to complain about the futility, he knew he had made the right choice. And while Andrea thought she was so cool with her "mosquito lab," who the hell wanted to cut up spit glands all day?

Chris, a second-year grad student studying the transmission of malaria from mosquitoes to humans, dropped to his knees to help with the mess. "How was your adventure?"

Why does everyone insist on calling my trip to a disease-infested camp in the middle of the African wilds an adventure?

"Yeah, it was quite the learning experience." Peter didn't want Andrea to know that he hadn't enjoyed himself. No doubt, she'd tell their advisor who had dispatched Peter to see the "true" effects of malaria because he had believed Peter was far too removed from the disease, too theoretical.

Peter thought back to the Kenyan hospital, to Malia, and to her mother, inquiring whether he believed. It didn't take much introspection to see he did not.

"Trivia night at Shay's," Chris said. "You coming?"

Typically, Peter was first in line for trivia night at the bar, but he was too tired. And he couldn't shake Malia's face from his mind.

One thing was now true: The illness wasn't just a puzzle anymore.

"I want to try a couple more formulations." He distractedly clicked open a file on the computer.

"Suit yourself," Andrea said as she and Chris headed for the exit. She hung the flyswatter back on the wall.

Peter frowned. Had the trip made that big an impression on him? Who actually changed in two months? Would one more late night in the lab cure malaria?

The African trip had been intense. *But I could use a little fun.*

"You know what?" He shut down the computer. "Wait up! I'm coming." As he grabbed his coat and shut off the lab's lights, he remembered the plea from Malia's mother, asking for his help, and the empty promise he'd made to try.

***

Amara set her daughter down in a small crib. Malia's fever had worsened since Paul left several days before. Whenever the fever did break, chills took its place, causing her to shiver despite a cocoon of blankets. When the fever returned, Malia's skin turned crimson as her body heated like a small fire in Amara's arms.

Amara dipped her nose into a colorful bouquet of flowers her brother had delivered. The arrangement's sweet aroma wafted hopefully, providing a temporary relief from the hospital's constant despair. Her brother was just exiting the tent, followed by the tribe's shaman, who had spent the night with Malia and the family. Amara considered herself wise for seeking counsel not just in the West's magic, but also in the ancient intelligence of the tribe's spiritual healer.

Throughout the night, the shaman had rocked the sick baby in his arms, blessing her while in a trance, humming prayers and chanting as he tried to draw the bad spirits from her body. Just before the sun rose, he had received a vision from the spirit world: an image of a young man carrying a gift for Malia and a boon for the hospital.

Amara knew it had to have been a vision of Peter, the young scientist who had left without a goodbye. The shaman was predicting his return.

***

Late for his rounds, Dr. Leon Becker approached the hospital with the heavy taste of liquor still on his tongue. Coffee in hand, he skimmed the daily report. Apparently, they'd lost a child in the night.

As he stepped into the tent, he passed the exiting shaman. Leon pitied the hopeful Kenyans who followed him, believing that a few waves of the witch doctor's hands would magically enable their loved ones' immune systems to outmaneuver malaria.

In many ways, though, he also envied the families of the sick and their unwavering faith. He'd yet to see hope change the course of the disease, but perhaps the delusion helped suspend rationality, providing its own kind of solace.

More than the families and their faith, Leon envied Peter Spaulding and his quick visit, his psychological distance from the sick and, most of all, his escape from Africa and the madness that had transformed Leon from idealistic hero to determined cynic these last three years, causing him to detach from the ones he'd once hoped to cure. Every day, he thought about going home, but who would do this important work if he left?

Shaking himself from his thoughts, Leon surveyed the tent, and his gaze landed on Amara. He walked over, said hello, and looked the child over. He tugged on her IV and squeezed the clear bag of antimalarial medication, which had no doubt lost ground to the parasitic infection. He made a few notes on Malia's chart, remarking that the disease had progressed classically. He suspected Malia's kidneys would fail soon, followed by anemia and possibly respiratory distress. Using his penlight, he inspected Malia's retinas for whiteness, which would indicate that cerebral malaria had set in. He made a note when he found them normal.

"Do you think the scientist who left will come back and help Malia?" Amara asked as he wrote.

Leon understood the reference to Peter, and the answer was no. The "advocates for the malaria initiative" never returned. Certainly not any from Harvard, who couldn't wait to leave the moment they'd arrived.

"Yes," he lied, faking a smile. "We spoke before he left. You and Malia made quite an impression on him."

"What is 'made an impression'?" Amara asked, looking confused.

"It means he thought highly of you and Malia."

A strong wave of self-hatred washed over Leon then. He hated the doctor he'd let this place turn him into. He hated his disillusionment, his excessive drinking, and the man he'd watched himself become. But he hated Peter more: his dispassion for humans and his ruthless pursuit of grades, degrees, and titles.

No, he wasn't going to lie for Peter Spaulding anymore.

Leon tore off his gloves. "You should know something. Do not put your faith in that man. He hated this place from the moment he arrived. And he is not coming back."

Flustered, Amara put a hand over her mouth. When Malia started to cry, she picked her up and turned to Leon in desperation. "B-but the vision…"

Leon snorted. "That man you call a shaman, who whispers chants over your sons and daughters . . ." Leon jabbed his finger at the tent's exit. "He won't cure anyone. And he *certainly* won't help your daughter!"

Lost in rage, he didn't try to temper his volume, which rose as he pointed at Amara. "To you, and all the others with misplaced hope, let me share *my* vision. Most of these children will die, including yours, and mark my words, you will never ever see Peter Spaulding again."

Amara's eyes filled with tears. The hope instilled in her by the tribe's shaman, her faith in Western medicine, and the motherly strength she'd nurtured throughout Malia's sickness all disintegrated, replaced by a profound sadness for her dying child and a hopelessness from which she'd never recover.

***

With a commanding lead in trivia night, Peter's team of Harvard doctoral students, affectionately known as the Mosquito Crew, was in good spirits at their favorite bar, Shay's Pub, as they relished the momentary respite from lab work.

"13.8 billon years," Peter whispered to Chris in answer to the trivia question the heavyset man on the stage by the bar had just read. Peter took a sip of his beer and sat back while Chris wrote the answer on an index card before handing the card to a waitress. The young woman delivered every table's card to the stage.

Still holding the microphone, the host straightened the cards and repeated the question: "Okay, the Big Bang took place how many years ago? Let's see what you all came up with."

He lifted the first card. "10 billion years ago." He slid the card to the back. "13.8 billion years ago." He read the next card and chuckled. "Okay . . . 25 years ago?" He shot a sarcastic look at the bartender. "Hey, Joe, no more drinks for the table that thinks the universe began in 1997."

The bar erupted in laughter.

The trivia host read cards from four more tables, including the Mosquito Crew's, then paused dramatically.

"The correct answer is . . . 13.8 billion years ago."

Everyone at Peter's table began clapping and laughing, excited over their fifth consecutive win. Chris offered Peter a high five.

"Are you getting a degree in physics too?" Andrea asked arrogantly, frustrated that most of the night's answers had come from Peter. He ignored her and took another sip of beer while the host prepared the next question.

Chris leaned toward Peter. "Ah, she's just pissed she has to clean up mosquito crap all day."

Peter chuckled. "Wouldn't theoretical physics be nice? All they need is a pad of paper and a sharp pencil. It takes me five hours just to prepare a single experiment."

"And ten seconds to watch it fail." Chris laughed.

"Funny."

"Ah, but they're theorists," Chris mused. "We're experimentalists. It's where the glory is."

"I don't know, man. I'm beginning to wonder if all this failure fulfills some dark psychological need." Peter sat up. "You know what I've been thinking a lot? Whether we've been mistaken in how we approach the fight against malaria."

"What do you mean?"

"The parasite is just too clever. Perhaps we can't really attack it head-on."

"You think too much, Pete." Chris slapped him on the back, then took a sip of his beer. "Tonight, just have a good time."

He was right; Peter always had a tough time shutting off his brain. It'd been even more difficult since returning from Africa. The puzzle had become an obsession. Malia had made everything so tangible, which made Peter's efforts that much more urgent.

The host began again. "Okay, ready for the next question, everyone? Here we go. In Ancient Greece, the storyteller Aesop wrote this popular fable to illustrate the moral 'slow and steady wins the race.'"

Andrea bounced in her seat and leaned across the table. "The Tortoise and the Hare," she stated with enthusiasm. "The Tortoise and the Hare!"

Chris turned to Peter, looking for approval. Peter nodded. The same answer had popped into his head, but stirred by the question, he'd remained silent. As he watched the woman collect their card, a jolt of energy hit him.

He spun in his seat. "What if we ignored infection cycles?"

"But that's the traditional approach," Chris answered, obviously disappointed the malaria talk was continuing.

"And after all these years of trying it that way, we still don't have a cure. What if we concentrated on the body's natural defenses?"

"But the parasite changes too fast for the immune system," Andrea chimed in.

"Indeed," Peter said. "It's just like the story of The Tortoise and the Hare. The parasite runs circles around the immune system."

"Strengthen the immune system?" Chris asked, his curiosity piqued.

"And make the tortoise as fast as the hare!" Peter catapulted from his seat. Euphoric, he ran for the door, weaving through tables. As he pushed open the bar's front door, the host announced, "And the answer is The Tortoise and the Hare."

***

Sitting in the driver's seat of a rental truck, Peter grabbed the foam box containing his prototype drug and pushed open the door. Stepping out onto the harsh Kenyan landscape, he marched toward the medical tent he had thought he'd never see again. Only a week before, just the thought of joining rounds in the hospital would have made him nauseous.

Now, as he walked toward the entrance with the foam box tucked under one arm, he felt useful for once. He'd spent eighteen-hour days in the lab after sprinting out of Shay's, testing a variety of formulations to boost the immune system's production of antibodies.

He ducked through the entrance and made his way toward Amara, relieved she was still there. She rocked in a wooden chair, gripping her unconscious child in her arms.

"You came back!" Her eyes held a mixture of joy and disbelief. She looked down at Malia. "You can help us now?"

Peter placed the foam box on the bed, lifted off the lid, and began unpacking its contents. He pulled out a syringe filled with a cloudy solution, cautious of the inch-long needle at the end. "Inside this syringe…"

"Who do we have here?" Dr. Becker interrupted, sauntering toward them. "Jonas Salk?" His voice rang with as much surprise as the woman's had, though his words were laden with sarcasm.

He knocked on the foam cooler as if it were a door. It was clear he wasn't happy to see Peter. In fact, he seemed downright hostile. In the two months Peter had spent in Kenya, Dr. Becker and he had gotten along well, but it was scorn that had bound them. They'd shared many meals criticizing the hospital and those within it, complaining about Kenya and sharing their contempt for the entire system. Misery loved company.

Now, Peter just pitied the tortured, beaten-down cynic before him.

"I've created a drug that I believe…"

"You've created nothing," Dr. Becker broke in. "You tinkered in the lab for a few days and came up with a potion that, in all likelihood, is ineffective and causes a host of side effects." He pointed at Malia. "This child is in a coma. She has cerebral malaria. Do you understand? It means she's going to die."

"I believe I can save her," Peter maintained calmly, trying to avoid a confrontation. He set the syringe on the bed. "This treatment doesn't directly attack the blood stage of the parasite's life cycle. Instead, it stimulates the immune system to manufacture more antibodies."

"So now you want to start injecting people with it, is that it?" Dr. Becker snickered. "I can only imagine what kinds of immunological reactions that stuff will cause. Did they even teach you about anaphylactic shock at Harvard?"

Peter's heart pumped faster. "Leon, please."

"You're all the same, you American students! You come down here, so idealistic, believing you'll change the world, hoping you'll cure malaria, of all diseases! I thought you were different. That you were a realist. But look at you! All pumped up with pride, thinking you've got the cure. And when it doesn't work, when it fails like the others have, what will you do? That false zeal you're feeling right now will vanish. You'll go back to your easy life, sipping beers and snacking on peanuts in Harvard Square, talking about how you took your shot once. And I'll be here, tending to the sick, watching this wicked disease evolve."

Normally, Peter would have engaged the doctor, but quarreling seemed trivial when so many around them needed aid. Dr. Becker shouted more accusations, his face enflamed, spit spraying from his mouth.

Suddenly, Peter pictured a reflection of himself. A self he might have become had he never returned to Kenya. Dr. Becker was right, the Peter Spaulding who'd gotten on that plane a week ago had hated this place, and he had wanted to escape. But he'd returned. And that life of chasing grades, fretting over getting published, and laughing away time at bars was over. Finally, he cared about the people his research might cure.

Furious, Dr. Becker motioned to a guard, a large African man with crossed arms. "If you think I'll just let you waltz in here and treat my patients with some cockamamie remedy, you've got…"

The doctor abruptly fell silent, his gaze glued to Amara, who held the syringe Peter had left on the bed. The inch-long needle was buried in Malia's arm, the plunger fully depressed.

Dr. Becker pushed Peter out of the way and ripped the empty syringe from Malia's arm. "Why did you do that?" he demanded, dumbfounded.

Amara stared at Peter. "Because I believe."

***

Peter watched Amara's face glow in the moonlight. She grinned at him and then nodded in the direction of the tribe's shaman, who led vibrantly dressed men and women around a blazing fire, twirling and singing in celebration of Malia's recovery.

"You saved my daughter," Amara said. "Just like our shaman said you would."

Peter smiled in contentment as he watched them dance. As the roaring blaze crackled, he stared into its hypnotic center, watching tiny bits of ash ignite, fly off, and dissolve in the star-filled sky.

Malia let out a healthy cry as she shifted in her mother's arms. It had been a week since her mother had given her Peter's drug. She had come out of the coma the day after it was administered and had improved every day since. Peter smiled as she whimpered, still awed by her recovery, which seemed like a miracle. In science, the path from theory to bedside was an arduous, unpredictable journey, yet in Peter's case, it had happened with blistering, unprecedented speed. He'd finally gotten that win he was looking for.

"Well, she'll live," Dr. Becker declared. He wore jeans and a blue T-shirt rather than his usual button-down shirt and white coat. "There's nothing I can do about that cry, though."

He grinned at his quip, and Amara and Peter chuckled cautiously. The doctor seemed sheepish, but they were still guarded since he had yet to apologize for his behavior.

"She experienced a few more fevers after she came out of the coma, but all in all, the drug worked." Dr. Becker shook his head and scratched his jaw. "I still can't believe it actually worked."

He interlocked his fingers and exhaled as if to say something, then paused. "You know, Peter . . . I just want to say . . ."

"I know," Peter assured when Dr. Becker couldn't seem to find the words. "And I'm sorry, too." He took a deep breath. "The infected aren't the only ones who suffer."

Dr. Becker nodded. "Your medicine might just put an end to that." He smiled. "What will you do now? Head back to Harvard? Accept praise for having created the drug of the century, the cure for malaria?"

"Malia's just one child," Peter protested. "We'll need more testing."

"That means years of planning, millions of dollars for research, large-scale manufacturing, and clinical trials."

"It won't be easy." Peter paused. "But I . . . have faith."

Dr. Becker nodded, looking impressed. "So, I got a call from your advisor yesterday. He wondered where you were. What should I tell him?"

Peter looked at Amara, the baby in her arms now sleeping. "Tell him thank you for sending me here. Tell him I've found all the humanity I need right here."

"You're staying?"

Peter looked into the bonfire and nodded.

"You'll need a good doctor to deliver all those shots."

Smiling, Peter stood up. "Let's talk about it over dinner."

"Just like old times." Dr. Becker grinned, but the expression soon softened. "One thing's for certain, Pete."

"What's that?"

"You made me a believer."

The Healing Book

The news of Laura's cancer had greatly upset her husband, Dr. David Mitchel, then a renowned cardiac surgeon in Boston. A man of action, a problem solver, David was frustrated that he had encountered a problem he couldn't seem to solve. Out of his depth, he sought out the best oncology specialists in nearby hospitals and threw himself into the study of metastatic breast cancer, spending late nights in his study hunched over scientific journals and textbooks.

David and Laura spent many meals discussing medical advances and experimental cancer therapies. The conversations fatigued Laura, who was a retired preschool teacher, but she agreed with David that they would fight her cancer with everything they had. They tried all of the available cancer treatments: chemotherapy, radiation, surgery, a cutting-edge immunotherapy trial. All interventions failed, however. CT scans showed the spread of tumors. Several months into the assault on the disease, Laura took David's hand one night in bed and told him that she wanted to discontinue treatment. David avoided eye contact, flipped over, and switched off the lamp. The next day, he burst into action.

Within a week, David had sold their Beacon Hill condo and bought a small cottage in Western Massachusetts. During move-in, David instructed the movers to arrange his study as it had appeared in their Boston home, with hundreds of books on several bookshelves, a laptop connected to a desktop computer, and stacks of notepads containing ideas about cancer treatments. That first winter night in the cottage, David worked in his study while Laura stared into the fireplace with a blanket wrapped around her shoulders.

That night, Laura thought about the nightmare David said he'd had right before he decided to uproot them and move across the state. In his dream, he had watched Laura die in his arms after failing a series of conventional treatments. It was then that he felt the pull against reason and science. The next morning, he committed to trying anything that might help him save his wife, even if that meant entering into the wilderness of alternative therapies, which he had always considered hogwash, even dangerous, given the lack of scientific evidence proving their safety and efficacy. David admitted that a man of science had become a man of hope.

David speculated that years of city living had overstimulated Laura's senses, keying up her body, making it vulnerable to disease by weakening her immune system and allowing cancer to develop unchecked by a strong defense. Tumors were always cropping up in our bodies, David had said, but if one's immune system was strong, they would be stamped out. If the immune system was weak due to the overproduction of stress hormones, however, a tumor could have the opportunity to grow and, if given enough time, threaten the whole system.

While the decision to relocate represented a change in treatment approach, David's skepticism of alternative therapies remained. It wasn't the doctor's style to consult "integrative" healthcare providers, and he and Laura certainly weren't going to travel to South America, or wherever, to experience the laying-on of hands from a shaman or faith healer. There would also be no talk of "sending love" to Laura's tumors or visualizing herself wrapping her arms around her traumatized childhood self that was supposedly the root cause of her illness.

First off, they would treat Laura's cancer with nutrition. "Let food be thy medicine and medicine be thy food," David said, harkening back to Hippocrates. It was no secret to either of them that the standard American diet, which included large quantities of meat, sugar, dairy, and refined foods, was effectively toxic and inflamed the body, damaging tissues and organs. And so, while listening to Mozart in their kitchen, they began to cook meals according to a plant-based diet, which were intended to give Laura's immune system the essential vitamins, minerals, fiber, and protein to battle the cancer. Since sugar was a proven energy source for growing tumors, they sought to starve the tumors by rooting out all sugar-filled foods.

A month into nutritional treatment, Laura's cravings for sweets had faded. She ate beans and nuts, organic fruits and vegetables, and lean meats sparingly. She drank copious amounts of water and drizzled foods with olive oil. She limited her consumption of red wine and drank several cups of green tea a day for its proven cancer-fighting properties. On Sundays, they fasted—a practice that had been shown to bolster the immune system and perhaps even slow the aging process by activating genes associated with longevity.

Since aerobic exercise was also good medicine, David and Laura took daily walks in the woods. They rescued a puppy and relieved stress by exploring trails behind their cottage together. In his reading, David learned that forests had been shown to produce a myriad of chemicals that were shown in some studies to relax the body and calm the mind. And so, he began referring to their walks as "forest baths." Most days, after watching the sun rise over the mountains, they would walk out onto their deck and do tai chi, which, according to traditional Chinese medicine, removed blockages in the body that caused disease by moving "life force" around various energy centers. After the light exercise, Laura found herself in better spirits. Afterward, she had less pain and would sleep better.

Each night before bed, Laura began to kneel near the fireplace and pray. Other than maybe relaxing her body, David saw little value in sending wishes into the air. He had never hidden the fact that he was an atheist, and Laura had always said that she too "lacked faith," or had at least found herself "unable to believe," and yet she didn't share her husband's strong convictions.

Sometimes, while wine-drunk, they used to speculate as to where humans "went" after death. David's position: the lights just went out. Laura wasn't so sure, though. Then, such speculations were mental play, good conversation, but death was no longer an abstraction now; it was on her doorstep. And so, Laura began to silently reexamine her beliefs.

On the days when her body ached and her thoughts swirled, a great fear of dying would take hold, and she would hope there was an afterlife, because at least that meant that this brief life wasn't the only life. "Don't we all want a little more time?" she thought. "Time to do the things we want to do? To spend more time with the ones we love?" Laura longed for a time when she could have breakfast with David without the shadow of her illness looming over them.

David wasn't the type to entertain existential conversations, so Laura poured her musings into a journal. In her notebook, she could ask questions that would otherwise alienate her from her husband. Laura had done some reading that said that journaling might help her process "stuck" emotions, which might be the root cause of her cancer. All Laura knew was that she felt better after expressing herself in writing. The hardest thing to manage was the fear her illness had brought, a ruthless anxiety about death that often woke her up in the early hours of the morning, her mind racing with worry.

Deep into winter, David began talking excitedly about bibliotherapy, a practice where literature was prescribed to ease the suffering associated with mental and physical problems. The ancient Greeks were the first to use bibliotherapy, referring to their libraries as sacred places of healing. After World War II, special libraries were even built in US hospitals where bibliotherapists matched fictional narratives with soldiers' problems.

Over time, the practice extended to the wider public and even became a profession. A bibliotherapist might prescribe Herman Hesse's *Siddhartha* to an overworked businessman dealing with a mid-life crisis. A dissatisfied lawyer could reexamine a life of striving for material success through the lens of Leo Tolstoy's novella, *The Death of Ivan Ilyich*. For those searching for meaning in a meaningless world, there was Albert Camus's philosophical essay "The Myth of Sisyphus," whereby the character Sisyphus eternally pushes a boulder up a hill only to see it roll back down after reaching the top.

David and Laura agreed that it was a bridge too far to assume that fictional narratives might slow the quiet spread of Laura's tumors. David viewed bibliotherapy through medicine's "three-legged stool." One leg offered drugs and medications. Another leg used surgery and other physical procedures. And the final leg included elements of self-care, like stress management, exercise, sleep, and bibliotherapy.

David talked enthusiastically about a study in which MRI brain scans had shown that the same brain regions are activated whether someone is reading about an adventure or experiencing it themselves. In all, reading as therapy could distract, teach, excite, calm, and even transport us. "Literature is medicine for the soul," Laura wrote in her journal.

In his study of bibliotherapy, David learned about a literary critic's mother who had apparently been "cured" by reading. As the story goes, the mother had been delirious in the hospital when her father visited and gave her a dozen adventure novels to read. It had taken the woman weeks to read through the books, but by the end, she was healed. So inspired by this case, David wrote a perspective piece for a medical journal, opening with a quote from Voltaire: "The art of medicine consists of amusing the patient while nature cures the disease." After that publication, he became obsessed with the mechanics of how books bestowed their healing properties. "The anatomy of bibliotherapy," he called it.

An amateur bibliotherapist, David also began "prescribing" books to Laura. While she preferred her cozy mysteries, Laura read the books her husband gave her. *War and Peace, Anna Karenina,* and *Moby Dick,* even adventure novels, like *Treasure Island* and *The Lost World.* David theorized that perhaps it was the mere escape that gave books and the reading experience most of their healing properties.

Laura did find that fiction provided a break from thinking about her condition. However, the minute she put her book down, Laura couldn't escape the gnawing suspicion that no treatment, conventional or otherwise, would remedy her illness.

As the snow swirled outside the cottage, Laura would read each night at the fireplace. In addition to distracting her mind, she found that the sound and rhythm of some books' prose had a calming effect. It was interesting to think that her actual physiology could respond to the cadence, syntax, and musicality of words. David shared research that certain works of literature contained prose that lowered blood pressure and reduced stress. Laura found passages in the novel *Lost Horizon* by James Hilton particularly soothing. In one part of the novel, Hilton describes the inhospitable, mystical Tibetan plateau using language that stilled Laura's mind:

> Without thought or knowledge, one could have guessed that this
> bleak world was mountain-high, and that the mountains rising
> from it were mountains on top of mountains. A range of them
> gleamed on a far horizon like a row of dog teeth.

After several weeks of using unconventional approaches to treat Laura's cancer, David and Laura were ready to check the status of her disease. They drove into Boston for a day of testing only to find that Laura's tumors had not spread or receded. Status quo. Laura now assumed that David's efforts would likely fail, and she probably wouldn't see another New England summer. The realization made her think that she had spent her entire life denying her own mortality. "It's a terrifying prospect: to die while the world goes on," Laura wrote in her diary, "and so we bury it, repress it, keep this inescapable fact at bay by busying ourselves in the world."

With oblivion more concrete than ever, Laura searched for literature that might help her reframe her view of herself and her place in the cosmos. One day, while reading Shakespeare's play, "As You Like It," a short speech took her breath away.

All the world's a stage,
And all the men and women merely players; They have their exits
and their entrances; And one man in his time plays many parts...

Laura was surprisingly comforted by the notion that she was like a character in a story. It was a relief to consider herself part of a grand cosmic narrative in which she entered into ever so briefly and then departed so others could continue the story. She had played a good part on the world's stage. She and David hadn't had children, but in many ways, the two- and three-year-olds in her classroom had been family. She had helped these children work through their emotions and tried as best she could to help them navigate the confusing and sometimes overwhelming realities of growing up. *What's wrong with passing now, having played such a wonderful part on the world's stage?*

When David wasn't working and Laura wasn't reading, they were watching funny movies; Groundhog Day was her favorite. Why funny movies? David had read the book, *Anatomy of an Illness: As Perceived by the Patient,* where the author Norman Cousins wrote about how he had cured a previously incurable autoimmune disease by binging on funny films. Cousins explained how humorous movies had provided much-needed amusement during his battle with his illness and allowed his body's own internal healing mechanisms to go to work.

Most days, David studied in his office. When Laura was so ill that she couldn't leave her bed, David would visit for a few minutes, wipe the sweat from her forehead with a warm towel, and then return to work. At times, it was inspiring to see David work so tirelessly in an attempt to heal her. Another part of her felt angry that David was often absent. Would she have been healthier had David shown her more attention, been more loving? Surely his presence would have eased her suffering. And yet, he remained locked away with his books.

His obsession with bibliotherapy growing, David embarked on an ambitious effort to write his own novel using what he was learning about how literature could heal the body and mind. A purpose-built fictional narrative, a "healing book," he called it. He closely studied the literary theories in *Poetics*, Aristotle's book on the craft of dramatic writing. One device, the philosopher wrote, was that effective fictional narratives presented readers with obstacles that produced a catharsis, from *katharos*, or clearing of obstacles. This clearing of obstacles provided a purging of emotions that led to a reworking of how the audience or reader saw themselves and the world.

David worked and Laura began to walk the dog alone. The morning walks weren't the same without her husband. What an elixir it had been to meander in the woods with David and laugh as the pup buried its nose in the snow, looking for a mouse that had disappeared. Alone one morning, Laura spent hours trying to catch the dog, which had run off. When she managed to grab the leash, an image flashed into her mind of David hunched over his desk, writing vigorously, and she began to weep.

David's book was written in piecemeal, chapter by chapter. Each night, Laura could hear the sound of her husband pounding the keys of his laptop from the bedroom. One night around midnight, she crept out of bed and peeked into his study to see him standing, scribbling on a pad of paper on top of a bookshelf, like a man possessed.

It wasn't long before David gave her pages to read. The early parts of his novel were a bit rough around the edges—too much "telling," not enough "showing," as Laura's English teacher used to say after reading her short stories in college—but the prose had an appealing lyrical style. Somehow, David had managed to pull off a neat trick. The voice in which he wrote was delicate, almost lilting. His writing style comforted her, and for many nights, Laura drifted off to sleep with pages in her lap.

As the weeks passed, the days began to warm and the snow melted, but Laura grew unexpectedly sicker. Her body frail and her mind often cloudy, she was now certain that the curtain would soon come down on her play. Early one morning, before the sun had risen, she rolled over in bed and thanked David for moving them to this beautiful part of the state. The rising and falling of the cicadas in their backyard was as good as any of Mozart's sonatas.

Laura tried to tell David that she no longer wanted a novel to soothe her worries; she wanted her husband by her side in her final days. There had been many lonely nights when she wished David would have finished his studies early, come to bed, and pressed his body against hers. That would have been a form of medicine, would it not? There's nothing cutting-edge about a hug, but it would have made her smile and feel warm and desired. An embrace wouldn't have taken away her cancer, but at least she wouldn't have felt so alone and cold during those long, dark winter nights.

David's book was nearly complete when Laura felt what she could only describe as a loosening attachment to her breath. She knew she had days, hours even, and yet David had drowned himself in his project. In a two-day writing frenzy, he finished his novel and rushed to Laura's bedside to read her the ending. Laura listened while David read, feeling tired, light, ready.

David's eyes welled up with tears, and he put the book aside and laid down beside his wife. He seemed to finally accept the fact that a book would not give Laura more time. Tears running down his face, David apologized for spending the winter buried in his work. Laura shook her head and told him it was all right. They may have been in separate rooms, but they were in the same town, under the same roof. The smell of him had never left her clothes. David shut his eyes tightly and said he was sorry for creating a healing book that didn't, in fact, heal.

Laura took David's hand and said that the books she had read, including her husband's novel, had comforted her and helped her fear death less. The literature she had been exposed to made her realize that she was part of something eternal, that while she would physically die, she could live on in David's heart and in the universal narrative in which humans continue to write as long as we are born. Indeed, David's book had not given Laura more time, but it had offered her comfort as she approached the end. His book hadn't helped her live; it had helped her die.

Early in the morning, David gazed at Laura softly and told her that he loved her and that he would miss her. Laura's eyes parted lazily, and she mumbled something that David couldn't make out. He was rubbing Laura's back when she drifted off, and her chest became still. David wrapped his wife in his arms and stared into the night sky until the morning came and the room filled with light.

Searching for Meaning in the Stars

Life is meaningless. The devastating realization came to me in winter, as I traveled from Boston, where I worked as a physics professor and mathematician, to my cabin on Lake Winnipesaukee in New Hampshire.

I'd left the city later than usual, and by the time I reached the lake, it was dark and snowing. There were no bridges or ferries linking the small island in the lake to the mainland, so I had to use a boat to get there. Crossing at night was dangerous, even without snow. I'd done it once before, navigating by a light from the only other cabin on the island, but this night was moonless and fog hugged the water, making it impossible to see much of anything. I did my best to steer toward the island, but it was only a dim shape in the fog.

Within minutes, I had lost my bearings. When the boat struck a rock, I jerked forward, hitting my head on the dashboard, and toppled to the floor. The boat lost power, and the running lights went out, throwing me into complete darkness.

When I woke, I didn't know how much time had passed, but the snow had stopped falling and a multitude of stars peeked through breaks in the clouds. At that moment, I felt like I had merged with the night sky. My sense of my body disappeared, and I was part of the heavens, connected to the cosmos.

For many, such a sensation might have made them feel connected to something greater than themselves, giving their lives significance.

Not me.

For years, I'd had the gnawing feeling that nothing mattered, but it hit a fever pitch that night. In that moment, I knew more clearly than ever that I was a tiny speck in a vast ocean of blackness. I was insignificant. A blip in the cosmic play.

It was terrifying.

As a theoretical physicist, I had a scientific view of the world and a cosmic view of human existence. From my perspective, humans were just bags of particles, whirling protons and electrons, governed by the physical laws of the universe. A young species, almost genetically identical to chimpanzees, we lived on a waterlogged planet circling a medium-sized star at the edge of a small galaxy in a cluster of thousands of galaxies, among billions of even more galaxies.

When I finally arrived at the island, I was shaken. Thinking about merging with the cosmos and how meaningless my life was, I couldn't sleep. How could I live with the knowledge? If life was so short and insignificant, why go on?

A few days into my stay on the island, I dreamed I was in college and decided not to attend my calculus class or do the assigned homework. I was aware I was damaging my grade by ignoring the class's requirements. My behavior continued, and by the end of the semester, I knew I'd failed calculus, devastating my semester GPA. Yet when my grades were released by my teacher, I didn't log in to the website to check them. I just carried on with my life, ignoring the matter

When I woke at three in the morning, I puzzled over the dream. What did it mean? Eventually, I realized it was an unconscious wish. I would *never* have been so neglectful in real life—I had always been studious in school—but in a dream, I could do anything.

But why was I fantasizing about avoiding my responsibilities?

I reasoned that my work to demystify the laws of nature and leave an enduring legacy had exhausted me. The dream represented a nihilistic wish to surrender all my striving. There was some appeal in giving up. I'd never thought about ending my life, but I recognized the allure of death. It was oblivion. The instant the lights went out, all my desires and dramas would disappear. In a strange way, there was comfort in the thought of leaving my struggles behind.

The next day, I called my primary care doctor.

"You likely suffered a minor concussion, but otherwise, you should be fine," he told me after I explained what happened.

"I think I'm having an existential crisis."

The doctor paused, likely not knowing how to respond. "I suspected depression, or seasonal affective disorder, but I can't confirm either based on your symptoms."

"What do you think I should do?"

"I'd advise taking a break from work for a while. Our minds and bodies have ways of telling us to slow down when we're pushing too hard."

Later that day, I took a stroll around the island, which was a quarter of a mile long and a tenth of a mile wide. Thankfully, most of the snow from the night before had burned away with the morning sun.

As I neared the only other cabin on the island, I saw a strong, stocky middle-aged man with a full beard and a bald head standing on the porch, his big hands wrapped around a cup. Mack was a local handyman and mechanic and the owner of the marina's gas station and convenience store.

"How are ya?" he called when he spotted me.

Usually, I'd walk over and chat for a while, but my mind still swirled from the prior night's dream and the accident a few days before. Instead, I waved and said only, "Good morning" before continuing on.

At the northern tip of the island, I sat next to a spruce tree. I brushed away a thin layer of snow and ran my hand through the spongy moss beneath. I reflected on the conversation with my doctor and realized my problem wasn't neurochemical or even psychological; it was philosophical. If I suffered from a "disease," it was an ailment of the soul. A crisis of meaning.

The religious people I knew got their values primarily from their faith, but I'd always relied on rational thinking and the scientific method to make sense of life. A scientist relied on facts, and there was no evidence to support the existence of a god.

While I couldn't delude myself, I acknowledged that by choosing not to believe, I had lost an essential source of guidance for navigating the complexities of the human endeavor. The sciences helped me explore the mysteries of our world, but they couldn't help me address the more significant questions my boating accident had raised.

Why was I here? What made life worth living? Would I go anywhere after death? In the face of these big questions, science, in all its glory, could do nothing. Science told me the hows, not the whys. I knew how the big bang had happened, but not why it had happened. I knew how evolution occurred through the process of natural selection, driven by random genetic mutations, but I didn't know why life had begun on our planet in the first place.

As a physicist, I'd spent my decades-long career obsessed with finding the most profound truths about the cosmos. I was no Stephen Hawking in terms of impact or celebrity, but I was a leading scientist, and my research, textbooks, and lectures had pushed the field of theoretical physics forward in significant ways. Yet now . . .

Why search for a unified theory of physics when our species may go extinct due to forces outside our control?

Even if we prevented our demise using technology, Earth had an expiration date. It was a cosmological certainty that in a few billion years, our sun would enlarge, engulf Earth, and explode. If our species was around and escaped that catastrophe, Andromeda, the closest galaxy to our own, was on a collision course with the Milky Way. If that wasn't bleak enough, the known universe was expanding so fast that in a thousand billion years, all the stars in our night sky would have died and gone cold.

If our species, planet, galaxy, and even universe had expiration dates, why play the game of life? Why pay taxes, teach, work, or love? Why not end one's life early?

The next day, I brought my boat to the marina. Though I'd gotten it running again after the accident, I wanted Mack to check it out.

"Of course," he said when I asked. "I'll look it over this afternoon."

"Thanks."

"Everything all right?" he added before I could leave to let him work. "You seem tense."

I told him about the dream I'd had, as well as an idea I'd been haunted by lately, which I'd read in a provocative book by a French writer. "This writer says the most vital question is whether life is worth living."

Mack's eyebrows raised. "In other words, whether or not we should kill ourselves?"

"That's right," I said. "According to the writer, answering that question is more important than knowing how many dimensions our universe has. From his perspective, humans crave meaning in their lives, yet the universe is indifferent to their desires. This leads to the 'absurd.'"

"You've gotta be careful with ideas like that, Alexander. I have a cousin who thought life didn't make any sense, that nothing mattered. He's now locked away in a psych ward, like the guy in that flick *One Flew Over the Cuckoo's Nest.*"

I nodded. The French writer warned that realizing life was irrational could lead to despair, but he also said we shouldn't stop at that insight. "He encourages us to fill the resulting existential void with a psychological revolt."

"What's that mean?"

"I'm not exactly sure yet. I need to figure that out."

Mack shook his head and laughed. "I think you just need a hobby, my friend. You're wound up pretty tight!"

I appreciated Mack's perspective. Like him, I had humble origins. We both came from small towns in New Hampshire, where many people were self-employed. When I was tired from hours of straining my brain with equations, I sometimes romanticized Mack's "simpler" life and grew nostalgic for my hometown. Sometimes, I'd whip up a little daydream about moving back home to start a small business so I could work with my hands and fall asleep every night in a tired body. Maybe I'd meet someone I enjoyed spending time with and open a bookstore or a bed and breakfast.

But alas, it wasn't my life. "What I could be, I must be." I was a man of science who had the tools to discover answers to complex questions.

When I returned to the marina a few hours later, Mack said, "Well, I've fiddled with a few things, and everything seems to be working fine. Just don't go hitting any more rocks, all right?"

I chuckled. "Roger that, Mack."

"And hey, if you want to come by my cabin this evening, I'd love to have you."

The invitation wasn't unusual, and I happily accepted.

At dusk, I took the narrow dirt path through the spruce and pine trees to Mack's cabin. He greeted me at the door with a six-pack of beer and walked me into his living room. Over the fireplace hung a framed photograph that caught my attention.

I nodded toward the picture. "What's this?"

Mack smiled. "It's called *Earthrise*. An American astronaut took that picture from a space capsule while he was circling the moon. You can see Earth rising above the moon's surface. Pretty cool, huh?"

"Absolutely," I said, staring at the image. It was enchanting to see Earth floating in the galactic blackness. There was our home, a magnificent small, blue rock where billions of us strove, fought, hoped, hated, and loved.

"It's amazing to think we're all living out our existence on this rock, just trying to add purpose to our brief stay."

Mack took a sip of his beer. "From this vantage point, there are no religions or nations, no democrats or republicans."

"It makes me feel insignificant."

"That's funny," Mack said. "It makes me feel special."

We walked out onto Mack's dock, where we chatted. Knowing what I did for a living, he often liked to ask life's "biggest questions," especially about the universe.

"You think there's life on other planets, Alex?" he asked at one point.

I shrugged. "With several hundred billion stars in our galaxy and a hundred billion galaxies within the universe? The chances are certainly high."

The next morning, I woke up and tinkered with an equation for a few hours. As I ate lunch, though, I decided to apply my intellect to something other than math or physics. I had thought my way into this crisis of meaning, so I could surely think my way out of it. To start, though, I needed more information.

After lunch, I picked up a book and didn't put it down until I'd finished it. For the next three weeks, I decided to take the advice of Mack and my doctor. I didn't do any math. Instead, I read books like a madman.

I started my quest for meaning by reading books that focused on understanding death and how to think about one's life knowing it had an expiration date. It soon became clear that humans were terrified of death. As an antidote, we busied ourselves in the meaning-making systems of our cultures to distract ourselves from the reality of our demise.

I, too, had spent my entire life repressing this fear. After all, what was more terrifying than knowing that one day, you would no longer be? With the accident, however, I could no longer deny reality and had faced the truth of my eventual demise. Facing the truth, however, came at a significant cost. Without denial, where could I find comfort?

No doubt there was comfort in believing a higher power could answer my wishes or I might go to a better place when I died. I'd certainly have company, as 89 percent of Americans believed in God, and 74 percent believed in life after death. I was well aware—albeit always amazed—that 25 percent of scientists at elite universities believed in God. Such belief kept my religious friends buoyant in times of struggle. Yet organized religion was of no use to me on this matter.

If I had been a younger man, I might have tried to relieve my anxiety by binging self-help books in a desperate search for a thought leader or guru who claimed to have simple answers to complex questions. I'd learned the futility of this strategy in my thirties. No gains were associated with it, and the gurus, motivational speakers, intellectuals, politicians, celebrities, and even therapists were just as much in the dark as I was on life's mysteries. Especially when they said otherwise.

My main preoccupation that winter was to understand what gave life meaning. I turned to those who had crossed this existential divide before me and who, in searching for meaning in their lives, had found a cure for their nihilism. Most of the books I read were written by philosophers and thinkers concerned with human existence.

I read a book by a famous author who'd suffered an existential crisis and fallen into a deep depression in his fifties after recognizing that none of his work mattered. In the writer's account, life seemed like an absurd joke. Knowing this, he felt he couldn't continue with the mundane tasks of everyday life. He'd finally concluded that working-class laborers seemed to live without the existential angst that afflicted the more educated or elite.

Mack confirmed this while we were sitting around the campfire one night. "I feel bad for people like you, obsessing over stuff like the search for the meaning of life. There's significance all around you! Look at my life. Fixing up boats contributes to the community. While customers wait, I tell 'em a joke or story to pass the time. And I'm on the town's zoning committee and am even considering running for sheriff someday."

I nodded, considering Mack's words.

As I continued to read, I realized I needed a new metaphor for life. A friend of mine thought of life as a journey, like a trek up a steep mountain along winding, sometimes perilous trails. I couldn't relate to that, though. It seemed inadequate.

The metaphor for life the French author proposed was the myth of Sisyphus, who had been cursed to push a boulder up a mountain, only to watch it roll down again every time he reached the top. But Sisyphus, the writer claimed, had learned to find some dark enjoyment in the monotony. He had been cursed, but every day, he had a job to do, and he did the best he could.

Was I not like Sisyphus? Every day, the same routine: wake up, shower, brew coffee, scribble in my notebook for hours, walk, read, sleep, and do it all over again. Could I, like Sisyphus, enjoy the struggle and find some dark happiness in the monotony? There were plenty of boulders to push in my field. Solving a complex equation was always a struggle, but it was invigorating when a problem cracked.

However, this parable still didn't help me understand why I should push boulders in the first place.

Moving on, I read books by a provocative philosopher with some exhilarating ideas. He created one thought experiment, "the eternal return," that urged readers to think about living their life repeatedly, the same joys and pains, in the same order, for eternity. If the thought of living every moment over and over again horrified me, then I hadn't become who I was destined to be.

Putting myself to the test, I realized I wasn't as dissatisfied as I might have guessed. In fact, I was rather content with my place in the world as a physics professor and mathematician. That said, if my life were to repeat endlessly, there were some changes I would make.

The ideas I encountered in my reading led me to make some of those changes. First, I spoke to the head of my physics department and requested a sabbatical for the spring semester. It took some convincing, as it was late notice, but I was granted the approval. Thinking I could live in my cabin, I put my Boston apartment on the market, and within a week, it was sold. Mack helped me fully winterize my cabin.

The day I moved all my belongings into the cabin, I was filled with joy. I'd always admired Henry David Thoreau and his experiment living in a small cabin on Walden Pond near Concord, Massachusetts. Now I was making my own experiment! I had the solitude to read, think, and work on my projects. I had enough savings to live comfortably, but if I needed funds, I could teach classes at the University of New Hampshire.

For the following month, all I did was read, work, and walk around the island, stopping to record ideas in a notebook. I was alone much of the time, but I seldom felt lonely.

Mack had become a friend, and I looked forward to his visits after he closed his shop for the night. Sometimes, we'd sit around a fire for hours, drinking beer and discussing whatever was on our minds. Mack liked to stargaze, so I'd bring my telescope to the end of his dock, and we'd examine craters on the moon. Sometimes, we'd see as far as Venus or Mars or even the moons around Jupiter.

Mack was always astonished by facts about space. When I told him our planet spun on its axis at about 750 miles per hour, and that Earth orbited the sun at 65,000 miles per hour, he rubbed his beard while he looked across the dark lake, lost in thought. One night, after a few beers, I told Mack about the books I'd been reading, and he offhandedly suggested I should write about what I had learned. It was a strange time in my life, and the idea of attempting to make sense of it through writing piqued my curiosity. With each day, I took the idea more seriously.

It was spring when I felt the welling up of a spiritual revolt inside me. A revolt against the despair of knowing the universe was indifferent to my desires and that a human life had no intrinsic meaning. The antidote, I realized, was to create my own personal significance.

For me, that involved engaging in projects and activities that energized me and gave my life zest. The field of physics had already given me these opportunities. Through my work, I expressed my unique talents and contributed to the advancement of knowledge. Perhaps, through my work, I was already rebelling against the meaninglessness?

There was no outside authority or standard to confirm whether this was true. No parent, teacher, politician, or God could know what the right choices were for me. It was something of a eureka moment to realize that each choice I made gave my life meaning. For me, a life dedicated to physics was a good life. The many authors I'd read had helped me come to this realization. Thinking my experiences could perhaps help others and knowing that storytelling and mythology had helped humans comprehend their existence for centuries, I took Mack's advice and began writing a book about my crisis.

All through spring, my daily routine involved waking up and writing feverishly until lunchtime. The manuscript began with the bleak certainty that our species was irrelevant in the vastness of the cosmos. To put things in perspective, I included the "cosmic calendar," where the time span of the universe—from the big bang 13.8 billion years ago to the present day—was overlaid on a single-year calendar.

On this calendar, the Milky Way didn't form until May, our solar system only coalesced around September, and single-celled organisms didn't show up on Earth until November. Dinosaurs appeared on December 24 and went extinct six days later. Astonishingly, modern-day humans appeared in *the last second,* at 23:59:59 on December 31. Dinosaurs lasted six days, and humans were only in their sixth second. If that didn't put life into perspective, I didn't know what could.

While I walked readers through the workings of the universe, the book was also part memoir and an attempt to answer the problem I'd set out to solve when I moved into the cabin: How did we go on living when life was brief and nothing seemed to matter? How did we accept Nabokov's description of a human life as "a brief crack of light between two eternities of darkness"?

Writing was philosophy in action. Every day, I brought order to disorder by transforming personal insights and ancient wisdom into sentences, paragraphs, and chapters. Writing was similar to physics: they both involved discovery. I developed a strong belief that if I got the correct words in the right order, then perhaps I could help readers make sense out of the chaos of their lives.

While I enjoyed the process of discovery in writing, it was challenging to transform vague impressions and feelings into coherent sentences and give the big mess of ideas form. Yet writing allowed me to think critically about what I believed and helped me in my quest to find meaning—and I would share what I learned in the book: We all had to make it up as we went. We found meaning in our lives by discovering our own reasons for living.

From this, I realized the book was my attempt at a second grand unified theory—not one that searched for laws transcending time and space but one encompassing the human endeavor. A guide for life.

As summer drew to a close, the crisis my boating accident had sparked in my soul was resolving. My voracious reading on the meaning of life and the self-reflection I'd done was providing diminishing returns. I knew I had to stop reading and thinking, and just live.

One night, as we sat around the fire, Mack suggested that perhaps it was impossible for humans to solve the physics problem to which I had devoted my life.

"Maybe no human can crack it," he offered. "Maybe humans are like frogs trying to understand geometry. Frogs will just never figure out geometry."

"Maybe the problem is beyond our cognitive capacity," I agreed.

"How's that search for the meaning of life coming?"

"I'm still unsure whether my life has meaning from a cosmic perspective," I said. "But it does have meaning from a terrestrial one—at the level of my local community and the people I know. Whether I have the ability to solve my equations, I've found my work life enhancing; it exercises my strengths and gives me a reason for being alive."

Mack tipped his beer in congratulations. "I knew you'd figure it out."

Beyond my work, there were countless reasons to be alive. Friendship gave life meaning. Creativity gave life meaning. Freedom gave life meaning. Watching the hummingbirds around the feeder was meaningful. That first sip of coffee in the morning was meaningful. An afternoon of reading in the hammock near the water was meaningful. Life was so short, but these things kept us alive.

At the end of the summer, I decided not to return to the university in Boston. I began a part-time teaching position at UNH. This gave me time to work on my equations and finish my manuscript.

When I did my first reading at a local bookstore, I shared the story of the night I crashed my boat and lost myself in the stars. I explained how that incident had prompted me to retreat into solitude and find reasons for living. After the reading, several people told me the book had inspired them to find meaning in their own lives.

After that summer, I no longer felt insignificant when I gazed up at the sky at night and lost track of my body and mind connecting to the cosmos. Knowing I would die no longer brought me dread. I knew my place in the world. I cherished the brief time I had to play my part on this planet.

Every day, I took my pencil and coffee-stained pages to my work desk to bang away at calculations. Perhaps I'd solve the problem and help us better understand our place in the heavens, or maybe I wouldn't. Maybe the problem was beyond my abilities. It didn't matter. I was working, participating, playing. I was alive.

Many months after the accident, I worked up the guts to take my boat onto the lake at night. The moon was out, and the stars were shimmering. In the middle of the lake, I dropped the anchor, laid on my back, and looked up at the sky.

Suddenly, I understood what the meaning of life was. Simply put, life itself had no meaning; there was only meaning *in* life. Meaning came from participating in life, even if you knew it was all fiction.

I came up with a new metaphor for living then.

Why not view my life and work on developing a unified theory as a sophisticated form of creative play? Why not see myself as a character in a novel overcoming challenges in pursuit of goals? It was an illusion, completely fake, but at least it was an illusion of my choosing. With this metaphor, life was a creative act, a work of art from beginning to end.

The Disciple

Gabby wouldn't have called it a cult. Desert's Gate was a community of like-minded people searching for purpose in their lives. She and a couple dozen other disciples lived in a house in Southern California. They abided by strict rules: no caffeine, no alcohol, no drugs, and sex only with the guru, Orion.

Orion was a charismatic man in his mid-forties, with a fit body and an air of superiority. Gabby and the other disciples would cook for him, give him massages, and read him Shakespeare while he soaked in a hot tub with a warm cloth on his forehead. On weekends, Orion would lead the group into a secluded part of Joshua Tree National Park to act as a medium for some higher power.

Gabby always eagerly awaited her turn.

When Orion called her forth, Gabby sat cross-legged at his feet and watched him close his eyes and rock himself into a trance. Suddenly, he became radiant, as if electricity ran through his nervous system. In an unfamiliar voice, he began to speak of an entity who watched over her and guided her through difficult times. The entity, a Native American chief wearing a large headdress, stood at Gabby's right shoulder.

"You are in a time of great transition, Gabby, but you are stuck, like a lion with its paw caught in a trap," Orion said, his voice mysterious. "American society is confused right now, ill-equipped to handle the pace of change and loss of faith in the wake of the rise in science and technology. But you, Gabby, have natural psychic abilities. You will soon lead a spiritual revolution."

Later that afternoon, Gabby received a video call from James, a former disciple who'd left the commune a few weeks prior. They'd kept in touch since he left through frequent texting, late-night video chats, and even old-fashioned letters. She often thought of James as her best friend, but he was much more than that.

James was convinced the Desert's Gate disciples had been brainwashed, and he'd been trying to convince Gabby to leave too, but she was resistant.

"I hired a private investigator to look into Orion's past," James said once they'd chatted for a bit. "Orion's a failed actor who did a stint in pornography. Then he got some certificate in hypnotherapy—no doubt to learn how to put people in a trance and control their minds."

James picked up a book and held it so Gabby could see. The cover bore the title *Confessions*, and Gabby could see Orion's name at the bottom. "This is his self-published memoir, which 'explains' how he communicates with the spirit world."

Gabby frowned but didn't say anything.

"Have you seen the videos?" James asked.

"What videos?"

"Hold on." James did something on his end, then nodded. "Check your email."

Gabby opened her inbox, found the email he'd just sent, and opened the attached file. It was a video of Orion and Gabby in the desert.

"This is one of the videos the PI found of our retreats."

Gabby watched with growing embarrassment as Orion placed his hand on her head and she began shaking uncontrollably. "How many more videos are there like this?"

"A dozen or so," James said. "They're all online. Desert's Gate has gone viral."

Gabby was ashamed to see herself under Orion's spell, but unusual things happened in the commune all the time.

"You need to get out, Gabs," James advised. "Orion is bad news."

Maybe he is, but . . .

"This is all I've known for twelve years. These people are my friends. We're practically a family."

"Just keep reading and watching these videos," James said. "There's going to be a lot of commentary on what the PI found. Please leave. If you need a place to stay, you can come here. For however long you want."

Over the next few weeks, the media wrote scathingly about Desert's Gate. But even faced with the impassioned pleas of her family, Gabby resisted leaving. What would she do without the routines and rituals of Desert's Gate?

It wasn't until Gabby told Orion she'd fallen in love that she made up her mind.

"Who's the lucky man?"

Gabby bit her lip. "He left a few weeks ago, James."

"You don't love me anymore?"

Gabby froze. She'd never loved Orion. She'd only done what she had for him, including sex, because he'd given her so much spiritually.

"Can James give you what I do?" Orion asked. "Can he fill that void in your soul like I can? We both know there's trauma yet unexplored. Psychic conflicts waiting to be resolved. Your paw is still caught in a trap. Let me show you how to remove it."

Confused, Gabby felt like crying. She'd spent years cleaning, preparing food for, and being intimate with this man. It had all seemed worth it for her growth. But now Orion claimed she couldn't be with a man she loved?

That was not okay.

"I'm going to leave."

"People are free to come and go as they please."

After all those years, Orion didn't even put up a fight. Gabby left the room and booked the next shuttle to Los Angeles.

She had sacrificed over a decade of her life to Desert's Gate. She'd abandoned her family and friends. She'd helped pay Orion's car payments, mortgage, and student debt. And that was to say nothing of the abuse Orion had inflicted on her and everyone in the commune, sexually and psychologically.

His intentions, she realized, were not for her spiritual development but for his ego.

Once on a shuttle bound for James's apartment, Gabby realized there were many false prophets like Orion—some with dangerous ideas and philosophies. What if it were her mission to find and expose them? Had Orion's revelation been correct? Was this her revolution to lead?

She knew just where to start.

"Stop the bus, please!"

The vehicle stopped. Gabby stepped out onto hot pavement and turned back toward Joshua Tree. Taking a deep breath, she headed back to Desert's Gate.

Cubicle

By the end of my second year of film school, I was still struggling to find my voice as an aspiring documentary filmmaker. Most of my classmates had already committed to an artistic style, and some had even begun film projects. They used many of the techniques we'd learned in class: on-camera interviews, voice-over narration, reenactments using actors or animation, and dramatic music intended to emphasize certain moments.

Perhaps I was a purist, but I considered such methods nothing more than parlor tricks. They cluttered up films and sometimes obscured the truth. Most of my peers considered themselves journalists, but my aims were novelistic. To make a film with all the subtleties and complexities of fiction. I wanted my film to raise questions, not just provide answers. To show what I'd observed in as simple terms as possible.

Yet no subject had ignited my passions. What did I want to highlight and show the world?

That summer, I interned part-time with the marketing department of Boston Health, editing videos that featured physicians and scientists talking about diseases and patients who had undergone successful treatments. A few weeks in, Kathy, the marketing content manager, called me into her office.

"Due to recent staff increases, we need more space," she told me. "We'll be assembling a dozen cubicles to make sure everyone has seating. How would you feel about working in one of the new workspaces?"

I hadn't worked in a traditional office setting before the internship, and I had never even heard of a "cubicle farm." I had seen a cubicle, though. Such a tiny space offered no natural light and seemed like a dreadful place to spend eight hours a day. Despite the question, though, something in Kathy's expression gave me the sense I didn't really have a choice in the matter. She'd already made her decision.

"Whatever you need," I replied.

Just as I was exiting her office, an idea struck me, and I turned back to face her.

"As you know, I've been hoping to make a film for my school thesis." When she nodded, I added, "What if I brought my camera into the office to film the assembly of the cubicles?"

She frowned thoughtfully. "I suppose that would be okay, but you'll need to clear the project through HR."

After three meetings and signatures on several official documents, my project was approved. The next morning, during the marketing department's weekly meeting of thirty employees, Kathy announced I would be making a student film about the office.

"Isaac will walk around with a camera," she declared monotonously. "If he asks questions, please answer them in a respectful manner, but do not disclose confidential information about our department or the hospital."

I stood. "Thank you for allowing me to observe your work. I'll do my best to avoid disturbing the environment or anyone. I plan to maintain a fly-on-the-wall approach. I only want to understand what it's like to work in a modern office setting as the new cubicles are being put together."

A marketing manager, Hannah, raised her hand, and I pointed at her. "Do you have a question?"

"Will you conduct interviews?" Hannah asked.

I shook my head. "I'd like to avoid on-camera interviews. I'd like to just film you going about your business and capture a story—if one develops."

She beamed. "How exciting!"

It took about two weeks for the workspaces to be built. The project was anticlimactic and decidedly uncinematic. So much so, I nearly abandoned it until I observed the interactions of employees working within the cubicles.

After a few days of gathering footage of the cubicle farm, it was clear most people stayed in one place most of the day, leaving only for lunch or to chat with a coworker in the breakroom or hallway. While one of the building's exits led to a path that wound through a private park, few folks took advantage of it.

The most surprising aspect, though, was the silence. The drop of a pin would have been clearly heard. To avoid distracting one another, many people chatted via the messaging tool on their computers. Even employees who sat a few feet apart communicated using the digital tool. And the moment someone passed behind them, they minimized the messaging tool as if they'd been caught doing something improper.

About a month into filming, I passed the cubicle of a bored-looking man named Jackson. I didn't know much about the thirty-something other than that he supervised a graphic designer and a copywriter. What made him so uninterested? Was something going on in his work life that I could explore? Curious, I asked his permission to film him.

Jackson shrugged, seeming indifferent to my request. Such apathy seemed to be his general approach to everything. Perhaps it was this too-cool-for-school quality I gravitated toward. Everyone else in the office walked the walk, so to speak, but Jackson seemed to be a free thinker. In an environment where conformity reigned, I sensed an independent thinker like Jackson might attract conflict.

I filmed Jackson for most of the week. Unlike others, who decorated their cubicles with pictures of friends or family, he had left the walls of his cubicle bare.

He seemed to prefer the lack of distraction, as he spent hours at a time hunched over a laptop, staring at Excel spreadsheets.

At one point, I asked Jackson to describe his role and the work he did: maintenance of the hospital's website, making updates and fixing glitches. That week, he was working on a project from Victoria, the department's vice president. The *US News & World Report* had ranked Boston Health thirteenth in the United States, dropping it from eighth the year prior.

"Lucky thirteen," Jackson noted with sarcasm.

I positioned the camera a few feet from his face. "What's your project?"

"Well, Victoria told Kathy to have me create a list of every place on the hospital's website where we say we're eighth and then change it to *thirteenth.*"

Out of nowhere, a balled-up piece of paper struck Jackson above the ear. I panned the camera toward the source to see his neighbor grinning from her chair. Christmas lights flickered on the walls of her cubicle.

"Your aim's getting better, Hannah," Jackson remarked.

"Lunch?" Hannah asked.

Jackson closed his laptop. "I'm starving."

Hannah looked at me and pointed at the camera. "You want to join?"

I agreed, eager to spend time in a more casual setting. The camera continued rolling as we strolled to the cafeteria, where we paid for our food and found a table. Jackson and Hannah agreed to me filming lunch, though others watched the camera with suspicion. I set the camera on a nearby table, hoping Jackson and Hannah would overlook it and act naturally.

A curious change transpired in Jackson right away. While he'd appeared bored and apathetic in his cubicle, his face brightened as he discussed a trade the New England Patriots had recently made and how it would benefit his fantasy football team. The change in his demeanor was fascinating. When Jackson talked about sports, he seemed so vibrant and full of life, yet he appeared deeply uninterested in his job.

"Do you like your job?" I asked.

Jackson shrugged. "I don't hate it. Any line of work comes with all sorts of crap. It's a job; jobs aren't supposed to be fun."

Having spent time with others in the department, I had the vague sense Jackson wasn't the only one who felt dissatisfied every day, year in, year out. Did they need money that badly? How did such widespread discontent manifest in the department?

The next morning, I strolled the halls with my camera, aiming to get a better sense of the environment in which the employees worked. The office walls were white and mostly blank. It might've made sense to display artwork depicting the renowned doctors, nurses, and hospital leaders who'd founded Boston Health and helped it thrive over its long history. It might have reinforced the values of the organization, instilled a sense of mission within the employees, and perhaps helped them find purpose in their work.

Yet most workers seemed to care more about what snacks were offered in the break room—mostly junk food. It seemed fashionable for people to concern themselves with trivialities and ignore big stuff that could help them become better workers.

As I was contemplating the bare walls, I noticed Hannah farther down the hallway, whispering with Claire, the graphic designer Jackson managed. Though Claire kept her voice low, I could just make out what she was saying about me.

"Watch out, ladies and gentlemen. Ken Burns, coming through."

I frowned at the reference to the famous documentary filmmaker. I greatly admired the man, but it was obvious Claire was poking fun at me. When I got closer, Hannah smiled innocently, as if they'd only been discussing the weather.

I hesitated, wondering if I'd misinterpreted Claire's comment. "Is there something you'd like to say about my film project, Claire?"

Claire pressed a hand to her chest, looking taken aback. "No, Isaac! We were just saying how much we liked Ken Burns's new documentary about Paul Farmer."

"Uh-huh." Not wanting to press the issue, I smiled and walked away, reminding myself I was a fly on the wall for this project, not part of the story.

The incident made me paranoid, though. Did others have a problem with my project? A few people had told me they didn't want to be filmed, citing a desire for privacy in their work lives, which I was happy to honor. Some employees even seemed to enjoy being filmed, as if the project might somehow make them celebrities. However, most barely acknowledged my presence.

A few of my classmates thought my project was a waste of time. One was filming graffiti artists in the streets of Somerville. Another was making a film about the oldest poetry bookshop in Harvard Square. They believed they were exploring more compelling topics with more fascinating characters.

While there was nothing wrong with their topics, I tried to explain how interesting my own subject matter was. To hold an audience's interest, every story needed conflict, and the modern office was chock-full of it. From a cubicle's claustrophobia and the mind-numbing monotony of assignments to the passive-aggressive behavior, gossiping, and politics that filled the office, most days, I had trouble deciding where to set my camera. Drama everywhere!

Yet I took my classmates' criticisms to heart. Feeling self-conscious about my project, I visited our professor, Venise. I ran the idea by her, and she asked me for some examples of what I'd been capturing around the office.

I started off with the staff meetings. "It's a bizarre dynamic where no one speaks up for fear of looking dumb or being seen as not following the rules."

Venise nodded. "Oh yes, that happens in academia too. Happens everywhere, really, so it'll be familiar to a broad audience. What else?"

"There's the office's break room. Coworkers spend a lot of time there discussing their weekends to avoid getting back to work."

Venise grinned. "Viewers will relish the subtext."

"Also, there's a spot at the edge of the parking lot where these two employees, Hannah and Claire, go to smoke and gossip about their coworkers."

"All good stuff." Venise paused thoughtfully. "Is there anything happening on an extra-personal level? To add an additional layer of conflict?"

I searched my mind. "Yeah, my boss, Kathy, said Boston Health isn't doing well financially. The department will soon undergo restructuring, which is probably the most dramatic event in corporate America. Everyone's afraid of being laid off, so people are defending their jobs, trying to justify their existence."

"This sounds like a great project, Isaac. I wouldn't listen to your classmates. Everyone's drawn to different topics. As an artist, you have to learn to trust your intuition. You want to make films about subjects you genuinely care about. If you feel drawn to this material . . . well, go make your movie, young man."

Venise's words lifted my spirit, and I knew I was committing to the right project, after all. "Hey, do you want to see some of my footage?"

"Absolutely!"

Pulling out my phone, I showed her footage where Victoria and Kathy discussed their plan to "exit" Jackson. I paused the video to describe how people in corporate culture seemed to speak a different language.

"They use terms like *stand up*, which seems to stand for starting something new; *socialize*, which means sharing an idea with colleagues; and *escalate*, which means bringing a perceived problem to superiors. When someone wants to distance themselves from an action that wounds their conscience, they often use a euphemism such as 'exiting,' which, in Jackson's case, means firing him."

"This will all play well on the screen," Venise said. "Viewers who don't know much about corporate culture will feel like they're witnessing another species of human."

"The drama doesn't stop there," I continued. "Everywhere you look, there are pockets of resentment, such as from the creative professionals, like graphic designers and copywriters, who have too many deadlines, are strained for time, and don't get recognized by the managers who assign the projects."

Venise raised her hands to calm me. "All right, Isaac, I get it. It's wonderful to see a student as passionate as you are. I have to teach in a few minutes, but here's a pro tip: The style of film you're aiming for is called *direct cinema*. You probably won't know what you really have until you go through all your footage. Finding your story will take a tremendous amount of editing. But the truth should reveal itself as you continue to gather and edit your material."

"That's my main insecurity over this project," I said. "I'm gathering so much material, I'm afraid I won't be able to separate the wheat from the chaff when it comes time to choose and assemble scenes."

"Understandably so. An audience won't want to watch ninety minutes of people sitting in cubicles gossiping and trying to game the hospital ranking system. They want to watch a movie. So create a *movie.*"

"But how?"

"A movie has a beginning, middle, and end. A documentary should be informative but also entertaining. When you reach the editing stage, find a dramatic structure within the material. It will help you choose and arrange scenes to create an entertaining movie."

By the time I left Venise's office, I felt much more comfortable with my chosen project and was eager to dive back in.

As the summer wore on, I continued capturing the subtleties and complexities of working in a modern office setting. I felt like I was observing a new species with strange behaviors and rituals.

Such behaviors included rampant complaining. The toilet flushed too loudly. The ID reader at the office's entrance didn't register fast enough. Employees couldn't park in the lot behind the building. On and on it went.

To perhaps distract themselves from their ennui, many employees occupied themselves with minutiae. They debated over who should water the plants and who should control the playlist during lunch on Music Thursdays—and whether Jackson choosing to play Bob Marley was a form of cultural appropriation.

Most employees finished their work by two or three in the afternoon, sometimes earlier. They couldn't leave until five, so they busied themselves by surfing the web or chatting. By the end of the workday, they looked exhausted.

It was evident most employees were miserable. Many felt their skills didn't match their responsibilities or their abilities exceeded the demands of their jobs. Though they earned respectable salaries, their jobs were, in a way, voluntary servitude. On camera, Hannah confessed to being a corporate slave. Jackson admitted to "living in the velvet ghetto," while his income kept him in "golden handcuffs."

During staff meetings, I'd often sit in the back of the room to record everything. The employees always spoke cautiously, presumably aware others were listening in.

Before one such meeting began, Claire turned to Hannah. "I heard you had a squabble with a doctor."

Hannah rolled her eyes. "Yeah. I asked this shoulder surgeon if she wanted to be in our video about the orthopedics department. She sent back a nasty email saying she wanted no part of our propaganda because she had patients to take care of."

"Yikes," Claire whispered. "What'd you do?"

"I forwarded the email to HR. Then I sent it to Victoria, who went over the surgeon's head and contacted the chief of orthopedics to urge the surgeon to participate."

"I assume the surgeon's joining now?"

Hannah nodded. "When I met her for an on-camera interview, I wore a short-sleeve shirt that showed the scar from the last surgery on my shoulder."

Claire raised her eyebrows. "You really showed her."

Across the table, Jackson frowned at the two women. I wondered if he thought Hannah's behavior was passive-aggressive or unprofessional.

Just then, Victoria sauntered into the conference room and sat down. She wore a dark-blue business suit and a stern expression. Some of the employees stared at her, waiting for her to begin; others stared at the table and peered at her out of the corners of their eyes. Everyone seemed conscious of the office hierarchy, making sure to be on their best behavior when someone at the top of the organizational chart was in their presence.

"Let's discuss our new *US News & World Report* ranking," Victoria said. "After all we've done to influence our ranking, it's unfortunate we dropped from eighth place to thirteenth. We need to redouble our efforts so Boston Health can be in the top ten again."

The group discussed several marketing strategies that could boost their ranking. An important initiative, they decided, would be to email more marketing articles to physicians each month.

When I caught sight of Jackson subtly rolling his eyes, I focused my camera on him. From previous footage, I knew he thought the email campaign was a fool's errand. As far as he was concerned, the hospital was simply spamming doctors with "journalistic-styled" articles containing physician quotes that bragged about Boston Health's medical services and scientific breakthroughs.

Jackson suspected doctors didn't respond positively to their emails. "Surely they notice the articles' clear bias," he'd said at one point. "If anything, they probably resent Boston Health for buying their email addresses." If so, the entire campaign might have had the unintended consequence of painting the hospital in a *negative* light.

From previous conversations, I knew Hannah didn't see it that way. She'd led various efforts to demystify the *US News & World Report*'s hospital ranking system to find ways of gaming it for Boston Health's benefit. She had admitted to me privately that she wasn't sure they could boost the ranking through marketing efforts, but she thought of herself as "a happy soldier," doing Victoria's bidding without objection.

Or as Jackson considered it, without "thinking critically." He believed the kind of obedience Hannah practiced was repugnant and led to groupthink and bad outcomes.

As far as I was aware, though, he hadn't voiced such thoughts outside our one-on-one conversations, likely because he was among the minority with such opinions. His objections might be an existential threat to the project, perhaps even to the jobs of people like Victoria and Hannah. Yet it seemed silly to overlook potential flaws in the initiative, as addressing them could improve the outcome.

Watching Jackson through the camera, I wondered if he would express his skepticism during this staff meeting. Every once in a while, he inhaled deeply or bit his lip, seeming to ready himself, but then stopped short. I kept him in frame, waiting for him to say something.

The conversation was wrapping up when Jackson began speaking abruptly. Startled, Victoria twitched in her seat.

"This whole initiative is ridiculous," he uttered. "Only a small aspect of the hospital ranking process can be influenced by marketers like us. Most of the score is determined by the hospital's results, not the opinions of other doctors, which is what we're trying to influence here."

An eerie silence fell over the room. Apparently, Jackson had committed a faux pas by calling the team's strategy and hard work into question. No one knew how to respond.

Victoria quickly took back control of the meeting and asked Claire to present her new design for the email template.

After the meeting, I set my camera up in the break room, hoping to observe the staff reacting to Jackson's behavior, but everyone just engaged in small talk. Some refilled their coffee or retrieved food from the refrigerator. I wondered if knowing my camera was present affected how they acted. Was their behavior "natural," or were they putting on an act for the camera? How would I know?

Either way, it probably wouldn't matter. Even if someone was performing for the camera, they would still be acting the way they *thought* they ought to behave. In this case, getting coffee and making small talk with coworkers.

Most people forgot about the camera. They came and went, chatting briefly about their family, a hobby, or their plans for the weekend. The weather always seemed to be a hot topic, especially with regard to how it might impact their weekend plans.

I found such conversations boring. When I wasn't filming, I was usually eager to talk about new projects, like the video we were producing to advertise Boston Health's same-day knee surgery. I'd interviewed several patients who had raved about their orthopedic surgeons and how satisfying it was to be able to leave the hospital on the *same day* as having the procedure.

Though I couldn't put a finger on why, it seemed that talking about one's enthusiasm for work was also considered a faux pas. People wanted to discuss subjects that helped them escape their duties, and work projects spoiled the fun. If someone wanted to discuss a work matter, it was customary to frame it in the context of a complaint.

Taking a break from filming, I went outside to get some fresh air. As I walked through the parking lot, I spotted Claire and Hannah in the smoking area, chattering excitedly. Knowing they would be gossiping, I ran back inside, grabbed my camera, and approached the women.

"Would you mind if I filmed you?"

Claire flicked ash from the tip of her cigarette. "It's fine."

Claire was usually guarded around the office. She was quiet in meetings, seldom sharing ideas or impressions. In private, however, she always bad-mouthed people, though she typically shied away from the camera, so I'd never captured this second identity. Perhaps because the smoking area was a place for gossip, Claire seemed to stop caring that everything was being recorded.

Claire took a drag on her cigarette. "Jackson is a total boob."

"Such a bad attitude," Hannah agreed.

Claire blew out a cloud of smoke. "Did he call me his 'logo lady' the other day?"

"Glad you told Victoria. Brave of you, actually."

"Oh yeah, he's in hot water right now."

I didn't understand why Claire didn't just express her discontent to Jackson himself and try to reconcile. Instead, she seemed committed to doing anything but engaging in a face-to-face confrontation.

"Victoria's getting HR involved," Claire added.

"Good!" Hannah snarled.

I found it ironic that Boston Health's marketing department was populated by communications experts, yet when conflict arose, they seldom communicated with each other, or if they did, they did so without effective resolutions. Rather, it seemed common practice for employees to weaponize HR against one another.

Claire beamed as she speculated that Jackson might be fired on Monday. Thinking such disciplinary action would be cinematic, I met with someone in HR to ask if I could attend such a meeting to record it. My request was declined, though they did say I could leave my camera in the room.

On Monday, I was determined to follow Jackson, though I was careful not to let on that a storm might be brewing. Curiously, he'd shaved his beard and seemed rather subdued. Did he suspect disciplinary action was coming?

Around ten, I visited HR to confirm I could film any meetings with Jackson. A middle-aged woman told me a meeting had been planned for before lunch, but she couldn't disclose any more details, and she swore me to secrecy. Before leaving, I situated my camera in her office, pointing it at the chair across the desk from her. I pressed the record button and left.

I ran back to Jackson's cubicle, set up another camera I had brought, and waited. Thirty minutes later, Jackson got a phone call that had his face turning white as printer paper.

"What happened?" I inquired.

Jackson's hand shook. "I was told to report to HR for a check-in with Victoria."

I followed Jackson, wishing him luck as he entered the woman's office. The HR professional was sitting behind her desk; Victoria sat across from her beside an empty chair.

I pulled up the video feed on my phone to watch the meeting unfold.

As Jackson closed the door, his eyes darted back and forth in angst.

The HR professional crossed her legs. "Please take a seat."

Jackson carefully took the empty chair. "Excuse me, am I being fired?"

The HR manager looked surprised by Jackson's directness. She glanced at Victoria, but the other woman remained silent. "Yes, your employment at Boston Health is no longer secure."

Jackson's fingers turned white as his grip on the arms of the chair tightened. He turned to Victoria, his face turning red.

Before he could say anything to her, the HR manager continued. "We've had several complaints—"

"Complaints? Who's complaining?"

"We're under no obligation to release the names of the staff members who reported you."

Jackson shook his head, looking dumbfounded.

"Several employees have said they are not comfortable in your presence. It's our judgment that you've created a psychologically unsafe work environment."

Jackson's mouth fell open. "So, that's it? You're firing me?"

"A security guard will accompany you to your cubicle so you can gather your possessions, but you won't be allowed to access any files." Moments later, the security guard arrived and escorted Jackson out of the room.

Following the pair, I filmed Jackson as he packed a box with office equipment and photographs. The guard then led Jackson to the parking lot. After loading the box into his car, Jackson turned to the office's windows and gave the middle finger to whoever might be watching. Then he turned to the camera, bowed, got in his car, and drove away.

On the last day of my internship, I met with my manager, Kathy. I was pleased with the work I'd done for the hospital. The video about same-day knee surgery had gotten a few thousand likes on the hospital's Facebook page.

"We've enjoyed having you, Isaac," Kathy chirped. "And truly, best of luck with your documentary. We can't wait to see the final product."

When I exited the building, Hannah was wiping tears from her eyes as she smoked a cigarette.

"It was a pleasure working with you, Hannah," I said, hoping to console her even as I said goodbye. "And good luck with your work on the *US News & World Report*."

"Whatever." She sniffled. "It doesn't matter."

I'd already packed the video gear into my car, but I pulled my cell phone from my coat pocket and motioned to it, indicating I'd like to film our conversation. Hannah nodded and took a drag on her cigarette.

"What do you mean when you say it doesn't matter?"

"Our work! None of it matters." She pointed to the building. "Whenever I think about how I spend every day of my life—whenever I think about my place in the world—I want to cry."

I'd noticed many employees had other careers or side hustles that offered the promise of better, more authentic lives, if only they would follow through. The copywriter brewed his own beer. Claire loved to bake and had always talked about opening a catering business. Even Victoria had made candles and sold them on Etsy.

"Is there anything else you'd rather do than work in marketing?"

"Sometimes I think about changing careers," Hannah admitted. "I wanted to be a midwife, but I'd have to go back to school. It would take time and money, and I have a mortgage, student loans, and a two-year-old." She blew smoke in the direction of the office. "Everyone in there did what we were supposed to do. We went to college, got a good job with a good organization, and started climbing the corporate ladder. But it was a hoax. A trap. A life sentence."

The sadness I felt for her in that moment weighed heavily upon my chest, but all I could do was wish her the best and hope she could find a better quality of life.

As I drove home, one thing stayed at the front of my mind: It was time to start making the documentary. That weekend, I organized the hundreds of hours of footage on my computer. The next Monday, I visited Venise's office.

"I want to thank you for all the advice you gave me this summer; it really helped. I've finished filming, and I'm going to start editing tonight."

"That's wonderful," Venise said. "At this stage, I always encourage students to develop a perspective on their subject matter."

"What do you mean?"

"What do you think about what you witnessed?" she asked. "How can you portray that without being too heavy-handed?"

I looked away as I considered the question. "I can't think of anything right now."

"That's totally fine. It'll come to you. It usually comes to me in a flash just before I get in the editing room."

Encouraged to forge a perspective on my material, I left the professor's office and strolled along the Charles River. As I considered my summer at Boston Health, I realized I did have a perspective on the material. Corporate America seemed like a soulless environment where people suffered countless indignities. People seldom said what they wanted, and those who tried to speak the truth were despised for their sincerity.

No one got along either. If they hadn't happened to work together, it was doubtful most of them would have spent five minutes together. No one enjoyed their work, and many were nihilistic about modern work life. And all the soul-crushing qualities of corporate America seemed to me to be embodied by the cubicle.

With that in mind, I decided on a title for my film: *Cubicle.*
I was so eager to edit the material, I neglected my homework for the entire following semester. It took me four months to finish the film. When I showed Venise the final cut, she was moved by its poignancy. "It's the best student film I've ever seen."

A week later, she called me back into her office. "I called a friend of mine who owns Somerville Theatre." She smiled. "Your film will premiere there, Isaac! It's scheduled to play during the holidays."

Incredible! I left Venise's office so energized, I sprinted back to my dorm. That night, I emailed an invitation to come see the film to friends, family, and of course, everyone in the office. It was Boston Health's movie as much as it was mine.

The night of the debut, I stood at the theater's entrance and greeted folks as they arrived. I sported a suit jacket I'd bought at a thrift store. I felt like a true filmmaker.

Hannah skipped through the entrance and shook my hand excitedly. "I can't believe I'm starring in a movie!"

"Easy there, Kim Kardashian," Claire uttered with her typical sarcasm.

The last to enter the theater, I chose a seat in the center and close to the wall to observe reactions.

The movie began with an establishing shot of Boston Health. It followed with shots of the marketing department and short vignettes of the staff working silently in their cubicles and mingling in the break room.

After the cubicle farm had been built, the film presented the point of view I'd developed on the subject matter by exposing the absurdity of corporate America: the mindless bureaucracy, passive-aggressive behavior, gossiping, emotional bullying, boredom, groupthink, conformity, and the disconnection—from natural light, from other people, and from themselves.

It quickly became obvious the Boston Health staff didn't like what they were seeing. Their concerned expressions said it all. They fidgeted in their seats, scowled in disgust, and swiveled their heads with contempt.

Some sank in their seats as they witnessed how they'd behaved. Hannah covered her mouth with one hand as she watched her passive-aggressive behavior toward the shoulder surgeon. Claire couldn't look at the screen as it displayed her being quiet in meetings but then gossiping behind everyone's back.

When the movie ended, my friends and family, who had no connection to Boston Health, began clapping. But nobody among the Boston Health group moved. The atmosphere in the theater was heavy. What was this feeling in the air?

Then I knew: shame. Everyone's behavior in the office had been presented so clearly; they were ashamed over the way they'd acted. Ashamed to be occupying their current place in the world. Ashamed to be who they were.

Until then, it hadn't occurred to me that my subjects might be angry with how they were represented in the film. I hadn't been heavy-handed. I hadn't interviewed scholars to comment on corporate America or gathered confessional interviews from employees to intersperse throughout the scenes to create drama.

I'd only stitched together real moments from these people's work lives. I had captured the truth. And now they hated me for it. Perhaps even hated themselves.

Suddenly, Victoria shot out of her seat, daggers in her eyes. She scanned the theater, and when she saw me, she pointed at me. "This is outrageous, Isaac! How dare you paint my team in such a negative light!"

Slowly, I rose from my own seat. "It wasn't my intention to portray anyone in a bad light. I'm a filmmaker. The artist's mandate is to tell the truth."

Before I could say any more, a man I hadn't seen enter the theater stood, lowered the hood of his sweatshirt, and removed his baseball cap. It was Jackson.

"You did it to yourselves!" he shouted. "If you wanted to be portrayed better, you should've acted better."

Nobody responded to Jackson's accusation. Instead, the Boston Health workers started leaving their seats, grumbling as they walked the aisles toward the exits. A few glared at me as they passed, but most avoided eye contact, sheepishly staring at the floor.

I wasn't proud I'd ruffled so many people's feathers, but I was happy I'd accomplished what I'd set out to do. I'd found a style of documentary filmmaking I loved. I'd discovered a voice of my own. And I couldn't wait to use my camera to tell more stories. No matter how hard to swallow they might be for those who took part in them.

A Case of Aphantasia

A few years ago, I began treating a thirty-five-year-old man whom I will refer to as Theodore. Theodore had a rare and only recently discovered condition known as aphantasia, which left him unable to visualize images in his mind. For example, if Theodore closed his eyes to visualize a sunset, he saw only blackness. About two percent of the population have aphantasia, but many—Theodore included—saw it not as a handicap but as a quirk of their imagination, perhaps not unlike living with color blindness.

Theodore did confess that it would be nice to picture a childhood memory in his mind's eye, like the face of his deceased grandmother. In fact, he believed that his therapy was often hampered because he could not call to mind images from his past. Theodore suggested that it might be easier to come to terms with his parents' divorce, for instance, if he could actually "see" the day they separated in his mind's eye.

When we first began therapy, Theodore had experienced paranoia over the security of his job as a copywriter for a major corporation. Despite being a high-performing and seemingly affable employee, he was anxious. A restructuring had taken place—several departments had been merged into one—and some employees had gotten the axe. Theodore feared he might be next.

I asked Theodore if he had ever been terminated from a job. Indeed, an old boss had fired him in a rather traumatizing fashion, and he claimed the event still haunted him to this day. He still feared that authority figures in the workplace didn't have his best interests in mind, and he would often interpret directives and constructive feedback as hostile. Such misinterpretations, as I saw them, would often lead to defensive reactions, usually outbursts of anger, which often damaged his work relationships.

Intending to learn more about aphantasia, I threw myself into the scientific literature to learn more about this newly-discovered condition. At the world's first conference on aphantasia in London, I attended a talk by Dr. Evelyn Banks, a psychiatrist from Envision Inc. She discussed a new technology called Mosaic that apparently gave aphantasics the ability to mentally visualize in a therapeutic setting. Dr. Banks was an older woman, in her mid-sixties, and she looked every bit an intellectual with her tortoiseshell glasses and black tailored suit.

Dr. Banks explained that the brains of people with aphantasia did, in fact, produce imagery, but for some reason, they didn't have conscious access to the images. She reminded the audience of psychiatrists that mental images were created in the occipital lobe, the brain's visual center located at the back of the brain. In normal brains, the images were then transmitted to the prefrontal cortex at the front of the brain, which was responsible for planning, decision-making, and problem-solving. In clinical trials, Dr. Banks and her colleagues had found that transmission of this signal was being interrupted in aphantasics, somewhere between the back and front of the brain. Mosaic didn't work by restoring this connection between the occipital lobe and the prefrontal cortex. Rather, it became the new "receiver" of the imagery, taking the place of the prefrontal cortex.

Thinking that Mosaic seemed to be the solution Theodore had been looking for, I eagerly asked if he would be open to trying the technology. We had built up a good deal of trust in our dozen or so sessions, and he consented without much objection. A few days later, I received a box from Envision. Inside, there was a USB drive containing a ten-minute video that provided instructions on how to use Mosaic with patients who had aphantasia.

In my next session with Theodore, I followed Dr. Banks's directions for using Mosaic to the letter. Adjusting my glasses to get a better look, I placed two silver strips, each about the size of a fingernail, at the top of his neck, just below the hairline. These strips, according to Dr. Banks, would detect brain waves associated with mental images and then transmit the signals through two wires to my computer for Theodore and me to view, as if we were watching television.

For our first test of Mosaic, I asked Theodore to visualize the day of his traumatic termination. He closed his eyes and tried to produce images in his mind's eye as he narrated his experience of that day. As expected, he reported seeing only blackness and a few spots floating behind his eyelids. To my astonishment, however, I could see everything on my computer screen, witnessing the day he was fired as if it were a film. Absentmindedly stroking my graying beard, I watched Theodore grab his jacket and then anxiously descend a few flights of stairs to an office on the ground floor of the building. He exchanged tense words with a blonde, heavyset woman and was escorted from the building by a security guard.

It was with childlike anticipation that I turned the computer monitor for Theodore to watch the visualization of his memory. To my surprise, he smiled widely. Then he sighed deeply, and his eyes welled with tears. It was a breakthrough—one of many we would have over the course of Theodore's treatment with Mosaic.

In therapy sessions, I am always searching for what the pioneering psychoanalyst Melanie Klein calls the *point of urgency*—an idea that is just about to leap from a patient's unconscious and into conscious awareness. I listen deeply to my patients, searching for and identifying their points of urgency. As gracefully as I can, I introduce the ideas into conversation so they may be taken up and integrated, no longer split off from their consciousness and bound to cause distress or dysfunction.

Several months into Theodore's course of therapy, I realized that one of his points of urgency revolved around women. Theodore was a handsome man with a lean build, brown hair, and strikingly blue eyes. He seemed to attract women with some ease, but he harbored a strong fear that they would eventually leave him.

When he was six, Theodore's mother divorced his father and left town for a year, leaving Theodore and his younger brother behind. I speculated with him on why his mother had left, and he suggested that, being in her early twenties, she had perhaps felt burdened by the responsibilities of parenthood. For years, Theodore had wondered whether his mother had even loved him. However, he told me it was more realistic that she loved him a great deal but was tragically unable to express that love in tangible, meaningful ways.

I helped Theodore understand that perhaps his fear of being abandoned by women stemmed from an absence of his mother when he was young and had been driven deeper by the death of his grandmother when he was a teenager. I was pleased that Theodore seemed to find solace in this interpretation.

About a year into working with Theodore, I took an unconventional tactic and reached out to Theodore's mother, Stephanie, intending to learn more about their relationship. During our hour-long phone conversation, Stephanie told me that they had been estranged for no particular reason. They had ultimately reconciled over her disappearance during his childhood, yet they had grown distant over the years anyway. No major event had happened between them. No bad blood. Just distance.

I asked her to elaborate, and Stephanie told me that her son's intelligence intimidated her. Theodore was smart and driven, and she feared she had nothing to offer him. In the rare cases that she reached out with a text or phone call, she worried that she might be bothering him, somehow pulling him away from his work, which seemed to be his highest priority. The inability to connect with her first-born seemed to cause Stephanie great distress.

With the advent of Mosaic, Theodore and I continued to witness crucial moments from his early years. Together, we watched the day his father told him that his mother was leaving. On the screen, we saw a young Theodore angrily pull at his hair until it stood straight up and then bury his head in his hands and scream.

We seemed to be making progress, until about a year into our sessions using Mosaic. Theodore began to report what I would refer to with colleagues as the "unintended consequences of artificial visual recall": involuntary images intruding into his conscious awareness.

One day, Theodore was waiting in line at the supermarket when images of his dying grandmother struggling for air in a hospital room rushed into his head, startling him. On another occasion, he experienced a rush of mental images from the time he left his mother's house to study abroad for six months. After saying goodbye and getting into his car to leave, he had stepped out once more, walked back to where his mother was standing, and given her one last hug.

When the intrusive images began happening with more regularity, our sessions shifted to the management of the mental pictures, which Theodore reported as increasingly burdensome. In therapy, it became obvious when Theodore's mind was overwhelmed with mental imagery. He might be in the middle of a sentence when he would shut his eyes and grit his teeth. Once, when a particularly intense rush of images took hold, he ripped the silver strips from the base of his scalp in frustration, stood up, and paced the room.

Seeing the obvious distress that Mosaic was causing Theodore, I suggested we discontinue treatment immediately. We were testing the boundaries of Mosaic, and I wondered if we were pushing it—and him—too far. Theodore insisted that we continue, however, telling me it was cathartic to relive these old memories and he'd never felt better, or healthier. I reluctantly agreed to continue using Mosaic, but I told him I would pull the plug if things got more serious. Looking back now, I should have put a stop to the use of Mosaic right there.

Though he didn't explicitly say it, it appeared as if Theodore considered his new visualization abilities a kind of superpower. Mosaic had helped him replace his aphantasia with its opposite state: hyperphantasia, the ability to see images in one's mind as if they were photographs. Theodore likened his hyperphantasic mind to a camera: he could create mental pictures rich with color and nuance, and he could move and rotate objects in space, with or without his eyes closed. Theodore reported that he would no longer watch a movie twice. Why should he when he could rewatch it in his mind?

Unfortunately, Theodore's extraordinary new capacity had come at an unexpectedly steep cost. Over the ensuing days, Theodore grew more distressed as visual images continued to intrude unexpectedly, with greater regularity and more vividness. He lamented that he was now *drowning* in pictures. The microexpression of an acquaintance or colleague could stick in his mind like a splinter, disturbing him weeks after noticing it out of the corner of his eye. He reported that he could rewatch these moments—any moment—as if they were scenes from a film. He could fast forward and rewind a visual memory, pausing on individual frames.

At that point, it was clear that we could go no further with Mosaic. Despite Theodore's resistance to doing so, I unplugged the machine and tucked it away in my office closet. I began our next session with an apology. I explained to Theodore that I was partly to blame for his troubling symptoms. I should have stopped the use of Mosaic much earlier, and I was sorry that I had not.

Upset, Theodore argued that there were always tradeoffs with technology. If humans wanted to fly, we had to accept that some planes would go down. The invention of the automobile gave us great freedom, yet many people died every day in car crashes. I agreed, of course, but I asked him to consider whether the benefits of using Mosaic to address his aphantasia outweighed the costs. He believed they did. I was of the opposite opinion. Regardless, my decision was final, and I was eager to return to more traditional therapy sessions. Unfortunately, I could not have predicted what happened next.

Even though we were no longer using Mosaic, Theodore remained a hyperphantasic. To my dismay, he continued to disconnect from reality during our sessions. In one session, Theodore was narrating a memory when his eyes drifted to the floor. When I asked him where his mind had traveled, he told me he'd just watched his sunglasses drop to the dirt—a memory from when he was a teenager. Not noticing they had fallen, his mother had accidentally stepped on and destroyed them. Though his mother had driven him to a store to buy a new pair, the memory seemed to have upset him a great deal. While Theodore watched the scene play out in the theater of his mind, his eyes welled with tears.

Desperate for solutions and hoping to gain others' perspectives, I published a case study about Theodore in a medical journal. Despite the possible damage it could bring to my career, I wrote about the costs Mosaic had presented and explained how my patient's condition continued to deteriorate even without continued use of the technology. I also described my troubling realization that the imagined world was becoming more appealing to Theodore than the real one.

To illustrate, I included a particularly poignant story Theodore had shared with me. During a walk, he had stopped to admire a tall birch tree. Within seconds, however, Theodore's mind had conjured up the image of a much taller, more robust, and more visually striking tree in its place, leaving the real tree an inferior version of the imagined one. Why focus on a real tree, I wrote, when the imagined tree was more beautiful? The real tree was bent in the middle, ravaged by invasive insects, and dehydrated from a hot summer, but the imagined tree was mightily tall and glowed healthily. The tree in his mind was perfect.

I was relieved, in one session, to hear Theodore explain that he was no longer as vulnerable to the mental health issues that had previously plagued him. Whenever he felt the sting of loneliness, for example, he would create a mental movie of times in college when he had felt a deep sense of companionship with friends. This might have manifested as enjoying meals in the college cafeteria or tossing a rugby ball with teammates. However, when Theodore confessed that the habit could have started because he was meeting up with friends and coworkers less often, I understood that real-life interactions weren't as pleasurable as the idealized past.

Theodore also believed that he was putting his newfound abilities to some positive use at work. If he felt bored at his desk, he told me he would mentally dislocate himself and slip into the imagined world. He once replayed a previous night's dream, in which he had taken the form of a seagull and floated on thermal vents high above the sand dunes of Cape Cod, occasionally spotting a crab and making the exhilarating dive toward earth for a meal.

In what turned out to be our last session together, Theodore was picturing his mother running down the stairs in a bath towel after a bookcase had caught fire in their home. His eyes snapping open, he exploded out of his seat and ran to my closet, going straight for the box that held my Mosaic machine. To my shock, he lifted the machine from the box and threw it at the wall, shards of plastic and metal flying in all directions.

I stood and walked toward Theodore slowly, holding my hands out to calm him. After a few minutes, Theodore relaxed and apologized, saying he would pay for everything. I assured him that insurance would likely cover the damages and offered to see him the following week. He agreed.

Still breathing heavily, Theodore fixed his hair, straightened his clothes, and left my office with his head lowered. Once he was gone, I retrieved my trashcan and began filling it with broken plastic and metal, circuit boards, and colored wires. Part of me was relieved to see the machine smashed to bits; I would never be able to reactivate it, no matter the temptation. With Mosaic officially gone, I looked forward to establishing a new normal with Theodore. To my dismay, I never heard from him after that session. He didn't answer my phone calls or emails.

He simply disappeared.

Several months later, I received a phone call from Dr. Banks, the psychiatrist at Envision Inc. She had read my case study of Theodore and wanted to know how long I had treated him using their technology. Once I'd answered her question, Dr. Banks informed me that Theodore was now in her care at the company and that I could visit him if I wanted. I was not told the reason for the invitation, but I sensed a desperation in her voice, as though she and others had failed to help Theodore and were grasping for an outside perspective. I told her I would be there in twenty minutes.

When I saw Theodore on the third floor of Envision, he was alone in the room, slumped in a chair. His face had grown scruffy, and an orderly informed me that he hadn't showered since he'd been admitted two weeks before. Though he sat in front of a television, Theodore's eyes were fixed on the corner of the room. I rounded the chair to see a string of drool hanging from his lips.

I greeted him but received no response. He appeared to be intensely preoccupied. I used a tissue to wipe the drool from his mouth and left the room to rejoin Dr. Banks in the hallway. She offered the possibility that Theodore had suffered a psychotic break. I hesitated to make any diagnosis at first; we were in uncharted territory. It was obvious that Theodore was lost in mental images. Whether he was reliving a memory or rewatching a movie, whatever he was experiencing had completely disconnected him from his physical environment.

Dr. Banks asked if I had spoken to others about Theodore. I hadn't said anything to anyone since he disappeared, which she seemed glad to hear. She led me to an elevator that took us one floor below ground level. I was invited into what looked like a hospital emergency room, a large open floor with exam rooms along the perimeter. I paused, uneasy, though it took me a moment to realize why. It was completely silent.

Dr. Banks slid open one curtain to reveal a young boy seated at the edge of his bed, staring at the ground in the same way Theodore had been looking at the corner of his room. Dr. Banks snapped her fingers in front of the child, eliciting no reaction.

She was treating about a dozen people like him, she said. No doubt there were more they were not aware of. She and her colleagues privately called these patients "the lost ones." After treatment with Mosaic, those who previously had been aphantasic had become hyperphantasics: off the charts in their capacity to form static or moving images in their minds. The technology was good, Dr. Banks gloated, but—she added with some uneasiness—they had not anticipated the repercussions of making it too good.

The lost ones weren't at the mercy of their minds. The mental imagery could, at times, be intrusive, but they could usually shut down the images. Instead, the lost ones had chosen to stay with their mental movies. Some lost ones, Dr. Banks explained, were wrapped up in memories from childhood. Some were binging on television shows. One man had spent hours mentally engaging in sexual acts with his female boss. Others played out fantasies of revenge; one woman stabbed an unfaithful lover, while one man smashed his car into another's during a bout of road rage.

Since I only had an average ability to visualize mentally, it had never occurred to me that someone might choose to live inside their head rather than engage with the real world. After some thought, though, I understood that within such a mental space, one could do whatever—be whoever—they wanted. In the real world, we paid taxes and bills and worked jobs for salaries that helped us buy things beyond necessities. In the world of perfect mental creation, one could lose forty-five pounds, smack an inconsiderate coworker across the face, or transform a traumatic childhood into a harmonious one. If one were so inclined, one could lift off the ground and fly around the city.

However, a person must still eat, drink, sleep, and use the bathroom. When

I brought this up, Dr. Banks assured me that if I stuck around the ward long enough, I would see the lost ones speedily visit the toilet or take a few bites of food before retreating to their rooms and back into the haven of their minds.

I left Envision disturbed, but I knew I had to see Theodore again, so I visited him the following day. I wondered if there might be a way to coax him out of the illusory world by reminding him of reality, so I brought an object that might trigger a thought perhaps more appealing than his dreams. When I walked into his room that day, I put a picture of his mother before him.

To my delight, his eyes focused on the image of him as an infant resting happily on his mother's lap. Theodore grinned and set the picture on his knee, but then his eyes fell to the floor and locked into place. I had lost him again.

I asked him to stay with me. To my surprise, he returned to the present and made eye contact with me. He said he had been spending a lot of time with his mother in his mind. He was not reliving experiences like the one in the picture but rather creating new ones with her. They would go on hikes together or sit around the fire in her backyard and share stories.

In real life, his mother was distant and unreachable, but in his mind, he could communicate his ideas and hopes to her. In his mind, she was available and loving. In his mind, she was the mother he had always wanted.

In some ways, that kind of imaginary play could be therapeutic. Such mental imagery was soothing, a form of self-care, but there was too much dysfunction to justify the possible benefits to Theodore's mental health. Like the other lost ones, he left his room only to use the bathroom, eat, or drink, after which he would retire to his room and dislocate from reality again. Not to mention, he was unemployed and in the full-time care of licensed mental health professionals.

After my second visit with Theodore, I requested that Dr. Banks release Theodore back into my care. Hesitant, she asked me to sign a confidentiality agreement stipulating that I not discuss what I had seen with anyone, under penalty of legal action. After signing the agreement, I left Envision with Theodore.

What I did next undoubtedly overstepped the bounds, perhaps even violated some code of conduct (many of my colleagues have said my license should have been revoked). However, I saw no other way to keep Theodore out of his imagination. I had grown attached to him. I liked him and hated to see him this way.

With Theodore in tow, I drove about three hours north to the White Mountains of New Hampshire and knocked on the door of his mother's house. A stocky woman with brown eyes answered. Once I'd explained to Stephanie that Theodore was among the lost ones, she seemed desperate to help and invited us in. Accepting the invitation, I walked back to the car and got Theodore. Once we were inside, he made his way to a nearby chair in the living room, reclined, and slipped back into the imagery of his mind.

Stephanie approached her son. She waved a hand in front of his face and was confused when she couldn't get a reaction. Then she became angry and turned to ask me how Theodore could just ignore her like this. Crying, Stephanie grabbed his shoulders, shook him, and to my astonishment, slapped him across the face. In that moment, Theodore began sobbing. But even with tears streaming down his cheeks, he remained absent, fixed in his imagined world. It was heartbreaking to watch.

Stephanie wiped her face with her hands and then knelt in front of Theodore. Gripping his face with both hands, she whispered a plea for him to come back. To real life. To her. An internal struggle took place then. Theodore's eyes went in and out of focus. He was with us, then he was gone, and then he was back again. The only explanation I could think of was that his consciousness didn't know where to land. It kept shifting from the mother in his imagination to the mother standing before him in the room. Faster and faster, he switched between them, searching for the love he needed.

I have come to believe that the two realities melded in Theodore's mind that day. He came to believe, in an instant, that the mother of his mind was the same as the one before him—that the detachment he had experienced from her had come about through no fault of her own nor of his own. That beneath the disappointments, insecurities, and failures of his mother was the loving mother his mind had conjured. The distance between the two mothers vanished, as did the distance he felt toward her.

They became *one*.

It was obvious from Theodore's expression that some battle in his mind had been won. Stephanie rubbed the back of Theodore's neck as he shook his head and stretched his arms up. As if he had been released from a long sleep, Theodore smiled in a way I had never seen in all the time I had known him. He asked his mother if we could all go outside and sit around the firepit in the backyard.

While his mother prepared chicken wings and mozzarella sticks in the kitchen, Theodore used newspapers and matches to start a fire in the pit. When Stephanie returned to the backyard holding a large plate of snacks, she asked Theodore if he wanted a napkin, but he didn't turn his head to acknowledge her. She glanced at me worriedly, no doubt fearing that her son had fallen back into the virtual world.

But the fear didn't last long. With his gaze fixed on the center of the fire, Theodore reached out to accept a napkin from Stephanie and then took the plate and thanked his mother. Biting into a mozzarella stick, he explained that he had pictured this very moment several times since developing his mind's eye, dreamed of it in great detail. Yet the crackling fire before him was far better than any fire he could have imagined.

Going Through the Motions

In a conference room on the bottom floor of the Fairmont Copley Plaza in Boston, "A Beautiful Day" by U2 blared through massive speakers on either side of a stage. The audience bobbed and rocked their heads to the music. They stomped the ground and shouted. The three-day self-improvement seminar was food for the soul; this conference room, a utopia; these people, their tribe.

Meanwhile, Graham sat in his chair and avoided eye contact with the plump middle-aged woman beside him, but she introduced herself over the music anyway.

"I'm Madeline," she said. "I've been waitressing at a small restaurant for over a decade now, but I'm finally ready to open my own seafood restaurant in Cape Cod. There's such a buzz in the air here. I feel so alive! Don't you feel it?"

Graham faked a smile and nodded. He couldn't judge Madeline for what seemed to be self-delusion, because he used to be just like her. A few years ago, Graham would've been hopping up and down to the music too. He would've collected business cards from fast friends and followed up by email at the end of the three-day escape. He might've sent them links to YouTube videos with speeches from movies and triumphant soundtracks playing in the background. The video of the life-affirming speech at the end of *Miracle* had been a long-time favorite.

For years, Graham had been a perpetual seminar-goer, a self-help junkie. He'd spent most of his twenties—even a small chunk of his thirties—gorging on personal development. Motivational books, inspirational movies, self-help audiobooks, and workshops had been emotional fuel. He'd read all the great motivation gurus: Wayne Dyer, Eckhart Tolle, Deepak Chopra, and even old-timers like Jim Rohn, Zig Ziglar, and Napoleon Hill. He could quote lines from James Allen's self-help classic, *As a Man Thinketh*: "A person is limited only by the thoughts that he chooses." Or perhaps Hill's *Think and Grow Rich*: "When your desires are strong enough, you will appear to possess superhuman powers to achieve."

Shaking off the memory, Graham searched the stage for movement as the lights dimmed. A slender man in his fifties with white hair, an impish grin, and a dark-blue three-piece suit strutted to the center. He raised his arms over his head and shouted, "Welcome to the first day of the rest of your life!" The audience erupted in applause. This was Max Title, Ph.D., psychoanalyst and author of the international bestseller *Why Say No When It Feels So Great to Say Yes?* Fifteen years earlier, Dr. Title had closed his clinical practice to write self-help books for the masses. Nobody quite knew how much he was worth, but judging by the houses he owned in Manhattan and Maui and the Aston Martin he drove, it was rumored he did all right for himself.

Dr. Title was born like all motivational speakers were created. He'd spent most of his life binging on self-help material. However, instead of using personal development books and audiobooks to become a better therapist, he'd consumed too many books, become obsessed, and sunk into the genre as if it were quicksand. He reached a critical mass of knowledge and then made the fateful decision to repackage what he'd learned to create his own self-optimization programs. And the anxious, the unhappy, and the lost flocked to Dr. Title to swallow his psychological elixirs at face value.

Once the crowd had stopped cheering, Dr. Title kicked off the first day of his Ultimate Life Design program. He started with the now-legendary story of how he'd fallen into despair in his early thirties, had an existential crisis, suffered a nervous breakdown in the middle of the night, and then—at rock bottom— experienced a profound post-traumatic growth. After his "awakening," the doctor spent a year meandering through public spaces in a perfect state of bliss. A voice told him to take what he'd learned to the people, so he rented out conference halls, rooms in libraries, and coffee shops and offered lectures on how others could "get the life they deserve." Graham had attended such seminars before, during which Dr. Title told rapt audiences they could attract anything: money, a promotion, a partner, a new car, a home, a new life. But only if they wanted those things like a drowning man wanted a gulp of air.

Filled with promise, Graham had done what Dr. Title and other gurus instructed. He'd dreamed big and wished for things with great desire. To Graham's disappointment—and later guilt, as he thought he must be doing something wrong—not long after he read a book or left a seminar, the emotional charge would diminish. To compensate, Graham would fill himself with more motivational fuel by ordering more books, watching more YouTube videos, or reading yet another how-to-be-successful article online.

But the world wasn't so easily conquered. The passive income wasn't flowing into Graham's checking account. That dream girl wasn't sleeping in his bed. He still lived in a 350-square-foot studio in a crummy part of Boston. Maybe he hadn't tried hard enough. Did he want his dream like a drowning man wanted air? Doubling down, Graham had made a vision board for his living room. He cut out pictures of men with six-pack abs and extravagant cars from magazines and pinned them to a tackboard. As months passed, Graham hoped to see tangible growth, but he only got the status quo. Dr. Title had promised to change his life, but Graham felt like he was running in place. Like drinking ocean water, reading self-help books had only made him thirstier.

Graham didn't realize it right away, but he had to fail spectacularly before his life improved. Puffed up on the confidence the self-help books had provided, Graham quit his job as a copywriter and drove across the country to Los Angeles to write screenplays. A difficult thing to accomplish, he soon discovered. Sure, some industry players had read his only script and said he had "talent." But talent, it turned out, did not a screenwriter make. The movie industry was notoriously inaccessible, Graham learned. It was tough to get meetings at studios, and producers and directors weren't exactly handing out writing assignments on street corners.

Graham stayed buoyant for several months, until the savings in his bank account dwindled. His lower back began to ache. He felt shaky, panicky. His mind was quick to worry, and he began to ruminate on his predicament, often catastrophizing. On a walk to the library one afternoon, Graham passed a homeless man in a public park mumbling to himself. Graham realized a thin line separated him from that man—separated sanity from madness. A few more missteps, and he, too, could become an invalid, perhaps homeless. One morning in his kitchen, Graham was preoccupied with back spasms when he began having trouble catching his breath. The panic attack landed him in the emergency room. A conversation with a social worker there made him realize that he'd lost his grip, become unsteady, unhealthy. After a few weeks, Graham took the advice of a psychiatrist; he abandoned his dreams and went back home.

With a new job, a routine, a salary, an antidepressant, psychotherapy, and new friends and romances, the panic receded, and Graham recovered. He got back on his feet. Yet something peculiar had happened. The motivational material that had fed Graham's soul had lost its potency; it no longer inspired him. Instead, Dr. Title's books and lectures felt out of touch with reality and triggered revulsion.

In therapy, Graham reflected on how unrealistic, and perhaps delusional, he'd been to think a few pictures from magazines tacked to the wall would make all his ambitions come true. He began to understand that it could take years, decades even, to get what he wanted. Moreover, Graham recognized that he should've planned his move to California better. He should've secured a day job as a copywriter before going to the West Coast, or at least kept the one he had in Boston and worked from home.

After returning from California, Graham caught up with an old friend from prior self-help seminars. His friend was excited about Brené Brown's book *Daring Greatly: How the Courage to Be Vulnerable Transforms the Way We Live, Love, Parent, and Lead.* But Graham discovered his friend hadn't achieved the dreams he had set for himself. Instead, he just registered for more seminars, purchased more books, and swapped more YouTube videos with other seminar-goers.

Paradoxically, Graham realized the folks who seemed the most fanatical about self-optimization were some of the most conventional people. In conversation, they could accomplish anything, but in their lives, they were risk-averse and played things safe. On the other hand, the people who seemed to be achieving their goals openly admitted their limitations, were full of doubts and fears, and typically felt like imposters in their chosen endeavors. And yet, they founded businesses, wrote books, exhibited their work, and had the most impact.

Slowly, Graham realized his old seminar pals weren't addressing the issues that might keep them from the "success" they craved. Instead, they zeroed in and obsessively focused on the positive. They deluded themselves with affirmations and vision boards while overlooking what subtly undermined them: an unexplored emotional life, a psyche saturated with conflicts and cognitive dissonances, an unexamined past littered with traumas. The fear of failure. The fear of success. The mom/dad/friend/partner/teacher who had made them feel unworthy/unloved/unwhatever.

Over time, Graham came to believe what Thomas Hardy once wrote: "If a way to the better there be, it exacts a full look at the worst." Instead of the self-help section of the bookstore, Graham began to find himself in the philosophy and psychology sections. To his surprise, the real self-help gurus seemed to be philosophers like Friedrich Nietzsche, a pessimistic, ailing man who stared reality in the cold, black eyes and urged readers to become who they were, break away from the crowd, and live boldly, dangerously. In the psychology section, he found Man's Search for Meaning by psychotherapist and Holocaust survivor Viktor Frankl, who proved humans couldn't live meaningless lives. And works by mythologist Joseph Campbell helped him understand that many people climb ladders that are leaning against the wrong building.

When Madeline tapped Graham on the shoulder, he realized it was intermission, and he'd missed Dr. Title's opening speech. Unsolicited, Madeline began painting a portrait of her future for Graham. She showed him a web browser on her phone displaying the domain name she'd registered for her soon-to-exist restaurant.

Graham reminded himself why he'd come here: To advise people like Madeline that they were delusional. To enlighten them about the too-rosy nature of Dr. Title's dream-achieving philosophy. The doctor's teachings didn't acknowledge the world's unfairness, its wild unpredictability, or its downright meanness at times. Dr. Title seldom talked about the single mother who worked two part-time jobs to stay afloat, the factory worker who'd lost his job due to the high-tech, globalized nature of the world, or the college graduate who couldn't even think about buying a house because of the $1,200 student loan payments they had to make every month.

That's right, Graham thought while Madeline prattled on about her lofty vision, *let's keep wishing for checks to fill our mailboxes. Let's visualize our hands wrapped around the steering wheel of our new Tesla. Let's repeat affirmations in the mirror like a mindless robot. You want more money? Just put a hundred-dollar bill in your pocket, and you'll "attract" the money you need!*

But Graham couldn't muster a response to Madeline's monologue. He told her he had to use the bathroom, and she shrugged, leaving to join a confidence-building group near the back. Why hadn't he just told her the truth? Why hadn't he told her that everyone at this seminar was being conned and that he'd had to fall flat on his face to realize that? He should have told her that Dr. Title and others like him made obscene amounts of money filling people's heads with cozy fantasies of becoming business tycoons and famous artists.

Then again, why couldn't Graham just avoid seminars like this? He might have, except people like Dr. Title would only continue their work, keeping people locked in self-delusion. Graham had left Plato's Cave, and he felt obliged to return to inform his shackled brothers and sisters that the world they perceived was an elaborate illusion. It was his responsibility to expose Dr. Title as the fraud he was, to prove to everyone that the emperor wore no clothes.

As "Live and Let Die" by Guns N' Roses blared through the speakers, Graham decided he needed a drink, something to dull his racing mind. Making his way to the hotel bar on the second floor, he passed a room where a group of attendees lay on yoga mats shouting at the top of their lungs—Dr. Title's patented "primal scream" therapy. Graham walked past another room, where he saw Madeline standing in front of a man holding a slim piece of wood, shifting back and forth and squinting.

Through the open door, Graham heard the coach instruct Madeline. "If you flinch, even for a second, your hand will bounce off."

Madeline took a deep breath, steadied herself, and thrust her hand down, splitting the wood in half. Graham heard her shriek, "I did it!" as he climbed the stairs. At the hotel bar, a few couples whispered together at tables or stared at their phones while they sipped cocktails and nibbled appetizers. Graham sat on a stool at the bar and ordered a beer. All this overcooked rhetoric about following dreams had offended his ears. He felt saturated with bullshit.

When the beer arrived, Graham took a sip and leaned back, trying to relax. But then Dr. Title pulled up a seat beside him. There he was, Captain Bullshit himself.

The doctor ordered a cocktail. Out of the corner of his eye, Graham watched him slip off his jacket and fold it over his stool.

"Are you enjoying the conference?" Dr. Title asked without turning.

A few awkward seconds passed. Graham thought about lying and saying something like, "These few hours have been the most inspirational I've had in years, worth every dollar." But only pre-California Graham would've said something like that. That man had been out of touch with reality. That man had been polite. That man hadn't rocked the boat. Post-California Graham had a compulsion for truth-telling and carried a verbal sledgehammer wherever he went.

Graham wiped his face with his hands and told the doctor the truth as he'd come to know it. "No. You're a con man, filling these people with nothing but temporary enthusiasm. You're destined to rip a hole in their gullible hearts. I should know. I've read everything you've ever written, watched all your programs, attended most of your seminars, but nothing has ever gotten me closer to my dreams. In fact, I used to think something was wrong with me since you make living seem so effortless."

Unfazed, Dr. Title asked him to continue. Graham brought up his time in California, how he'd failed to break into Hollywood as a screenwriter. His chronic low-back pain. How he had to crawl back home with his tail between his legs and relapse into his addiction to a salary.

Graham shook his head. "It's all bullshit, what you feed these people. Your rhetoric only fills people with illusions and makes them strangers to themselves. How long until the euphoria of these 'breakthroughs' fades? How long until these folks feel guilty that they're not responding to your program?"

Dr. Title nodded absently. "If that's how you feel, why come to this seminar at all?"

Graham gritted his teeth. "Because someone has to stop con artists like you. I came to alert other attendees that you're full of crap and that they're wasting their money and time on a professional liar."

The doctor didn't seem alarmed, just curious. "What do you believe in, Graham?"

"What's that got to do with anything?" Graham demanded. "Why do I need to believe in something? Why should I cling to an ideology, deity, or school of philosophy? I've searched for meaning in science and philosophy and even some religions, like Buddhism, but I've found nothing but disappointment. Hell, most teachers, scientists, and leaders I've come across have somehow let me down. Their perspectives have been incomplete, at best, and at worst, they've lied to try and manipulate me."

Increasingly, Graham found it difficult to find comfort in such an erratic world. No platitudes from Dr. Title or anyone else could soothe his worries over financial institutions eroding people's investments with service fees, big food companies mass-producing toxic food, or pharmaceutical companies trying to convince people they were prone to diseases that the companies' pills could keep at bay.

"Why do you think you broke down in California?" Dr. Title asked.

Graham admitted he hadn't seen reality clearly at the time. He hadn't been completely delusional to think he could move out to California to break into screenwriting. He had simply been naïve enough to think that creative writing could support him so early in his career. Graham had self-published two novels and had many essays and articles published. With a strong portfolio and some confidence, he'd felt ready to leave the workforce and write full-time. But while he'd had a decent start, he later realized that every young artist needs a day job while they learn their craft.

It was a tough lesson to learn.

When Graham had moved home for stability, he normalized. With a regular salary, he had felt more secure. His back had stopped aching, and he'd no longer needed pills to keep panic at bay. "I lost the ability to deceive himself," he told Dr. Title. "I can no longer be fooled. I've become resistant to self-help. Immune to bullshit."

"What about hope?" Dr. Title said. "What about dreams?"

Graham explained that his newfound realism hadn't taken away his ability to envision a better future. He could still use his imagination to write fiction, and he had even started his third novel during an MFA program in creative writing. A long-time fan of investigative reporting, he'd also developed a deeper interest in journalism. A couple years after returning to Boston, Graham changed careers from writing copy for businesses to writing feature articles for a small magazine. It paid half what corporate writing paid, but the work seemed unbiased and more meaningful. It wasn't the propaganda he used to write before California.

The cost of such devotion to reality, though, was that Graham occasionally struggled to remain buoyant. In some ways, he'd lost the ability to have faith. With nothing and nobody to believe in, how did one live a meaningful life?

Dr. Title nodded in silence and pulled out his phone. Graham took a sip of beer and watched the doctor scroll. Moments later, the doctor passed the phone to Graham. On the screen was an excerpt from psychiatrist Irvin Yalom's *Existential Psychotherapy*: a suicide note written by a patient suffering from a so-called "disease of despair."

Imagine a happy group of morons who are engaged in work. They are carrying bricks in an open field. As soon as they have stacked all the bricks at one end of the field, they proceed to transport them to the opposite end. This continues without stop, and every day of every year, they are busy doing the same thing. One day, one of the morons stops long enough to ask himself what he is doing. He wonders what purpose there is in carrying the bricks. And from that instant on, he is not quite as content with his occupation as he had been before. I am the moron who wonders why he is carrying the bricks.

Graham shook his head in shock. As he returned the phone, he realized he used to be one of those morons, and now he doubted the point of carrying the bricks. He'd questioned his place in the world—rejected so many beliefs without replacing them—and he was still in a tailspin.

"You've changed so much in the past couple of years," Dr. Title said. "Your old beliefs no longer apply. Perhaps it's time to replace outdated philosophies with new ways of thinking." Dr. Title nodded to Graham. "You, my friend, have to create a new set of beliefs that suits you. You have to invent new rules and discover new values to navigate the choppy waters of life."

The doctor took a sip of his cocktail. "The people who come to my seminars are at different stages of life, but you are more advanced than most. You've transcended my teachings, but now you're stuck in limbo. I'm not the guru for you, Graham. You have to become your own guru now." Dr. Title smiled. "Isn't that what all the great teachers and thinkers have tried to do for their followers: To awaken them to the powers they already have inside themselves? To encourage them to listen to their hearts, walk their unique paths, and become who they are and live accordingly? As Nietzsche once said, 'One repays a teacher badly if one always remains nothing but a pupil.'"

"You're right," Graham said. "I've shed my skin; I just haven't formed new skin. But there are so many schools of thought, so many religious and secular ways that claim to know how to live a human life. In what—or in whom—should I believe? There must be an ideology, a luminary, or a God to whom I can dedicate myself?"

"The answers are not in a book, young man," Dr. Title said. "You won't find them at a seminar or even from a guru like me."

Graham felt confused, agitated. Abruptly, he jumped off his stool, mashed his teeth together, and balled up his fists. "I just want to feel!"

Dr. Title lowered himself from his seat and stepped in close to Graham. He placed a hand on Graham's chest. "Did you feel that? It was a release of energy, wasn't it? Something just got dislodged. That was your soul speaking."

Graham stepped back and lowered his gaze. Had he been searching for answers in the wrong places? Maybe the answers weren't in the mind but in the body. Not in his head but his heart. Perhaps he couldn't think his way out of discontent. Maybe Graham had to *feel* his way out.

Graham's thoughts began to coalesce. He'd always been active, a lifelong athlete, fidgety whenever he had to sit still for long periods. Teachers had never been able to get him to relax in class. An athlete in high school and college and on into adulthood, he had kept his body fit with spin classes, yoga, and weight training. He'd always felt the most expansive, most alive, while moving. There was something deadening about working at a desk all day. It felt anti-instinctual, even alien.

In a fervor, Graham motioned for the bartender and paid his bill. Then he turned to Dr. Title and thanked him for his time. He'd come to the seminar to expose the doctor as a fraud, but ironically, the man had inspired him to discover who he really was.

Dr. Title gulped down the rest of his drink. "You will become one of the greats. I know it."

Bursting through the bar's exit, Graham broke into a slow jog down the sidewalk. A few minutes later, with sweat dripping down his face, he came upon a cramped subway train. As he ran alongside it, Graham examined the inside of the car, pitying the passengers who were crammed into the small space like sardines.

That night, Graham couldn't sleep as he mulled over his conversation with Dr. Title. Was Dr. Title right that Graham couldn't think his way out of his slump? Were the answers bound in his joints and ligaments, coursing through his veins? What did feeling one's way out of existential angst look like, anyway?

The next morning, Graham attended a yoga class in a hundred-degree room. He felt his hamstrings loosen as he bent forward in the sticky atmosphere. Sweat poured off his body to create a puddle around his yoga mat. Graham synced his movements with the others. He stood up straight, raised his arms over his head, and stared at the ceiling. He lowered his arms, bent over, jumped back into plank, lowered himself to a pushup position, and twisted into upward dog.

A half-hour later, while lying in Savasana, Graham felt relief wash over him. The movements, the yoga practice, had felt cleansing. No longer was he confused or preoccupied with questions that had whipped him into a frenzy the day before. Contemplating this, Graham had an idea. What if he developed an original routine, a new path toward healing that others could follow?

Back at his apartment, Graham began researching movement arts. He launched into an in-depth study of familiar activities: yoga, cycling, swimming, and running. He dove into uncharted territory to study different dance styles, like salsa and interpretive dance. He read books by choreographers and watched interviews of dance instructors on YouTube. He attended ballets, Cirque du Soleil, the Blue Man Group, and even a cheerleading competition. At work, he watched YouTube videos of whirling dervishes and tribal dance rituals.

Graham recorded all his observations into a note-taking software on his phone. He felt like an anthropologist, seeing the limitless possibilities of the human body for the first time, learning the myriad ways it could bend, twist, rotate, and flip.

In one video, Graham watched an elderly woman with arthritis dance with a shaman in Africa. He was astonished when they cut to footage of the next day that showed her walking up a flight of stairs with no pain. How had the healing ritual worked? He didn't believe the shaman had removed a malevolent spirit from the woman's aching joints. And yet, the ritual somehow had shifted her biochemistry toward recovery.

Continuing his exploration, Graham began participating in obstacle course races that required participants to pay large sums of money and then suffer for ninety minutes. In his first race, Graham leaped into frigid water, crawled through mud, and ran through hanging wires that delivered ten thousand volts of electricity.

After months of study and practice, Graham had a routine that consisted of thirty-three maneuvers. The sequence was a mix of yoga, dance, and basic gymnastics. Each movement took about a minute, making the whole routine just over a half hour. Graham felt great after finishing the routine. There was something cleansing about the repetitive motions. The routine had a meditative quality, too. The concentration the movements required stopped his mind from drifting, forcing him into the present. The thirty-three maneuvers became his daily ritual. His mantra. Graham didn't have a rational explanation for why his routine felt so good. Perhaps it was the release of endorphins, the so-called "runner's high" that can come after vigorous physical activity. Eventually, Graham stopped trying to figure out why his routine worked. It made him feel great. Wasn't that enough?

At the gym, a friend saw Graham practicing his maneuvers in one of the studios. Intrigued, he asked Graham to teach him the sequence of thirty-three movements. It took the man about four days to learn. After doing it for a week, he told Graham he felt more energetic, lighter, and more joyful. He invited Graham and about a dozen others to perform the practice in his living room.

A week later, Graham was teaching the routine to another group. The practice seemed to appeal to white-collar workers—the desk warriors. "My life is comfortable and safe. Boring!" one woman confessed. "I waste every day sitting in front of a computer screen, lost in a digital world." Spending her days in front of the computer screen at work, the TV screens at home, and the phone in her hands, she had forgotten what the real world "felt" like. She had lost track of her senses, but the maneuvers brought her back in touch with them.

It took most people about a week to learn Graham's routine if they practiced two or three hours a day, but there were those who took months to grasp them.

Most loved how challenging the set of maneuvers were. The routine encouraged them to push their limits, making them feel invincible and giving them a sense of accomplishment.

Many participants reported the spontaneous remission of certain chronic health problems, from autoimmune disorders to lifelong allergies. Whatever the healing mechanism was, it was unclear. A physician thought the sequence might activate anti-inflammatory hormones in the body but confessed the benefit could be the placebo effect. A physical therapist suggested the movements no doubt released tight ligaments and tendons. A traditional Chinese doctor thought they activated meridian points, restoring the flow of energy, or chi. An acupuncturist claimed they opened up energy centers.

As the popularity of the routine spread throughout Boston, Graham developed a new philosophy to accompany it, something to replace the self-help industry's ineffective rhetoric. A new set of values had coalesced in Graham's mind that were loosely based on ideas put forth by existentialist philosophers like Friedrich Nietzsche, Søren Kierkegaard, and Jean-Paul Sartre. Graham had read these thinkers with great enthusiasm, as well as novels and plays by Albert Camus, Franz Kafka, and Fyodor Dostoevsky.

Most of the people drawn to Graham's routine were like him in that they looked to science rather than a higher power or religion to answer the mysteries of the natural world. But science couldn't answer many of the questions that religious traditions aimed to: *Where did I come from? What should I do with my life? What happens after I die?* Graham's new philosophy aimed to make sense of human existence by helping find meaning in a universe that was almost certainly indifferent to his actions and desires.

One night, something unexpected happened as Graham was teaching the movements to a crowded living room in Brookline. Graham started articulating his new system of beliefs out loud. As Graham led the group through the thirty-three movements, he spoke a new gospel while the trainees moved in perfect synchronization.

"Life is short, my friends. We have an average of seventy-nine years on this planet. We will age fast; our beauty will fade; our bodies will weaken and start to ache. You and I and everyone we have ever known or loved will get sick and die. Such truth is inescapable. Please, do not take solace in the possibility of an eternity in some blissful heaven. Otherwise, you will miss the life you are living now. This is the life you have now; do not waste it. Be who you are today. Do what you want now."

Graham paused to lead the class into position number seventeen. He moved into a deep lunge and reached his arms out in front of himself. Once in the position, he held his body rigid. "There's no predetermined path. Our purpose hasn't been written in the sky. Your genes don't determine what you do; your parents, teachers, or religious leaders can suggest how you should live your life, but you don't have to follow their suggestions. No book can tell you who you are, and no higher force weaves your fate. You are responsible for your own destiny. You make the choices that shape your life."

As Graham settled into position number twenty-four, he spotted a woman at the back of the room struggling to stand on one leg. He locked eyes with her and nodded encouragingly. She stabilized.

"To those who might anguish upon hearing all this, supposing that life is futile and the universe indifferent: do not despair. Fill this existential void with a personal revolution. Engage in rigorous self-study. Build yourself a set of ethics like a patchwork quilt. Live by a code of values and fulfill the individual purpose you have chosen. Let your true nature bloom. Only then can you live an authentic life."

Without Graham's knowledge, a video of that session was uploaded onto YouTube. In three days, it got more than a million views. The producer of a talk show called Graham to discuss the movements and philosophy and ask him onto the show. Graham agreed and performed his routine for a national audience. His appearance whipped the press into a frenzy. Journalists called the school of thought Maneuverism.

Pundits tried to account for Graham's rise in popularity. A renowned trauma researcher speculated that the practice might help individuals release painful experiences buried in their subconscious. On a radio program, a preschool teacher called in and claimed the movements were healing because they weren't *meant* to heal. They were a form of play that most adults had forgotten how to do.

Graham began traveling across the United States to teach Maneuverism to professional athletes and celebrities who paid lavishly for his teachings. As part of the instruction, Graham reminded his students that each of them was the only one who could give meaning to their life, that only they could manufacture their life's purpose. He advised them to stop looking for meaning in places other than their hearts. The answers to the biggest questions could only be discovered by looking inward, he assured them. He urged them to avoid mindless careerism, moneygrubbing, sex, booze, or whatever else they used to avoid the terrifying certainty of nonexistence. He directed them to stop pretending that they would live forever.

A year after Graham first appeared on TV, he opened a studio in Boston. Several months later, he launched another in Los Angeles. He taught hundreds of trainers to share the routines with thousands. These trainers memorized the movements and quoted Graham's philosophy as they led their classes. The studios filled with people twisting and bending their bodies as they acquired new knowledge. Eventually, Graham's ideas extended to Europe, South America, and beyond.

White-collar professionals flocked to Maneuverism in droves. When pressed for answers, most of these people couldn't say why they gravitated to the school of thought. Many office workers said they had spent years in front of their computers, writing emails, updating documents, and building digital products. Yet at the end of the day, there was no sense of accomplishment. While a bricklayer could admire a wall they had built and a fisherman could still smell the ocean on their salty hands, office workers had nothing to show for their work at the end of a workday. Digital advertisements and blog posts couldn't be carried like a hammer or a bucket of paint.

Maneuverists, on the other hand, could pick calluses off their palms after a month of going through the motions. As their bodies hardened, their spirits soared. Maneuverists preached that they didn't want more stuff in their lives—smartphones, mountain bikes, subscriptions to new streaming services. They just wanted an experience that made them feel alive. They wanted memories that wouldn't fade. They wanted stories they could tell their friends and family.

People from all walks of life visited Maneuverism centers. They had lost loved ones. They had beaten cancer. They were ready to change their lives. Much ink was spilled about how the movements tapped into the human need for ritual, but Graham knew they provided whatever was desired. The thirty-three movements became a canvas for people's desires, grief, ambitions, and sorrow. Some joined the school as a way to stay fit. Others admitted the routine was just fun. Some wanted to escape boredom. Many just wanted a place to forget themselves and their problems.

In what can only be described as humblebragging, many people shared selfies of themselves performing the maneuvers on their social media accounts. The images showed them mid-kick, mid-spin, or upside down. Some looked determined, others peaceful. Some painted their faces or bodies. Some did the movements in costumes; a few groups performed them in the nude. Many individuals changed their profile pictures to show them posing in the exercises, making them instant celebrities.

A couple of years after founding Maneuverism, Graham began organizing flash mobs to perform the routine at locations throughout the United States that were mired in conflict or in need of what many Maneuverists called "a spiritual catharsis." Large groups of individuals performed the movements synchronously in front of corrupt financial firms on Wall Street, on the street in front of the White House, along picket lines at corporations that were oppressing their workers. The media flocked to cover these mass events, bewildered even as they endorsed the events as the citizens' right to organize and protest peacefully. One person told the reporters they weren't protests but group prayers.

As it turned out, those words came from a familiar face: Madeline. She and her husband, Bob, had both taken up Maneuverism. When they met Graham at the flash mob at the White House, Madeline greeted him enthusiastically.

"You know, Dr. Title's teachings are good, but yours are so much better. Remember that restaurant I told you I was going to open up?" She shook her head. "I never did. But I did quit my waitressing job. And then Bob lost his factory job assembling pickup trucks." She huffed. "We've both become obsolete in this fast-moving and unpredictable economy. Expendable."

It became clear to Graham that Madeline was one of a growing number of people who believed the routine emitted healing energy, especially when performed in large gatherings, in much the same way groups who meditated as one believed they could make the world a more peaceful place.

"Your philosophy addresses what I've been missing," Madeline said. "It's something I can believe in. And now I get to take part in a cleansing in front of the White House! It's so empowering! I feel like I can finally be of service again."

By this point, Graham had become an institution, the center of a colossal corporate machine. He published a book on Maneuverism called *Going Through the Motions*. He gave commencement speeches, appeared on Saturday Night Live and talk shows, and made specials for streaming platforms.

Some claimed that Graham had founded a religion. Some alleged that Graham had reached the top of Maslow's hierarchy and had become self-actualized, as the Buddha had done under the Bodhi tree. For many, Graham was the picture of human flourishing, as described by the Ancient Greeks. He was Nietzsche's Übermensch, or superman—a self-determined man who lived by his own code. For some, it wasn't a stretch to call Graham a modern-day prophet. Others believed he'd founded a cult, not unlike L. Ron Hubbard's Scientology.

While touring in Boston, Graham rented the same conference room at the Fairmont Copley Plaza in which Dr. Title had held his conference when he inspired Graham's awakening. As he walked onto the stage to start his speech, Graham saw Madeline sitting in the front row, beaming.

Standing in the bright spotlight, Graham didn't speak right away. Instead, he looked out over his disciples and caught and held several people's gazes. He thought about how badly most people needed an ideology or a school of thought to follow, how desperate people could be for guidance as they struggled to make their lives meaningful in an incomprehensible universe. Graham had to invent a new school of thought just to understand how easily people would cling to a dogma or faith that claims to have the answers to unsolvable questions.

But why was his school the "right" school? Why was his way better equipped to help people navigate the challenges of life?

Then Graham saw Dr. Title standing by the exit with a proud grin. What did he think of Graham's worldwide success? Did he take pride in having sparked Graham's spiritual revolution? Were they competitors now? Did Dr. Title even care?

Whatever the answers, at that moment, Graham realized that Maneuverism had been the perfect school for him given the circumstances of that particular time of his life. The movements had helped him get back on his feet after stumbling in California. They had helped him shed the angst of years of office work that had atrophied his body and deadened his spirit. Maneuverism had led Graham to discover himself when he was lost.

At that moment, it occurred to him that Maneuverism had served its purpose. It had allowed him to turn inward during a time of great change and discover his unique motives for living. Now, though, Graham had outgrown the school he had founded.

Just like that, at the peak of his wealth, fame, and power, Graham decided to walk away from it all. With hundreds of people and dozens of his trainers waiting for him to speak, to give the command for them to start the movements, Graham thanked everyone for attending and proposed they find their own meaning now.

"You must avoid schools like Maneuverism," he told the rapt audience. "You must be skeptical of leaders who claim to have simple answers to complex questions, even me. Stop clinging to dogma, please, and find out what works for you. I'm not your guru. You must do it alone, as I did. You must become your own masters now."

Amid the silence of a stunned audience, Graham walked off the stage and out of the conference room. He ascended the stairs and walked through the bar where he and Dr. Title had chatted a few years ago. He crossed the street and walked to the small park between the Boston Public Library and Trinity Church. Under the summer sun, Graham lowered himself to the grass and lay on his back. He put his arms behind his head and watched clouds pass across the blue sky. At peace, he breathed deeply, closed his eyes, and enjoyed the warmth.

When a shadow darkened his space, Graham opened his eyes to see Madeline standing over him. She took a seat beside him, crossing one leg over the other. Graham propped himself up on his arms.

"Everyone is confused and waiting for you to return," Madeline said.

Graham shook his head. "I'm not going back."

Staring toward Trinity Church, Madeline nodded. She seemed to accept his decision. "What will you do next?"

"I just want to lay here for a while," Graham answered.

Madeline thought for a moment, then shrugged. "I'm going to go back to the conference. Maybe we are all just running away from reality in there, but it feels good to work on myself with a community of like-minded people. I respect your wish to break free of dogma and gurus but living so sincerely isn't possible for me. I find comfort in a system with defined rules and rituals. It's too hard to live with my eyes wide open. I think a little self-delusion is necessary for me."

Before starting Maneuverism, Graham might have considered such willful ignorance repugnant. But he'd changed. It was distressing to accept that life had no intrinsic meaning, that every human being had the freedom to do whatever they wanted, that people lived and died, yet the play went on. Most people needed limitations on their possibilities. Too much freedom—too many choices—was paralyzing for most.

Graham knew there was comfort in following someone who claimed to know how to live. There was comfort in believing that the answers to life's biggest and most mysterious questions were known. And what was wrong with seeking comfort in a life riddled with challenges and hardships?

That was how Madeline had chosen to live her life. Graham understood it, respected it, and admired her for making that decision.

As for Graham, he didn't really know what he would do next. But for the first time in his life, that was okay.

Chasing Fireflies at Midnight

I had just finished dinner when I received a phone call from a nurse at Maine Medical Center. She informed me that my grandmother was in the intensive care unit and might need dialysis. My grandmother, Anne, didn't have COVID-19, thankfully, but her kidney disease had advanced, according to the critical care physician, who wasn't hopeful about her prospects. As soon as I got off the phone with the nurse, I left my apartment in Boston to drive up to Maine.

When I entered her room a few hours later, Anne's skin was pale, and she was having trouble staying awake. The doctor had just given her an anti-anxiety medication, which made her drowsy, but she insisted on talking with me, wanting to know how my latest article was coming along. I told her I had submitted the final draft to my editor and that the story was going to be the magazine's cover story. Anne smiled, clutched my hand, and closed her eyes. I sat back in my chair and wondered how much longer I would have with her.

I hadn't been close to my grandmother growing up, and in my twenties, I was so focused on the future that I charged forward, trying to find my place in the world. I didn't pay much attention to family history as the idea of digging up the past seemed like a waste of time. Meanwhile, Anne researched our family's lineage, read history books, and visited our ancestors' graves. She mapped our heritage exhaustively, while I ignored it.

It was only a few years earlier, sometime in my thirties, that I realized learning more about my past could help me know not only where I had come from but also where I should go. Recognizing this, I began trying to get to know Anne better and encouraged her to share stories of her life.

Every few months, Anne would send me mini pieces of memoir that captured slices of her life: Dropping out of college after getting married. Going to graduate school in her late thirties to study public policy after a divorce. Meeting her second husband and becoming politically engaged in the seventies. The excitement of the feminist movement and the thrill of becoming a democratic delegate for Massachusetts. My father moving to New Hampshire after high school to become a "mountain man" and start a construction business. Through her, I learned that I came from a long line of rabble-rousers—the origin of my revolutionary spirit.

Anne thought of these as her piecemeal memoir. We both acknowledged the essays probably wouldn't find publication, but that was never the point. She just wanted to record the past for the family, and maybe for herself, too. And because neither my father nor my younger brother seemed to have any interest in learning the details of her life, I would have to become the family historian.

It's unfortunate that few seem interested in Anne's stories. She lived a common life, but every life has extraordinary bits when examined closely. How my father takes for granted the traits he inherited from his mother! Indeed, he values education highly and pursued an associate's degree in adulthood to better himself. Yet he forgets his mother pursued a master's while raising him. When Anne's second marriage fell apart, she packed up her belongings and drove from Boston to Los Angeles to start a new life. My father, brother, and I fancy ourselves risk-takers, yet we forget Anne's pioneering spirit runs through our veins.

After a year of struggling to secure employment, Anne was considering returning home to Boston when she found a job as a city planner in Los Angeles. She's now been retired for almost twenty years, but to my surprise, she looks back on her twenty-year career as a city planner with some regret. She considers her pension vital, but what she always wanted was to become a journalist.

Anne's city planning office stood across the hall from the offices of the *Associated Press*. She revered the *AP* for its top-notch journalism, but she never found a way in with them. In fact, she had sophisticated ways of talking herself out of such a career path. She wasn't a natural storyteller, she convinced herself. She wasn't resilient enough to pursue a story when doors were slammed in her face. She wasn't a bulldog like the reporters in her favorite movie, *All the President's Men*. She thought she was too gullible to see through the subjects' lies. So for twenty years, Anne worked on the wrong side of the hallway.

Though she has never admitted it, I think my grandmother envied my writing career. I wasn't the type of "balanced" journalist Anne had wanted to become, though. I was a science writer for a biomedical research institute—a hired gun for a development team at the Galen Institute in Cambridge, Massachusetts. Everything I wrote was designed to raise money for scientists' research projects. I wrote and edited grants, proposals, and letters to grant-making institutions, philanthropic groups, and wealthy donors. I interviewed scientists and wrote feature articles.

I enjoyed the work, but like my grandmother, I revered journalists. I admired them on *60 Minutes* for speaking truth to power during difficult times. I'd been romanced by movies like *Spotlight* and *The Insider* that depicted investigative reporters exposing deep injustices in society.

Haunted by my grandmother's cautionary tale of working close to the *AP*'s office, I decided to try my hand at freelance journalism. I wrote and eventually published a few pieces of literary journalism in consumer magazines. The writing and rewriting with editors took immense effort, and the pay wasn't as good as corporate work.

Thinking I could perhaps merge my commercial and journalistic interests, I pitched the idea of writing a feature article to the editor of the Galen Institute's magazine, *Cellular*. No doubt the editor thought I was a hack who couldn't write objectively, but he was impressed enough by my clips to let me take on the piece. It was one I had wanted to write since my arrival at Galen two years prior: a story about a plant biologist at the Institute who studied how and why fireflies lit up, a natural phenomenon called bioluminescence.

When I told Anne over the phone that I was writing an article about fireflies, she said that she'd always been fascinated by the insects. When she was a child, she and her father would use nets to catch them late at night. In retirement, Anne became something of an amateur scholar on fireflies. She regaled me with facts about the fascinating creatures.

Apparently, fireflies use quick flashes of light to communicate with other fireflies. The flashes also ward off predators and help the fireflies find mates. Each firefly has a distinct courtship signal, with males being the primary signalers. The females remain grounded during the males' courtship displays. If a female likes a male, she responds by flashing back. The females prefer males who give off longer-lasting flashes. A pair will flash back and forth until they've mated. Once they do, they stay together all night. It's as if the flashes are love songs, my grandmother supposed.

As I began writing the article, I immersed myself in the scientific literature the lab had produced. The lab's mission was to explore the biochemistry of plants from all over the world. The lab studied the dizzying array of chemicals plants used to defend themselves against threats, like other creatures, droughts, and lack of light.

I was working on the article one weekend, when I took a break to read Anne's most recent memoir pages. It was then that I sensed we might not have much more time together. She was eighty-three and suffered from various health issues, including chronic kidney disease. She wrote in her piece that she hadn't realized how vital kidneys were until they became deficient.

She also found it strange to be living in Maine because she had lived in Southern California for most of her adult life. She would have spent the rest of her life in California, except she fell and fractured a hip, stripping her of her cherished independence. After the injury, my father convinced her to return to the East Coast. Eventually, Anne decided to move to Kennebunkport, Maine, a charming town she'd always adored and visited whenever she came to see us. In summers, my father, brother, and I would ride bikes around Kennebunkport, stay in a local bed and breakfast, and visit Sharon's Seafood restaurant for lobster rolls.

A week before visiting Anne in the hospital, I stood on the lawn of Acadia Senior Living, and we talked through her window. Since the COVID-19 pandemic began, safety measures have kept people at a distance from high-risk populations like the elderly, as eight out of ten deaths have been among adults over sixty-five.

She had spent the last year mostly cooped up in her room; I had been sequestered in my apartment, working from home. A year into the pandemic, we chatted about "caution fatigue" and how tired we were of isolation. The toughest thing about the pandemic for Anne was not being able to touch anyone. She said her "touch tank" was low, and she just wanted a damn hug. She seemed melancholy, even depressed, and had been relying on her anti-anxiety medications to sleep every night.

Most of all, Anne was bored. She was tired of tinkering with a memoir that would never be published and no one but her grandson would read. She was on her third book about kidney disease and hadn't read for enjoyment in months. And the assisted living facility was getting on her nerves. The mind-numbing chair yoga each morning, the painting classes, the daily ritual of gathering around the television and watching *The Price is Right*. Until she moved into an assisted living facility, she had assumed a love of bingo was a myth; it wasn't. Sunday bingo was like Christmas for most of the residents.

The pandemic had made her living conditions insufferable, Anne told me through her window. Most residents were glued to their televisions or computers all day, soaking up news reports. During socially distanced meetings, people worried about the virus and how their health issues put them at risk. Anne said she'd lived a long life and had gotten her fill. If the virus got her at eighty, so be it.

The sense that Anne needed a project—an adventure, something to take her mind off the pandemic—led me to visit her facility in the middle of the night. With a ten o'clock curfew in Boston, I should've been home like everyone else. Yet I drove an hour and a half north to break my grandmother out of Acadia, dressed in dark jeans and a black T-shirt to avoid being seen. It was midnight when I arrived.

After parking the car, I tiptoed to her window and tapped on the glass. The curtain slid aside on the second knock, and my grandmother appeared in the window, rubbing the sleep from her eyes. She glanced at the clock on the wall. "What the hell are you doing here so late?" she asked shrilly.

"I'm getting you out of this prison to go on an adventure." I reminded her of our last conversation and of how fed up she was with the living conditions. I, too, had been feeling cooped up sitting in front of the computer all day and gorging on the news at night. I had lost touch with the natural world. I felt I'd lost touch with myself.

Anne protested, reminding me of the curfew. The risk of infection.

"It's midnight," I said. "Not another person in sight." I pulled a fresh mask from my pocket for her. "There's enough hand sanitizer in my car for the population of Switzerland. And we'll be home in a few hours."

"I don't like surprises," she said when I dodged her question about where we were going. She eventually agreed, though, and went to get dressed.

Ten minutes later, Anne appeared in the window. Holding her legs and then her lower back, I carried her through the window and placed her on the ground. I helped her adjust her face mask and then led her to my car. "Stay low and keep your voice down," I said as we began to cross the lawn.

Suddenly, a set of automatic lights illuminated the lawn, and we ducked behind some bushes. A window snapped open, and a man with snow-white hair leaned out. "Who's out there?"

When he spotted Anne, she stepped out from behind the bush. "I'm with my grandson, Hank."

"What about the lockdown? And the curfew?"

"Go to bed, Hank. If I'm not back in time for chair yoga, cover for me."

On the highway driving north of Kennebunkport, Anne told me about Hank. "He's one of my only friends at Acadia. I don't much care for the guys he associates with, though. They're lazy. Every day, Hank and four others meet for coffee: same time, same table, same orders. Such a waste of time, idly passing the hours talking about politics or bragging about their kids' accomplishments." Anne's days were different. She took classes on politics and history, organized the Acadia Book Club, and had video conferences with the League of Women's Voters in Los Angeles.

Dodging another question about where we were going, I turned left onto Laudholm Farm Road and took another left onto Skinner Mill Road. Minutes later, I parked in the lot at Wells National Estuarine Research Reserve, a 2,250-acre network of trails that hugged the Maine coast. I hopped out of the car and circled around to open the door for Anne. I squirted a glob of sanitizer into her hands while she fumbled with her mask. I offered to help, but she said she could do it herself. Opening the trunk, I put two nets in my backpack. After clicking on a flashlight, I studied a paper map. Laudholm Beach was less than a mile away.

I led Anne past a visitor center and onto Knight Trail. We walked the wide, grassy path. Grasshoppers chirped all around us, and waves crashed in the distance. We took a right onto Barrier Beach Trail, passing an estuary that emitted a pungent odor of sulfur. We kept moving, and the woods opened out to a parking area. From there, we followed a boardwalk to Laudholm Beach.

I kicked off my sandals, putting them in my backpack, and offered to put Anne's shoes in as well. When her shoes and socks were off, she pressed her feet into the cool sand. The soft crashing of waves was exciting, and the salty air was invigorating. The nearly full moon lit up the beach. We walked along the shore, admiring the darkened houses along the coast.

As the beach turned to rocks, I led Anne to a grassy meadow. "Wait. Watch." She didn't understand until we spotted a faint, eerie glow.

Anne's face brightened. Letting out a giggle, she scurried toward the flickering insect. When she was a foot away, the green glow stopped, and she paused. The glow appeared a few steps farther away, and she skipped after the firefly, around a sand dune. I followed, pulling a glass jar from my backpack.

Anne stepped in close to the firefly and cupped her hands together, but she missed the light. The next time, the beetle was in her hands. She watched the firefly crawl across her palm as it blinked. Removing the lid, I nodded for her to drop the firefly in the jar.

"Did you poke holes in the cover so the fireflies won't be hurt?"

I nodded that I had.

She placed her hand over the jar, gave it a tap, and the firefly fell to the bottom. I handed her a net, and we continued along the beach.

Just then, sparks of light rose all around us, and the beach became luminous, ethereal. Filled with awe, we laughed and used our nets to sweep the insects out of the air. After twenty minutes, the jar was glowing with fireflies.

"It's likely filled with mostly males," Anne said, examining the jar. "They'll glow all night if we add more females."

To find females, we searched the grass for glows that lasted longer. Soon, we had caught a handful of females, and Anne guessed the jar was filled with about a hundred insects. She pulled a few leaves from a shrub and put them inside, explaining that food would also help keep the fireflies blinking all night.

We strolled toward the ocean and sat down on a beach towel. The fireflies flitted across the glass jar in front of us as waves crashed in the background. When I pulled two sandwiches from the backpack, Anne unwrapped the tinfoil to find a lobster roll from Sharon's Seafood. She smiled widely, and we ate in silence. Once finished, Anne balled up the tin foil.

"Thank you for breaking me out of Acadia. This has been so exciting. I'm getting cold now, though, and I think I'm ready to go home."

On the drive back, Anne held the glass jar in her lap, mesmerized by the twinkling insects. Back at the assisted living facility, I picked Anne up and slid her back into her room. She gave me a hug through the window and then asked me to wait. After a moment, she returned with a binder.

Anne passed the binder through the window. "This is my research on fireflies."

I flipped through the pages, briefly stopping on an article to read a headline or a passage Anne had highlighted. There were dozens of articles and notes she'd taken. I stopped on what looked like a transcript of an interview.

"A few weeks ago, I interviewed an entomologist from Harvard," Anne said. "Anyway, I knew that I'd never get around to writing something. I want you to have the research. Hopefully, you'll find it useful."

A few days later, I was working on my firefly article at home. The research my grandmother had collected was extremely valuable. It detailed the courtship behaviors of fireflies, as well as how other animals, like deep-sea creatures, had evolved the ability to glow in the dark. Anne had dug up news reports that proved firefly populations were dwindling in the United States due to development that encroached on forests, fields, and meadows where fireflies lived. The light pollution produced by humans also disrupted firefly populations by obscuring the signals they used to find mates.

These articles became background for my piece; I cited a few studies and used a couple of quotes from the entomologist. In my interview with Galen's plant biologist, I had learned that the scientists had successfully sequenced the insect's genome and had finished several experiments that revealed the basic chemistry involved in the firefly's bioluminescence. According to the biologist, bioluminescence had likely evolved to ward off predators and then evolved into a way to attract potential mates.

When I visited Anne after she was admitted to the ICU a few days later, the nephrologist said her kidneys had begun to fail and she didn't have long. When I got to her room, Anne's eyes flickered open, and she smiled. We talked for a few minutes, reminiscing about our adventure. Opening my bag, I pulled out a jar of fireflies I had collected the night before.

She examined the jar and then asked, "How is the article coming?"

I told her the article was finished, and that I'd used a lot of her research to write it.

"I'm proud of you," she said, a smile spreading across her face. "I'm glad someone in this family became a writer."

From my bag, I also retrieved a copy of the new issue of *Cellular*. I had worked with an illustrator to create the cover art. It had a beautiful graphic of a firefly in a meadow at Laudholm Beach. "Check out the article," I urged.

Anne flipped the magazine open to the article and paused. Next to my name was hers. It had always been a dream to see her name in print. Her eyes welled with tears, and she didn't say a word. I sat in my chair, watched the fireflies flicker in the jar, and let her read the story we had written together.

Trail Magic

"Dr. Stowe?"

Looking up from the notes in my lap, I found a young woman with long brunette curls hovering uncertainly in the doorway of my office. "Yes?"

"The receptionist told me to come back. Said you were ready for me?"

I glanced at the clock and waved her toward the sofa chair across from mine. "Of course. Tristen, isn't it?"

"Uh-huh."

She hunched down in the chair, her head lowered. The posture reinforced the notes I'd received from her primary care physician, who had expressed concerns over Tristen's possible depression.

"Can you tell me what's going on, Tristen? Feel free to express whatever you're thinking or feeling. This is a safe space; I won't judge."

"Where do you want me to start?"

"Just tell me your story."

"Well, I grew up in Florida and started college there. However, I moved to Boston to finish my undergrad and got my master's in media science from Boston University. I've been working as a researcher at a digital marketing agency in Cambridge ever since."

"And how's work going?"

"I have so much to do, I feel like vomiting."

I frowned. "Do you often feel nauseous?"

Tristen grimaced. "Not really." She waved her hand dismissively. "I'm a bit prone to hyperbole sometimes."

I raised my eyebrows. Whether or not she'd been exaggerating, the demands of her job clearly overwhelmed her.

"You work quite hard, don't you?"

Tristen chewed on her lower lip thoughtfully. "Have you ever heard the term *kuroshi*?" I shook my head. "It's Japanese; it means 'overwork death.' Some people in Japan work so hard, they die."

"Do you feel like you're suffering from *kuroshi*?"

Tristen shrugged. "I have this recurring stress-dream where I'm meeting with my team and I'm so exhausted, I pass out and hit my head on the table. When I lift my head from the table, all my teeth have been knocked out."

I hummed. "Have you had thoughts about harming yourself or others?"

She snorted. "I'm too busy to kill myself."

When I didn't laugh, Tristen glanced away. After a long moment of silence, she began to speak softly.

"I've always been fascinated with Japan's suicide forests. Sometimes, when I'm not feeling well, I like to drive out to Concord and walk around Walden Pond. There's a path I've found that leads to a small field about halfway around the pond. There, I think about not being alive."

Tristen's fascination with suicide was troubling. It was obvious that work stress was affecting her mood, but I wanted to dive deeper and explore the possibility of hidden traumas that might also be contributing to her depression. As our first session came to an end, we agreed to meet every Thursday.

I realized early on that Tristen's distress stemmed from feelings of alienation and purposelessness. As a therapist with existential leanings, I felt uniquely suited to help her discover a sense of purpose and meaning in life. To address her self-concept problems, I needed to help her answer two questions: Who is Tristen? What does she want?

A few weeks in, we talked about the idea of the "true self."

"I never know what people mean when they talk about 'finding one's true self,'" Tristen lamented. "What is it, really? How do I look for it? How do I know if I've found it? And what if I find my true self but don't like her?"

"I don't think there's actually a true self to find, per se," I replied. "According to the existentialist school of thought, we create who we are through the choices we make. We can't choose our parents or where we're born, but it's our responsibility to find our window of freedom and stretch toward it, to choose who we become."

After a moment of silence, Tristen nodded slowly. "Window of freedom . . . I like that."

By the end of the session, I felt like we had made good progress, but Tristen expressed impatience. "Shouldn't I have had some kind of breakthrough by now, like he does in *Goodwill Hunting*?"

I shook my head. "Movies like that are dramatizations of the process. And even if they were accurate depictions of someone's experience, not everyone's journey is the same."

Her impatience stuck with me, however. I decided to begin the next session by addressing something I'd been thinking about since I'd first met her.

As Tristen settled into the chair across from me, I readjusted my wire-rimmed glasses. "Tell me, do you think you have a good understanding of who you are?"

"You're asking who I think I am?"

I smiled. "Yes. Give it a shot. If someone asked you, 'Who is Tristen?' what might you say?"

She thought for a moment. "I don't know, honestly. No one's ever asked me that before." She lowered her eyes to the ground, and silence fell over us for a few minutes.

Finally, she lifted her head. "This is kind of silly, but I have this metaphor I sometimes think about." I nodded encouragingly. "Okay, in this metaphor, I see myself as a dung beetle rolling a little pile of poop into a ball, and the ball just keeps getting bigger and bigger as I roll it."

I stroked my beard. "Why a dung beetle?"

She shrugged. "Because of all the bullshit we deal with every day."

"What kind of bullshit?"

She waved a hand to encompass everything. "Everywhere you look, there's bullshit. When I was in college, it took the form of constantly striving for perfect grades, trying to look cute for boys I didn't even like, and sucking up to professors to get strong recommendation letters for grad school."

"And in adulthood?"

"I roll dung day in and day out."

"Tell me more about that?"

Tristen leaned forward in her seat, her expression coming alive in a way I hadn't seen before.

"Dung is striving for all these bullshit American milestones: Get some job you hate. Marry someone you can tolerate. Have kids who will nearly bankrupt you. Buy some cookie-cutter house in the suburbs. Drive a hybrid SUV. Save for a retirement you won't get to enjoy, because you'll drop dead from a heart attack in your sixties."

"Tell me how you really feel," I joked.

Tristen's expression turned stern. "How I *really* feel? I feel like most people die at twenty-five but don't get buried until they're seventy-five."

In our next session, we veered onto the topic of spirituality.

"Did you grow up with a religious affiliation?" I asked.

"I was raised Catholic. My parents were super devout and took me to church every Sunday. I guess I'm a lapsed Catholic."

"What kinds of beliefs do you hold now?"

Tristen frowned. "I'm not sure. Nothing from a traditional religion, I know that much." She paused for a moment, before shaking her head. "It's a tough question. What about you, Dr. Stowe? What do you believe?"

Typically, I'd keep the conversation focused on my patient, but I thought my perspective might help in this case. "I'm an atheist. I take a cosmic perspective on life."

"What do you mean, 'cosmic'?"

"Have you ever seen a picture of the Earth from the perspective of space?"

When Tristen shook her head, I indicated a framed photograph on the wall. Turning to look over her shoulder, Tristen stared at it as I explained more about it.

"In 2014, this photo was taken from the surface of Mars by the Curiosity Rover. It shows Earth as a tiny blue spec floating in the inky blackness of space."

Tristen shuddered and turned back around. "Truly the stuff of nightmares."

I laughed. "It reminds me that humans are but one of millions of species on a small rock in a galaxy among billions of galaxies in an infinitely large universe."

"Doesn't that make you feel insignificant?"

"It does, yes, but I also feel like it's an honest reflection of reality."

Tristen frowned. "How does that affect your beliefs?"

"It changed me quite profoundly. In my twenties, I subscribed to Buddhism and even some New Age theories, but as I started to look at my life from this cosmic perspective, I gravitated more toward the philosophical tradition of existentialism."

"Existentialism? I feel like you've mentioned that before."

I nodded. "It's a philosophical and literary movement based on the premise that a human life is meaningless. Or rather, there is no intrinsic meaning to our existence."

"That's pretty bleak, don't you think?"

I shrugged. "Believing your life has no meaning isn't the most uplifting idea, sure, but that realization is just the beginning. Once you accept that you aren't here for a specific reason, you can find your own unique reasons for living. We become the architects of our lives. With each choice, we make ourselves into what we choose, shaping our futures."

Tristen sighed. "It's still low-key depressing."

"Admittedly, it took a while for me to get comfortable with the idea of life having no meaning, but you get used to it. I like that it puts all the responsibility on each person to create their life. I'm happy to talk further if you're interested."

"No offense, Doc, but that's a pass for me."

I chuckled. "Fair enough."

The next few sessions were spent filling in the blanks of Tristen's personal history. It wasn't until our tenth session that we hit upon a deep wound.

Ever since she was little, Tristen had known she was attracted to women, but queer folks had been bullied in her high school. She admired classmates who had come out, but she hadn't been brave enough to follow their lead.

"Did your parents know you were gay?"

"I wasn't bringing home boyfriends, but we couldn't talk openly about things like that. The church didn't exactly look kindly on the gay community."

"Did you ever tell them?"

"I worked up the courage eventually."

"How'd they react?"

"They said I was confused and refused to talk about it ever again. I can still remember my father saying, 'You've made the wrong decision.' As if my sexuality were a *decision*."

"How did their reaction make you feel?"

"It destroyed me! My grades took a nosedive. I dropped out of swimming and drifted away from friends."

Tristen paused and swallowed.

"What else?" I prodded.

She broke eye contact. "I didn't really want to be around anymore."

"Is there a specific memory you have in mind from that time?"

"Yeah. One day, I walked into the middle of the woods near my town. I found a soft bed of moss to sit on and watched the sun set behind the treetops."

She hesitated. I didn't want to push her, so we sat in silence for a minute or so.

"I pulled out the bag in my pocket," she finally said, "and dumped the pills I'd been collecting into my hand. I was crying so hard, I could barely see what I was doing."

Her eyes welled with tears.

"But then something unexpected happened. A fox leaped onto a nearby log and stared at me. We just looked at each other for a bit. Then it made its way toward me, until I could touch its soft fur. It let me pet it. It was so sweet."

"What happened after that?"

"The fox scampered off. I dumped the pills back into the bag and drove home."

Tristen took a shuddering breath and scrubbed at her eyes. I offered her a box of tissues, which she used to dry her face.

"I applied to college in Boston the very next day," she said once she'd regained her composure. "I needed to get away from my family and the world I'd grown up in. Even with the drop in my grades, I was accepted into Boston University, where I majored in math and computer science. That's where I got my academic edge, striving to become a perfect student, pushing myself and working long hours."

"Rise and grind" was how she approached school—and now her workdays.

"What do you think drove your high-achieving behavior?"

Tristen didn't even hesitate. "The need for perfection. Ever since I was young, I wanted to be perfect: A perfect student. A perfect athlete. A perfect person."

I reminded her that she was doing all right, having a master's degree and working as a researcher for a successful company.

She frowned. "I still feel like I come up short everywhere, like whatever I do isn't enough."

"Do you think this feeling of inadequacy is perhaps driving you to strive and overwork yourself into cycles of burnout?"

Tristen stared at the floor. I let a moment of silence pass before I asked what she was thinking.

"My twenty-fifth birthday is coming up. I'm worried about it."

Assuming Tristen was worried about entering a new decade, I thought we might have a conversation embracing a new phase of adulthood or even aging. I quickly learned the anxiety was for a different reason.

"I made a pact with myself when I was eighteen: if I still felt at twenty-five how I did at eighteen, I would end it."

"By 'end it,' you mean take your life?"

Tristen nodded solemnly.

"May I ask how far away your twenty-fifth birthday is?"

"It's next month."

"Do you still feel like you did when you were a teenager?"

She shrugged. "Moving here, I changed in a lot of positive ways, but I still feel like I'm carrying around this load."

Glancing at the clock, I realized we were out of time. "Would it be okay if we talked about this more next session?"

Tristen shrugged. "I guess."

Over the next few days, I worried about Tristen, troubled by her words. She took an antidepressant and was in psychotherapy with me, but I wondered if I could be doing more for her. Looking for advice, I called my mentor, Ruth.

"It sounds like she's exhausted from overwork," Ruth said once I'd explained the situation.

"What's the treatment for exhaustion?"

"Well, what's worked for some patients is a period of rest and reflection. It sounds like Tristen could use a break."

"From work?"

"From everything: work, the demands of modern living, the city, herself."

"What should I do if her suicidal ideation escalates?"

"If it gets to the point where she's planning an attempt, instruct her to go to the hospital immediately. Tell her to have the doctors call you to let you know she's been admitted."

"And if she won't go to the hospital?"

"You can send the police to her home—and you should."

I thanked Ruth for her advice and wished her well.

In our next session, I jumped right in with a big question, hoping Tristen and I could eventually talk about how she might be able to take a break. "What do you want out of life?"

Tristen gave me a perplexed look. I kept my expression as sincere as possible, and she rolled her shoulders. "I don't know. Good health, happiness, financial freedom, a woman I'm crazy about. I'd like to move up at work and . . ."

"What is it?" I asked when she remained silent.

"I've been thinking about your beliefs. I've been reading about that philosophy of yours, existentialism. It bummed me out."

"How so?"

"If nothing matters, if our lives are insignificant, why do anything at all? Why get out of bed every day? Why go on living?"

"But if life's meaningless," I countered, "that means it's up to you to give it meaning, right?"

Her face remained expressionless. "I guess."

"Do you have a sense of what gives your life meaning, Tristen?"

She crossed her legs and stared out the window. "My work gives my life purpose, and my friends are great, but—"

She stopped short.

"What is it?"

"It's nothing."

"Go on, please."

She grinned. "There's always been something I've wanted to do but been too afraid to talk about, much less do."

"What is that?"

Her face brightened. "This might sound crazy coming from someone who was raised in Florida, but I've always had this crazy dream to hike the Appalachian Trail. All two thousand one hundred ninety-three miles of it, from Georgia to Mount Katahdin in Maine."

I sat back, intrigued. "What's stopping you?"

Tristen sighed. "Work takes up all my time. I have too many responsibilities, too many people depending on me. But I often fantasize about dropping everything and hiking the AT. Sometimes, I research the logistics for fun."

We spent the next few sessions analyzing her desire to hike the AT. There were many practical concerns holding her back. For one, she felt leaving her job, even for a short leave, would upset a lot of people, her coworkers and bosses alike.

I thought about how Tristen had put her trust in me, and I hadn't offered a lot of practical solutions, which was what she wanted. I often reminded her that therapy was a slow process. Often, it could take years to heal.

I was planning to burrow deeper into Tristen's sexuality in the next session, but she never showed up. I called her several times, but the calls just went to voice mail.

My worry grew with every rendition of her voice mail's greeting. It had been a few weeks since Tristen first mentioned her pact to kill herself on her next birthday if nothing changed. While a glance at her chart assured me it hadn't passed yet, I couldn't shake the fear that she had decided not to wait.

Ruth had told me to send Tristen to the hospital if her suicidal ideation solidified into a plan, but what if I couldn't get Tristen on the phone? Should I go ahead and call the police, ask them to visit her home? What if she wasn't there?

The more I thought about it, the more certain I felt that she wouldn't be. She had often talked about visiting the forest near Walden Pond—her own "suicide forest." I shuddered.

It wasn't something a therapist should do, but I decided to go looking for Tristen myself. I needed to make sure she was okay, but I didn't want to call the cops on her. I told the receptionist to reschedule the rest of my appointments and jumped in my car. I turned onto Route 2 and drove west. Twenty minutes later, I arrived at Walden Pond.

From the parking lot, I followed a path around the pond. About half an hour into the walk, I took a narrow path deeper into the forest just south of Walden Pond.

The sun was starting to set when I reached a small field. I paused to watch the sun sink beyond the trees. Out of the corner of my eye, I spotted someone sitting on a stump near the edge of the field.

It was Tristen.

I approached her slowly. As I came closer, I saw that her hair was messy and her eyes were red and puffy. Clearly, she'd been crying.

"What's wrong, Tristen?"

She showed no surprise at my presence. She just stared across the field as she answered me. "My birthday is next week, and nothing's going to change." She sniffed loudly.

I wanted to help, but I didn't know what I could offer besides more talk, which she already thought wasn't productive enough. I had to try, though.

"Tristen, I'm worried about you. I think you should go to the hospital. They can—"

She snorted. "They can what? Keep me from killing myself?" She shook her head. "That's not why I came here, Dr. Stowe."

I bit my lip, unsure whether I believed her.

Seeing my skepticism, Tristen reached into the pockets of her jeans and pulled the insides out, indicating she hadn't brought pills with her like she had when she was eighteen. "I just wanted to get away from everything, you know? I was hoping the forest could . . . I don't know. Help?"

Clearly, she was struggling, but she didn't seem to have a plan. It was a bit of a gray area for me as a therapist, but if I wanted her to trust me to help her, I had to trust that she was being truthful with me.

"All right. I believe you." She eyed me warily, but I continued. "And I believe I can help you find a way to feel better. I don't know how yet, but I'm certain I can. I just need you to trust me."

Tristen scowled. "Why should I, though? You thought I was planning to kill myself today, even though I told you my pact was for my birthday. For that matter, you don't even think life is worth living! What's the difference if I die next week or in a few decades. We'll all be forgotten only years afterward anyway."

I exhaled slowly. "I think you're really overwhelmed and feeling trapped by your circumstances. Maybe I can help you feel free."

The word *free* seemed to register with her. She glanced at me out of the corner of her eye. "Free to do what?"

"Whatever you like. To live your life how you want to live it."

She wiped her eyes and stared at the setting sun. When I held out my hand, she shook her head and slid her hand into mine. I helped her off the stump, and we walked out of the field without saying anything. Only once we reached the parking lot did I ask her to come see me the following day.

When she agreed, I couldn't have been more relieved.

When I got home, I threw myself into research. I only had a week left to help Tristen, so I dug into the most cutting-edge approaches to healing. Eventually, I began reading about psychedelics, some of which were being used to promote psychological healing.

"There's a resurgence going on with psychedelics," I told Ruth. "I was thinking we might try giving Tristen mushrooms in a controlled medical setting?"

"What makes you think it'll work?"

"Honestly, I don't think Tristen has a serious psychiatric condition. She displays characteristics of depression, of course, but there's plenty to depress Gen Z. She's anxious, but who isn't anxious in her generation?"

"What do you think is going on?"

"She's struggling with the kinds of self-concept issues we all deal with as we come of age and struggle to figure ourselves out. Perhaps a psychedelic could allow her to go deeper inside herself and discover something therapy can't get at."

The next day, when I proposed the idea of using a psychedelic to aid our therapy, Tristen put up no resistance. "I attended Burning Man last year and took a few mind-altering substances with friends."

"Did you have any insights while you were out there?" I asked.

She nodded. "Oh, yeah. I was in the middle of this crazy desert, with wind and dust swirling all around me, and I felt like my mind had expanded to the size of the moon. I felt an overwhelming connectedness to the world and everyone in it. Unfortunately, the feeling wore off hours later."

Focusing on me once more, she asked, "Why a psychedelic, though?"

"Psychedelics have been shown to ease fear and anxiety and have been helpful in folks with depression."

"Okay. Which psychedelic are you thinking?"

"I'd like to try magic mushrooms, if you're open to it."

Tristen shrugged. "Groovy. What's the procedure?"

"I'll administer the drug in an exam room here at the center, so you would hallucinate in a controlled setting and we could provide medical supervision."

"Like my trip sitter."

I chucked. "Something like that."

"How much would I take?"

"I'll base the dosage on factors like your age, gender, and weight."

Tristen shrugged again. "Okay, let's do it."

When Tristen returned the following Monday, I guided her to an exam room for the procedure. Inside, a nurse smiled and stood up from the chair he'd been sitting in.

"Hi, Tristen, I'll be here to make sure you feel comfortable and that everything goes smoothly during the treatment."

"Thank you for your service," Tristen quipped.

At my invitation, Tristen hopped up on the bed against the wall. I held out a cup for her to take.

"Is this the magical elixir?" she asked.

I nodded. "We prepared the mushrooms as a tea."

As she took the cup, she joked, "You know, I'm more of a coffee drinker, Dr. Stowe." Lifting the cup and inhaling the steam, she crinkled her nose. "The worse it smells and tastes, the better it's supposed to work, right?"

I smiled. "Please feel free to drink it at your own pace. As you do, I'll tell you a bit about what you're likely to experience during the session."

Tristen nodded and took a sip.

"So again, the reason I suggested we try this approach was because I feel you might benefit from a new way of looking at yourself. A psychedelic can alter your consciousness enough to do just that."

Tristen took two gulps.

"You can think of normal, everyday consciousness as your ego," I continued.

"Your ego is your sense of 'I,' but it's different from what most of us perceive as our 'self.' This experience should help you step outside your ego and see yourself anew."

Tristen raised her eyebrows skeptically but finished the tea in one final gulp.

I took the cup from her. "Now just lie back and try to make yourself comfortable."

As she did, the nurse slid pillows under her head and legs, before spreading a blanket over her and tucking her in. As Tristen rolled her head on the pillow and closed her eyes, the nurse lit a candle on a table beside the bed, and I dimmed the lights. Finally, the nurse started a soothing song playing from a speaker in one corner of the room.

Ten minutes went by without anyone saying anything.

Eventually, Tristen spoke up. "Um, I don't think it's working."

"It can take a while for the drug to work its way into your system."

Another ten minutes passed.

When Tristen spoke, her voice wobbled. "Okay, something's happening. I'm in the feels now."

"How so?"

"It feels a little like being high on weed, but there's more depth to it. It's like I'm experiencing the world on another wavelength or something."

The nurse stood up. "Would you mind if I shone a light in your eyes, Tristen?"

Tristen shook her head, and he flashed a penlight in her eyes. "Pupils are dilated. The drug's starting to take hold."

"Just go with the experience, Tristen," I urged. "Don't resist any feelings that come up for you. And keep describing what you're experiencing."

"My senses are heightened." Tristen lifted her hands and examined her fingers. Slowly, she slid them down the wall. "How often do you think about your fingers? They're so underappreciated. They do so much work and get so little credit."

Hoping to steer the conversation toward a more meaningful topic, I spoke Tristen's name softly.

"Mm-hmm," she mumbled, her eyes once again closed.

"Would it be okay if we talked about something from one of our previous sessions?"

Looking like her mind was elsewhere, Tristen nodded slowly.

"Do you feel like you're holding back parts of yourself?"

"Yes." Her face scrunched up. "I'm always playing nice, trying to please everyone, not really saying what I want to say, not really being who I want to be."

"And who do you want to be?"

"I don't know. Not who I show everyone every day."

I sensed Tristen might be coming close to a realization, so I brought the conversation back to the life metaphor she'd shared with me.

"We've talked about how you feel like a dung beetle pushing around a pile of dung that keeps accumulating more and more dung. Can you tell me more about that?"

"I just wish I had more time for myself. I'm always drowning in obligations. Everyone wants a piece of me: colleagues, friends, family. I just want to be free."

I ran my hand through my beard. "What does being free—"

Tristen's eyes snapped open and darted around the room. "Where's my phone?"

I asked the nurse to grab Tristen's phone. He grabbed it from the desk and handed it to her. She frantically typed and scrolled, before showing me the screen. She pointed to a photo of herself. She sat at a table in a fancy restaurant, surrounded by other people in business suits.

"Look at me! I'm grinning like a moron. What a phony!"

"Tell me what's happening, Tristen."

Instead of answering me, she tapped the phone's screen and shouted, "Delete."

She tapped the screen again. "I'm deleting all this bullshit, that's what's going on. It's dung, all of it!"

I positioned my body so I could watch as she scrolled to another photo. "Delete." Another. "Delete." Again and again. "Delete, delete, delete!"

Tears welled up in her eyes as she navigated to the social media platform's settings. She hovered her finger over the screen for a moment, then hit *Delete profile*. She slumped into the bed, closed her eyes, and continued to cry.

I leaned over her and calmly asked, "How do you feel?"

She exhaled deeply. "I feel like I just stopped rolling the dung."

"And what does it mean to stop rolling the dung?"

Opening her eyes, she stared at the wall. "I know what I need to do."

I asked her what she meant, but she refused to say. "I'm not going to tell you. I'm going to show you."

Our next session was the day before Tristen's twenty-fifth birthday. I was tense, not knowing what to expect. My worries faded, though, when she marched into my consultation room and announced, "Guess what, Dr. Stowe?"

I grinned. "What?"

"My paperwork went through yesterday for a six-month leave of absence to hike the Appalachian Trail!"

My grin widened. "No way!"

"It's the best birthday a girl could ask for."

"That's terrific, Tristen!"

Giddy with excitement, we spent the rest of the session discussing her plans. I was amazed by how much her appearance and disposition had transformed. Her face was animated, and she waved her hands around as she spoke.

At one point, Tristen pulled out her phone and showed me an app called Far Out.

"You can follow me on the trail. I'll write mini stories every day on a blog."

"Of course I'll follow you. I'm so excited for you."

Two sessions later, we agreed it would be our last session. I felt like I'd done my job. Tristen no longer needed a therapist. She no longer needed me. In the words of psychoanalyst Donald Winnicott, "We all hope our patients will finish with us and forget us, and that they will find living itself to be the therapy that makes sense."

A couple of weeks later, Tristen left for Georgia to start her long-distance hike.

Her first blog post showed her on the summit of Springer Mountain, the first achievement of her great adventure.

In the photo, Tristen wore a new pair of sunglasses. They were circular, with a bright-blue tint that reminded other hikers of Janis Joplin, the "OG hippie."

Tristen named her blog *Trail Magic*, after the concept held by the long-distance hiking, or thru-hiking, community that the trail always provided just what a person needed when they needed it. "The trail provides," as the saying went. Usually, what a hiker received was a person they met along the way, known as a "trail angel."

In one social media post, Tristen described what trail magic meant to her.

"If I'm exhausted and feel like I can't go another mile, what I need to keep going will find its way to me. Whether it's a cold drink, a hot dog, or an uplifting exchange of stories with a fellow hiker, Trail Angels can be found all along the journey. Trail magic is serendipitous yet all around us. It is the embodiment of 'the trail provides.'"

As many long-distance hikers did, Tristen hiked off and on with a similar group of people: her "tramily." Everyone in her tramily adopted a trail name. Tristen's was "Head Empty." A fellow hiker, Amber, had chosen the name because Tristen seemed to empty her mind while hiking.

As time went on, Tristen appeared to become intimate with Amber. One day, she posted a video in which Amber sat on her lap as their tramily sang John Denver's "Take Me Home, Country Roads" around a campfire.

As the weeks passed, I made checking her blog a daily habit, even as I focused on my other patients and continued building my practice. Seeing Tristen doing so well was an enormous source of happiness and pride.

About five months into her AT journey, however, Tristen stopped posting to her blog. For the first couple of days, I passed it off as just her missing a post. But as more days passed with no update, I began to worry. Had there been an accident?

After a week of no blog updates, Tristen called me, her voice heavy.

"I left the trail. I dislocated my knee on challenging terrain in the White Mountains of New Hampshire and had to be airlifted to a hospital. I only had about three hundred miles to go to get to Katahdin."

"I'm so sorry to hear that, Tristen. I know how much this hike meant to you."

She blamed work for causing the accident. "The day before the injury, I got an email from my boss that the team was in a major crisis and he needed my help."

"How did you respond?"

"The last thing I wanted was to go back to Boston: back to office life, days packed with meetings, sitting in front of screens, and giving presentations all day. But my team was in trouble and needed me. The next morning, I couldn't stop worrying, and that's when I tripped on a root." She groaned. "So much for 'head empty.'"

Concerned the demands of work life and the annoyances of city living would overwhelm Tristen again, I asked if she wanted to continue therapy.

She agreed.

That night, Tristen posted a picture showing her and Amber on a dirt trail from behind, holding hands. She captioned it, "I miss the natural harmony of living in the woods. I miss waking up with the sunrise and winding down after sunset. I miss the trail's rhythms. I miss morning coffee before a long day. The scenery. Laughing around the fire with my tramily. With Amber."

In therapy, Tristen admitted to uncontrollable bouts of crying and difficulty getting out of bed every day. She was devastated that she hadn't finished the AT by reaching Mount Katahdin. Now, she felt like a prisoner to her job. She had even broken up with Amber since Tristen couldn't bear to watch Amber finish the hike.

"I wish you'd never told me about existentialism, Dr. Stowe," she complained in one session. "If you're right, we're all at the mercy of random cosmic forces we can't control. It seems like a curse to have even be born."

I tried to explain that my view of existentialism could be used to inspire her to invent her own reasons for living. Instead, her worldview had become nihilistic. Life seemed to have no purpose or value anymore.

Worried by Tristen's state of mind, I recommended we meet three times a week. I thought this would offer her the best chance for recovery. We needed to unpack her perceived failure of not completing the AT and develop a coherent narrative that would give her a sense of control over those painful experiences.

If nothing else, Tristen needed someone to hear her story. She needed to be alive in someone else's mind—my mind, as it were. Ruth told me how she tried to interact with grieving patients: just be there, hold space, and listen.

In our next session, Tristen recalled the first night she had spent with Amber.

"I was lying in her arms before the sun came up. It was so warm and cozy. I could've stayed there all day. I'd never felt anything like it. It was so nice to hold someone—a woman—and to be held. For so long, I had so much love to give and no one to give it to. Now Amber was getting all that love."

When Amber posted on social media that she had summited Katahdin, finishing the Appalachian Trail, Tristen sank deeper into depression.

"It's devastating what happened to her," Ruth said when I called seeking her professional opinion. "She had a chance to enjoy life, find some peace, and feel free, and then it was snatched away again."

"What do you think I should do?" I asked.

"This is a serious situation, Malcolm. I would start with upping her dosage of Zoloft to two hundred milligrams. If she even hints at suicide, get her to the hospital right away. Honestly, I'm surprised you didn't do it at Walden Pond."

I accepted the rebuke and agreed with her recommendations. As I got ready for my next session with Tristen, I was prepared to discuss changes to her medication. Those plans fell apart when she barreled into my office, sat down, and eagerly leaned forward in her chair.

"I went back through my old blog posts, Dr. Stowe. It was nice just to remember how I felt while hiking. But more than that, I had an epiphany. I was reading a post I'd written about existentialism, where I mentioned that you had introduced me to the philosophy."

"I remember you saying it was a bleak and uninspiring perspective on life."

She nodded emphatically. "Yes, but last night, I realized what my philosophy is—and it gave me some hope."

I shifted in my seat, eager to hear more. "Go on, please."

"Existentialists seem to believe there's no order or reason to the universe and that events just happen randomly. That humans are this cosmic joke, and we're all just desperately searching for meaning in a meaningless universe. I've been looking for a different way of thinking: A perspective that allows for meaningful coincidences. A universe where we're connected by something we can't necessarily see, hear, or feel."

I stayed silent for a few moments, stirred by Tristen's words. It was true that in the existentialist tradition, there was no meaning to life, nothing really mattered, and we were all just making it up as we went. I'd been able to find some dark empowerment in that way of thinking, believing I was the inventor of my life. Tristen hadn't been able to do that, and I now wondered if she was worse off for meeting me.

"Do you think my perspective brought you down?" I asked.

"Initially, yes, I think it did. But I think it also inspired me in a paradoxical way."

"What do you mean?"

"I rejected your worldview at first, but that rejection prompted me to go looking for my own meaning for life. Eventually, it helped inspire me to hike the Appalachian Trail, and that's where I found community, belonging—and love."

I grinned. "I didn't realize how unpopular my belief system was until I met you."

Tristen laughed. "I'm not saying your choice to see life through the existentialist lens is wrong. What you believe is valid. It just didn't work for me."

"Please, tell me more."

"You're a man of science, Dr. Stowe. You don't believe in God or an afterlife or ghosts or astrology or tarot cards, because there's no scientific proof that such things are real. But what if there are aspects of reality that science can't yet understand? What if science doesn't yet have the tools to understand what we deem supernatural or inexplicable?"

"You said you found a philosophy you like?"

Tristen nodded. "I realized what I believe while I was hiking. I believe all things—animals, plants, the water in the lakes, rivers, and oceans—are all connected by something we don't yet understand. And I think humans, with all our intelligence, curiosity, and technology, are here to witness it all."

"Is there a name for this belief?"

Tristen looked toward the window. "You know, Walden Pond is where Henry David Thoreau did his famous experiment to live in the woods by himself for two years, living off the land. I just finished reading his book Walden. Now I'm reading Nature by Ralph Waldo Emerson, Thoreau's mentor. They were transcendentalists."

"And what do they believe?"

"They thought spiritual matters couldn't be understood through reason but through self-reflection and by trusting one's own intuition. They thought there was only so much you could learn from studying, reading, and thinking logically. Sometimes you can learn more in the woods, just trusting your own inner voice."

"And what is your inner voice telling you?"

"I can't stop thinking about the Appalachian Trail. I realized what had made me happy about the AT. So much of my struggles revolved around how disenchanted I am with American society: our fetish with productivity, how we work ourselves into cycles of burnout, and our desperate need to leave the madness behind. While hiking the AT, I felt at peace and totally free. I felt like I could breathe for the first time in my life."

"So what are you saying?"

"What if I finished my journey, starting the trail where I left off in New Hampshire?"

"What's stopping you?"

She folded her arms over her chest. "I'm afraid I'll fail again. I shot my shot—and missed."

"Well, I hope you'll find the courage to begin again. It doesn't have to be a once-in-a-lifetime chance."

When Tristen didn't show up for our next appointment, I knew I had to heed Ruth's advice and call the police. Before I did, though, I decided to check Tristen's blog, just in case. The post I found made me so happy, my eyes filled with tears.

> *I was driving home from therapy this afternoon when I spotted my round, blue-tinted sunglasses sitting on the dashboard of my car. In that moment, I knew I had to finish my hike to Mount Katahdin.*
>
> *That decided, I didn't go home. Instead, I drove north to the White Mountains of New Hampshire to buy the gear I would need to finish my journey. I messaged Amber to let her know, and she met me at the trailhead.*

A week later, Tristen posted a picture of her and Amber at the beginning of the section of the AT that sliced its way through the rugged mountains. In the post, she narrated their first few moments on the trail.

> *I pulled out my sunglasses and proudly put them on. Amber glanced back at me. "Let's go, Shades. We're burning daylight." It was then I knew that Amber had given me a new trail name: Shades.*

To finish her post, Tristen wrote that she had initially resisted existentialism, until she realized what I had always been trying to say: Her identity was just a collection of the choices she made. She was free to do whatever she wanted, free to go wherever she desired, and free to become whoever she wanted to be.

"Thank you, Dr. Stowe, my Trail Angel."

Acknowledgments

Thank you to everyone who read early drafts of these stories and provided thoughtful feedback and suggestions. Some of these folks include: Al Leftwich, Mark Jednaszewski, Monika Kalina, Rob Hickey, Denise Ferazzi, Marissa Grunes, and Sam Cooke. Thanks also to the following faculty members of the Solstice MFA program: David Yoo, Laura Williams McCaffrey, Sandra Scofield, Steven Huff, and Robert Lopez.

A huge thank you, as always, to my longtime editor, Tod Tinker, for his keen insights, smart editing, and meticulous fact-checking. Thanks also to Elvira Mac for line-editing a few of these stories when they were in their embryonic stages.

I'd like to thank some of the healthcare providers I've met over the years who've helped influence my thinking about health and disease and the role of the physician in healing patients both physically and emotionally. These doctors include Zacharia Isaac, MD and Daniella Sarno, MD of Brigham and Women's Hospital; David Elpern, MD, a dermatologist in Williamstown, MA; and Jeffrey Millstein, MD, who I had the pleasure of meeting at one of Columbia's Narrative Medicine conferences.

Given how much this book is focused on emotional and psychological healing, I'd like to express my deep gratitude to my former therapist, John Grillo, LICSW, who spent several years helping me look inward and reflect on myself and my life. The insights we discovered in our sessions helped me better understand who I am and what I want, and ultimately became the stuff of fiction.

Dustin Grinnell is a fiction writer, essayist, and marketing writer. Previously, he's worked in writing roles for Brigham and Women's Hospital, Whitehead Institute for Biomedical Research, Charles Rivers Labs, and Bose Corporation. He's currently a full-time content marketing manager at WuXi Biologics.

Originally trained as research scientist, Dustin worked at a small biotech company after graduating Wheaton College (MA) and then earning his master's in physiology from Penn State, where he conducted human-performance research at the Noll Laboratory. With a background in science and medicine, he brings to bear in his writing a fearless curiosity and a passion for rigor. As a writer of creative nonfiction, he's published articles about the secret life of a con man, a woman in a BDSM relationship, and a winner of the Extreme Mustang Makeover. He's profiled the inventor of bungee jumping and interviewed scientists who visited Bermuda to unearth a new model organism. In 2019, he detailed his own experience with psychosomatic symptoms.

As for his personal adventures, Dustin has climbed Mount Kilimanjaro, run the Paris marathon, hitchhiked across New Zealand, and backpacked through Britain, Spain, France, and Costa Rica. These expeditions have been featured as essays in the Sunday travel sections of media outlets, such as the Boston Globe, Philadelphia Inquirer, and Living Now Magazine. He has won two Solas Awards for Best Travel Writing and an honorable mention from the North American Travel Journalists Association Travel Media Awards Competition. His essays were brought together in his book, *Lost & Found*, a collection of twenty-three essays in which he writes about discovering amazing places—and bit by bit, himself.

A writer of science fiction, Dustin is the author of three novels in his "Human 2.0" series that explores the science and perils of enhancing our biology to make us superhuman. *The Genius Dilemma* (2013), his first novel, explores man's obsession with progress through cognitive enhancement. *Without Limits* (2015), the second in the series, explores man's inherent desire to cheat via a nanotechnology-based performance enhancement technology. His novel, *The Empathy Academy* (2022), which was published by Atmosphere Press, delves into the use of a gene-hacking technology to correct predispositions to unethical behavior in adolescents.

Dustin holds an MFA in fiction writing from the Solstice MFA Program at Lasell

University, a BA in psychobiology from Wheaton College (MA), and an MS in physiology from Penn State.

Connect with him on Twitter, Instagram, or TikTok and read his writing on DustinGrinnell.com.